Reunion

Reunion

With best wishes to
my friend, The Bear,
to Erin and the family
Jim George 11/2012
(from the Batcave
in Austin)

James Kennedy George Jr.

authorHOUSE®

AuthorHouse™
1663 Liberty Drive
Bloomington, IN 47403
www.authorhouse.com
Phone: 1-800-839-8640

First published by AuthorHouse 12/30/2011

ISBN: 978-1-4685-2968-5 (sc)
ISBN: 978-1-4685-2967-8 (hc)
ISBN: 978-1-4685-2969-2 (ebk)

Library of Congress Control Number: 2011963087

Printed in the United States of America

This book is printed on acid-free paper.

Contents

Acknowledgements

FOR MANY YEARS, this story has been in my head. It has proved difficult to present itself in a fashion suitable to be told. In the words of today, I am told I am the adult son of an alcoholic . . . told that there are effects and impacts. The meaning of that was unclear to me until I attempted to write this book.

This work is fictional, but is based on the era and culture of Princeton, West Virginia in the 1950's. The events depicted reflect the high school activities all of us experienced, to some extent, and the characters are composites of various people, real or imagined, from that generation. Certainly we came of age during a momentous time of social change, both the strong impact of desegregation as well as the music of our generation, at the very onset of the rock and roll revolution.

Many people gave unselfishly of their time and counsel to assist and guide me. First and foremost, my family: my wife, Diana; our three children, Juliet, Jimmy, and Chris; as well as my sister, Sally George Vance, and her husband, Dan Vance. Each read the book and contributed to its final form.

The John Rogers Book Club, my long-time book club in Austin, opened my eyes to literature, and the members read a too-early version of the manuscript, providing much-needed and very candid advice. Three editors, Mindy Reed, Susan Luton, and my daughter, Juliet George McCleery, reviewed the manuscript and helped me at both the micro, technical level, as well as the macro level, to fashion the story as (hopefully) a writer, not a technical industry executive. The Writers League of Texas has served up numerous writing seminars and resources. Several people read the book critically, some numerous times, and offered not only extensive constructive criticism but also encouragement and enthusiasm. Those included Jim Parnell, Trent Miller, Joe Hart, Lonnie Dillard, Tom Dillon, Dave Sumner, Paul Torgersen, Bill Stephenson, Shanny Lott, Diane Umstead, and Stewart Vanderwilt. Shanny Lott, a distinguished Austin artist and sculptor, did the cover artwork.

Thanks to all,

Jim George
Austin, Texas
November, 2011

Part 1

"Left to itself, history would forget, but fortunately there are novels—loaded with emotions, swarming with faces, and constructed with the sand and lime of language."

Louis Chevalier
"The Assassination of Paris"

Chapter 1

BUDDY'S PHONE CALL started it. "Jimmy!" He gushed when he talked. Lots of air. I could almost feel his breath through the phone.

"Buddy, Buddy Lewis?"

"Of course," he said. "Come on now. You-all still in Austin?"

"Sure are."

"We had a meeting of the reunion committee last night. It's on for September. You and Callie just got to come back for this one. It's going to be great. Jimmy, I can't wait! The weather ought to be good. The trees should show some color."

Buddy the Oldies King.

"I can't wait for you to hear my new tapes Friday night!"

The very thought started a flood of memories: crisp clear nights, familiar faces, lilting accents that to this day mark the speaker as "from there," winding valleys with chords of mist over the creeks in the morning, unending mountain scenery teeming with the finest hardwood stands in North America. Not all the recollections were positive. Old brick buildings in a decaying downtown, declining since the mall arrived back in the 1970's. A Wal-Mart Supercenter at the other end of town cemented the downtown's complete collapse a few years ago.

Buddy's phone call started our planning. Callie, my wife, is a year younger but knows the group almost as well as I do—in some ways better. She has a good memory for names and faces, and quite a few of her friends dated guys in my class. She was a really good dancer. In fact, she won the Best Dancer award for girls when she was a senior. So any reunion was fun for both of us.

That night, we got out the annual from my senior year. Eleven black kids were pictured out of 212 photographs. Back then, the polite word among the white kids was "colored."

There must be a Ph.D. thesis somewhere on high school reunions. Ours certainly has changed quite a bit over the years. The first one was a contest of who could show off the best business card title and wear the best suit or dress. At the end of that weekend I had a pocket full of business cards—some form of "junior manager" or "administrative" this or that—and tossed them out as we left. The atmosphere at the 10-year reunion seemed to be all about achievement . . . who could climb the ladder of success fastest. It seems silly looking back.

It was at the 15th that things got wild. A girl from Florida, whom I recalled as smart but reserved, got looped and danced the pole dance without a pole. Several attendees had a continuation after-hours party. The attention to, "look at me, I'm doing well," was ending. People started coming alone.

At the 20th, people started coming with spouse number two, or even three. On good behavior, each introduced their guest or new spouse around. No more interesting debauchery, all well behaved. Now they were all about their kids, sometimes very young kids with family number two. Inevitably, these spouses were from somewhere else and, for the most part, came because they felt they had to.

The primary cultural bonding was always the time transport of music. Buddy's tapes would be the constant backdrop for Friday night's mixer with lots of, "Hello, it's nice to see you again," while squinting at the name badges—lots of table-hopping and talking.

"Saturday night's the big program with the meal and the band," I said to Callie. "They've booked Coverall. Buddy says they can do all the oldies."

"Is Buddy still playing drums with them?" she asked.

"No, he stopped after his heart attack several years ago. But I'll bet they ask him to sit in."

The next day I called to book a room.

Chapter 2

MORE VIVID MEMORIES, etched-in-stone experiences, remain about my classmates than about my own parents. Mom and Dad both are gone now. Mom is a painful hole in my life. I miss her. Dad is another story.

I had only a piecemeal understanding of my parents as real people. We never had an adult-to-adult relationship. Most everything I know is from memories of childhood discussions and old photographs.

My older sister, Susie, and I got a bit of oral history from Mom's side when she would tell us "when I was a little girl" stories to our delight. Daddy never said much about his youth. But some of our aunts filled in a few things, with sparse detail and politically correct backfill. A handful of old snapshots indicate both of our parents were attractive people. She grew up in Danville, south of the Bluegrass area of Lexington. People in Kentucky have deep roots. Mom attended Centre College and then Norton Infirmary in Louisville to learn medicine. Armed with a fresh RN certificate, she took a job in public health nursing in eastern Kentucky, the epicenter of all the hillbilly jokes, working with the people who lived in the hollows and the coal camps. She was parked beside the highway one day looking at a map, uncertain of the way back to Paintsville, in one of those peculiar coincidences in life when Jim Jackson, then about 30, was returning to his room after making the rounds for the GMAC automotive credit business of General Motors. His route included the GM dealers in eastern Kentucky. He had an impressive way of speaking, good timing, pleasant and resonant.

In a brief memoir he compiled later in his life while undergoing treatment in an alcohol-rehab center, he wrote, "I saw a young lady pulled over by the side. I stopped to see what her trouble was and found that she was a young nurse with the health department who had been in that area only for a short time and was not familiar with the roads. She turned out to be Sara and we later on became good friends."

I always got a kick out of the statement that "she turned out to be Sara." As if she was someone else earlier in her life! His notes moved right past this fortuitous introduction and the revelation that they became good friends, and jumped right onto a climactic, "Sara and I kept in touch with each other pretty closely and in 1941 were married in Paris, Kentucky." She gave up her nursing career and the couple moved to Huntington, West Virginia. A year or so later, Susie entered the world.

Mom always was close to her brother, Carter Clay, who went on to become the quintessential "doctor everything" in Danville, where he developed a wonderful practice and lived in the finest home in that genteel southern college town. I remember it as a magnificent, stately, old brick structure with two large stories, a dank basement (into which I rarely ventured) full of huge horseflies in the heat of the summer, and a wondrously full attic (they do not construct houses that way anymore) full of dust, cobwebs, and mysterious old trunks. Large old trees full of frisky brown squirrels, set back from the traffic of Lexington Avenue, surrounded the manse. The first floor was dark and formal, with beautiful antique furniture, pictures of Kentucky cardinals and famous racehorses, as well as detailed family crests. So many framed pictures.

Uncle Carter had everything a man could wish for, apparently, except real happiness. Later, he fought addiction for drugs he prescribed to himself, and divorced after an absolutely scandalous affair with a vivacious local woman—the two eventually married and remained happily married the rest of their lives. Mom's other brother, Uncle Tim, was a self-made man who left home at a young age, got into sales, became a zone manager for Chevrolet, and lived in a swanky part of

Cincinnati. Mom would forever be their little sister, and both brothers adored her. No man could have lived up to their protective expectations. Photographs of her as a young woman show that she was beautiful: lovely rectangular face, high forehead, and a classic Roman nose.

The Jackson family was as tightly bound to Virginia as Mom's family was to Kentucky. Dad completed high school in Saltville, Virginia and attended VPI, as Virginia Tech was known then. However, a combination of Depression-era financial problems and his lack of passion for his studies resulted in his withdrawal at the Christmas break of his sophomore year. The family lost the farm. Dad came back and went to work for the CCC in Virginia. He never went back to college, but he had ability with numbers as well as smooth people skills. His resonant voice was one of his best assets, and he never corrupted the language.

My father's paternal grandfather was Worthington Winfield Jackson. An icon displayed in his Confederate officer's uniform in a large charcoal drawing that hung in the most prominent location in our modest home, he was involved in some of the worst fighting at the "point" during the first Battle of Cold Harbor. Right in front of him, the New York Seventh Heavy Artillery Battalion broke through the Confederate lines, over six miles long defending Richmond, with a focused charge at first light. The fighting was hand-to-hand, charge and counter-charge. Smoke obscured everything. Heavy cannons fired at point-blank range. When the carnage at that location ended, the Federals had broken through, but they were repulsed 30 minutes later when Confederate reinforcements counterattacked. Both armies ended up where they began, only 100 yards apart. Casualties were great on both sides. My great-grandfather was shot and bayoneted in the first charge. He would have been finished off with a second bayoneting, but a comrade next to him killed the Union soldier with a single blow to his head, swinging his rifle as a club when the ammunition ran out. Jackson was carried behind the Union lines after the initial charge, laid out as a prisoner, in all likelihood to die from his wounds. Miraculously he survived and spent the next year at Fort Pulaski, a Union prison near Savannah, Georgia. After an unsuccessful escape attempt, he and the others were recaptured and sent to a Federal POW prison near Baltimore, where he remained until the war ended. He returned to Princeton, which mostly was burned to the ground, now no longer in Virginia, and moved across the new state border to Smyth County, Virginia, where the war hero built the original family farm and prospered in a hamlet named Broadford, on a river crossing not far from Saltville, one of the primary salt producing sites of the Confederacy.

Later, Dad's mother, now quite elderly, lived in Charlottesville, Virginia, with his sister, my Aunt Margaret. She and her husband owned two apartment buildings directly across Jefferson Park Avenue from the University of Virginia campus. They maintained a formal lifestyle in what seemed to me to be a museum of a home in a fashionable unit in one of the two buildings. "Granny" Jackson had bristling stiff facial hair that scratched me when I was presented to her to be hugged, as she was maintained in formal taxidermy-like condition by the oldest of her seven children.

The families had little in common, but Mom and Dad appeared to be living—if not outwardly loving—proof that opposites do attract. One advantage for Mom was that her second-born had been me, a real living and breathing boy, the only male descendent of Dad's family with the Jackson last name, the designated "keeper of the flame." That was very important to the stately Virginians.

From the time he was a teenager, from what I was told, Dad loved to drink. Aunt Molly, Dad's youngest sibling, recalled the day he and a friend drove the family's new Buick off the road coming down from a moonshiner's still up in the mountains west of Marion, Virginia. Somehow neither boy was hurt, although the car plunged down a mountain side through the dense woods. The family never came down hard on him for this or later episodes. No one seems to know why.

In a strange dynamic, the Jackson clan felt Mom was too "social" for Dad, while the Clays never accepted Dad as financially good enough for Mom. I grew up in the crosshairs of an acceptance contest on both sides of the family.

Throughout, an unpleasant memory persists: Dad calling out when he was drinking. He would holler the name "Joe" over and over. "Hey, Joe." I heard it a thousand times. "Joe, come over here. Joe, set 'em up. Joe . . . Joe." It never seemed to stop, ending only when he finally fell asleep at our small kitchen table, in a smoky drunken stupor.

Fortunately, Dad never was violent, either sober or drunk. If he had been, I'm sure Mother would have left him. He was a mushy, slushy drunk. As the sales manager for Gibson's Motors in Princeton, he cleaned up well every morning—six days for work and Sunday for church. He looked good in a tweed sport coat and nice shirt and tie, and if there was a splitting headache and low rumbling in his ears, he never let on. He had a facile gift of gab, was honest in his dealings with people out at Gibson's, and folks kept coming back to trade cars with him. His pleasant, even elegant, southwestern Virginia tinge served him well. After work he would drift into his alcoholic world, where the Elks Club offered small-time and sometimes more than small-time gambling, a bar, and kindred souls. The Elks and similar "brotherhoods" were the only game in town for booze at a bar.

"I'll go to the national Elks home in Winchester, Virginia, when the time comes," Dad used to tell Mom, Susie, and me. There was no mention of how Mom would fit into the equation or where the money would come from. Susie and I still recall those conversations with some shallow amusement.

Chapter 3

CALLIE AND I usually drive back by heading up the familiar Interstate route that skirts Dallas, on to Little Rock, and over to Memphis to spend the night. Then it's the full length of Tennessee through Nashville, Knoxville, and finally Bristol into Virginia's southwestern corner and up into West Virginia's "Four Seasons Country" where, as self-described by the city, Princeton is benefiting from both the tourist business and the booming demand for coal nearby in the mighty Pocahontas coal seam.

The town's older residential sections were built in the 1930's. To this day, they appear unchanged to the casual eye, tucked among and sheltered beneath mature oaks and maples, sturdy deciduous specimens in the prime portion of their geographic range.

The summers and falls are wonderful, cool and pleasant, especially as evening progresses. It's good to be back. We've made the customary stops at family members and are heading over to the reunion at last. In the older residential areas, the best homes, those of the doctors, lawyers, and business owners, are handsomely constructed with large lots and mature trees. The neighborhood where I grew up consists of solid homes, built of brick, not as large, with small yards and fewer large trees, definitely less leafy. The home on North Walker is still there. The new people have a flagpole now. They cut down that huge blue spruce, the one Mom picked out as a live Christmas tree in 1958. The pretty little thing would become a behemoth, over 70 feet high by the time her health began to fail. The neighborhoods remain much the same until we reach the Thorn Street Bridge, which crosses over the N&W Railroad tracks and Brushy Creek. That creek used to rampage and flood the low-lying area, Stumpy Bottom, at least twice a year before the Army Corps of Engineers dredged out a deeper channel. East Princeton, on the other side of the bridge, is a collection of smaller, mostly wooden homes, usually painted white. The Stumpy Bottom flood plain itself has a smattering of uneven wooden homes as well as trailer homes and dilapidated buildings.

At the Athens Road intersection, we turn left onto Route 20, which must have been an Indian path as it still follows the top of every hill and ridgeline between Princeton and Athens.

"Slate Gaskins and his wife should be here this weekend, don't you think?" I ask. "Didn't they have a baby on the way the last time we had one of these?"

"Try five years before the last one," Callie says quickly. "That little baby would be almost ten now."

Slate was the lead guitar player and one of the main singers in the band. The prototypical high school leading man, he wore his longish hair in a duck's-ass, a blond James Dean, with blue eyes and the painful, soulful look of the time. He also played football, an end, and was a serious student as well. His senior bio in our annual listed his ambition as an engineer. Sure enough, he studied mechanical engineering at Virginia Tech and became chief engineer at a large manufacturing company.

"He was a good guitar player."

She nods. "And a great looking guy as well."

Slate could do the guitar player moves. Someone who looked like that just had to be a lead guitar player in a band. He always fronted the band, on the right.

Buddy was the drummer and the emotional heart of the band. He always sat in the rear, the domain of all drummers. Thomas Jefferson Lewis III, Buddy, the quintessential good guy. Everyone loves Buddy. He's retired from a job with the state . . . something concerning business licensing. Underneath that easy, outgoing appearance, he's recovering from a severe heart attack three years earlier. He even quit smoking, a lifelong addiction.

After desegregation became the law and was implemented at Princeton High School in the late 50's, Arcie Peterson came into the picture. Arcie, friendly, outgoing, polite, theatrical, and devoted to music, joined the band our junior year. His senior class bio listed his ambition as orchestra leader, and his photograph featured a beautiful smile and hair which was long, glossy, and held in place by one of the hair pomades popular with the black students. He had the best voice in the band, but if someone was away, he would bring that instrument from his collection and play their part. If everyone was there, he was the lead singer, stationed front and center.

The band. Two words, so many experiences.

"Slate, Buddy, and Arcie all will be there. They never miss a reunion," Callie says as we come into Athens. A sign at the one and only traffic signal points to Concord University, a small liberal arts college, just up Main Street a quarter of a mile from Route 20.

We slowly pass the intersection and start down the long hill, leaving town to the north. The highway drops sharply until we reach the valley, cross a clear stream, and head up the next hill until we approach a level plateau. The butterflies in my stomach shift around—only 20 minutes away now.

So many churches are out here, practically one after another. Most are well maintained, rural, and small. Some are on the wane, with a few overrun with weeds, no longer active at all. In this area the ratio of churches to other structures is appreciable. Religion is big business.

A road sign indicates Pipestem State Park two miles ahead. The butterflies crank it up. Finally, the tall stone marker, an Indian motif, signals the park entrance. Driving into the park itself, we quickly gain elevation on the quintessential park lane, winding, well maintained, and nicely mowed on both sides. Clusters of small cabins sit among the trees along with classic park-like heavy wooden signs with the letters honed out, emblazoned with honey-gold letters announcing the hiking and horse trails that curve off in various directions.

A road off to the left leads to the signature tramway, a heavy-duty cable car system built in Switzerland. Each car carries up to six people, suspended from a huge stranded wire cable as thick as a man's wrist that runs supported by tall metal stanchions set into massive concrete foundations traversing all the way up and down the mountainside. As the car pivots on its suspension joints, it sucks any feeling of stability out of your gut as you approach the river and the 1,000-foot-deep gorge.

The main lodge itself soon comes into view. We park beside a car from Georgia and walk toward the lobby and the main unloading area, underneath a protective roof.

"Well now. Lookie who's here." The raspy voice is shaped by years of smoking. "It's Jimmy and Callie."

Instant recognition. "Marnie Bowland, you don't look a day over . . . let's see, how old are we now?"

Marnie Bowland, now Marnie Bowland Santoro, rail-thin, still has a laughing come-hither look, although her sun-creased face shows overexposure to the Florida sun. She always was, and continues to be, a smart and trendy dresser. Marnie used to live with her single-parent mother in a small garage apartment. We were in the same grade in Mercer School when I arrived in Princeton during the summer of 1954.

She ran with a different group of girls and had a "bad girl" swagger. I still think of her every time I see a rerun of *West Side Story*. Marnie would have been a perfect WASP version of that sexy Puerto Rican strutter. She was a Su Wan, one of the two Princeton High School girls' social clubs.

Marnie can see through lies. "I have a very good bullshit filter," she would say. Both Callie and I like her realness and earthy candor. She's comfortable in her own skin.

We catch up briefly but are excited and ready to check in.

"Hello and welcome to Pipestem," the young woman says. The accent definitely is local.

"We just drove all the way from Texas. Glad to be here!"

"Well, you-all are here. Glad you made it. Your room is all set. Number five thirty-five, a non-smoking room with a king-size bed. Enjoy your stay here with us." She hands me a green plastic fob with the number 535 emblazoned, along with a large, old-fashioned metal key. No modern programmable computer room keys here.

Our room is old, just off the elevator, the very first room, boxed in by an ell of the building. It peeks out beneath an elevated passageway one floor higher in elevation. The net result is claustrophobic, with the brick building wall on one side and the walkway overhead blocking out the sky. We can see the mountains on the other side of the gorge, but it's like looking through a horizontal periscope. The effect, along with the dampness of the room, is smothering. Callie's disappointment is apparent.

The reunion instructions state "Appalachian casual." What's that? Musket and coonskin hat? Overalls? Brogans? Let's see. Do I feel more self-confident or less? Do I need to make what people call a statement with a new sports coat or shoes? Is this a jeans and tennis shoes sort of event? Do I give a shit? I've been through a wide range of these phases over the years, ranging from new suits all the way to jeans and a casual shirt. Tonight is a jeans night.

The mix of voices and Buddy's 50's and 60's rock and roll music gets progressively louder as we walk toward the meeting room. Buddy and I both like the oldies and R & B stuff.

"Are you O.K.?" I ask Callie, who looks wonderful. "Do I look good enough to walk in there beside you?"

She laughs reassuringly and takes my hand.

At that exact moment, Buddy Lewis pops out of a side door. "Jimmy! You made it."

"You personally are responsible for us being here," I have to shout over the music. "Looking good. How's it going?"

He's all revved up. "Do you like the music? I got this off a golden hits CD I bought at a doo-wop concert in Charleston. You wouldn't believe it! Twenty-five acts, all fifties or sixties groups. You know, the good ones!"

Right then, Buddy's tape segues into "Come Go with Me."

"You hear that? The Dell-Vikings . . . . They were there! Right in front of me. I heard them do this in person."

Buddy is even thinner than his usual trim self from before his heart attack several years back. He still wears large, plastic-frame, dorky glasses and has most of his hair. He looks good. It's the voice, that unique soft hollow voice, the accentuated lilt. That's his trademark, along with his nickname. Has anyone ever called him Thomas Jefferson Lewis the third?

Someone did a lot of work on the handouts. The class reunion book is bound with plastic coils and has all the addresses, phone numbers, and so on. There are biographies toward the end. It looks interesting, but there isn't time to check it out then because Buddy has us by the arm and we're swept into a swirl of people, all looking familiar yet strange in the dimness.

The next three hours are a constant stream of oldies music and one person after another forming back into my consciousness. Before I know it, my legs are wooden and someone motions us to a food table, which by that time is thoroughly picked over: sliced pepper pieces and celery ends, as well as cheese bits, all of them dried out. I exchange hellos with Slate Gaskins and see Donnie Davis, our class president. Marnie Bowland (I stopped using the girls' married names) is bobbing around, connected to an adult beverage. Someone turns on the lights. Only 10 or so of us are still in the room. All of us are from out of town, staying at the lodge or a nearby B&B, so none of us have to drive back (with the exception of our lovable music man) over those curvy roads after several hours of schmoozing and not a little drinking. The lodge finally has a non-smoking policy, so I don't have to squint through a haze of smoke and later try to sleep with that familiar burning sensation in my chest.

"What's the plan for tomorrow night?" I ask Buddy as Callie and I help him pack up his stuff.

"Tomorrow is the main deal. There'll be a program, and I think you-all will be impressed. Coverall is the band. A cover band . . . get the name? But they're good."

"Is that the band you played with?"

"Yeah, but I had to quit when I ran into the health problems—you know, the heart attack. Oh, they want me to sit in on a few songs tomorrow. Jimmy, I haven't played a lick in a year! Can you believe that? I hope I can keep up."

"You're the man," I crack. "Don't overdo it. Pace yourself." We start toward the door. Then, "Will Arcie be here tomorrow? Arcie Peterson?"

"There's only one Arcie," Buddy counters. "Well, sure. They asked him to do some old soul music. He's got a CD out. It's been out a while, but he's still pushing it. Yeah, Arcie's got the big-time guest spot!"

"Arcie sent me his CD about Nine-Eleven," I mention.

"Arcie never gives up," Buddy says. "That's for sure."

Part 2

PRINCETON, WEST VIRGINIA

"Our childhood . . . the imprint we get . . . it takes a long time to grow our way out of it."

Rodney Crowell
February 9, 2011
"Fresh Air" Interview with Terry Gross on National Public Radio

Chapter 4

THIS PART OF West Virginia juts down deep into Virginia. It was part of what used to be Western Virginia before the Civil War. The new state seceded from the Old Dominion (it was called the Referendum on the Dismemberment Ordinance) in October 1861, and the final boundaries weren't agreed upon until the final state Constitutional Convention of April 1862. By that time, the young men of the area already had voted with their feet, and nearly all of them enlisted in the so-called southwestern Virginia battalions in Lee's Army of Northern Virginia. The men who enlisted from Mercer County, Virginia—those who managed to survive the war—came home to Mercer County, West Virginia.

Princeton is the county seat of Mercer County. It's only 10 miles away from Bluefield, its larger arch competitor, which didn't exist when Princeton first was settled. But when the huge Pocahontas coalfields were discovered along the border of southern West Virginia and southwestern Virginia, the Norfolk and Western Railroad chose a valley with blue flowers, a place that be would named Bluefield, as a major repair and maintenance location. The "shops" grew large with good union jobs. The city boomed not only as a center for heavy industry maintenance and support, but as an administrative and financial center as well. Coal was transported by rail to the ports at Norfolk and from there on to the great industrial centers of America and Europe. Bluefield had one FM and two AM radio stations, as well as Channel Six, WHIS-TV, the NBC affiliate in southern West Virginia. Prior to that, local people had to erect tall towers to pick up television from Roanoke, Bristol, Charleston, or Huntington. The *Bluefield Daily Telegraph*, the main daily newspaper in the area, was a staunchly Republican paper in a solidly working class Democratic political area—"a mouthpiece for fat cats," as Daddy used to say.

Our Boy Scout Troop 66 was selected to help direct cars into the VIP parking area the day the West Virginia Turnpike opened all the way south to Princeton in November 1954. *The New York Times* ran a story that day entitled "Road to Nowhere," but that didn't dampen anyone's enthusiasm. We scouts were dressed in our olive brown uniforms, including our formal merit badge sashes. Troop 66 was headed by a wiry man named Roland Carter, a typesetter at the *Daily Telegraph* and a Korean War veteran. He had never talked about it to us until one night after a scout meeting. He got into a reflective mood and told us about one major battle in which the Chinese sent wave after wave after wave of their soldiers up a hill toward his line, which was anchored by a 50-caliber machine gun, his machine gun. The bodies piled up in grotesque stacks. He aimed the gun right at the top of the layer of the dead, sweeping the barrel from right to left and back, and caught the Chinese as they climbed over. His machine gun glowed red-hot from continuous firing.

"I never could understand why they kept coming," he said.

Troop 66 was a terrific scout troop in my eyes. We numbered only 10 or 15, didn't get into serious outdoorsmanship, and rarely did much hiking or overnight camping. We were "book smart" scouts, as opposed to "outdoors savvy." I zipped right up through the ranks and achieved my Eagle Scout award. The evening one other boy and I received our Eagle pins was a significant event in our community: the *Daily Telegraph* sent a reporter, and our photos were in the paper the next day. Our parents were present, of course. Daddy always showed up for any recognition shots. It was good for business.

Some of the kids called our troop the "Jewish Troop." I didn't know what "Jewish" meant at the time. I was aware that there were people called Jews, but for me the term was bland and non-emotional. Mom or Dad never said a word on the subject. Princeton and Bluefield both had fairly prominent Jewish populations. The families had immigrated into the area from New York in the early 1900's. They seemed to blend in well. They lived like everyone else, and to me they were different only in the sense that a similar immigrant population from Lebanon was in terms of appearance and last names, which certainly were different from the Scots-Irish surnames of the region. The Jewish boys in town all were in Troop 66. None of them wore different clothes. All were good students. None were athletes. Their names had the distinctive sound of eastern European origins, and the families' dark hair and facial features differentiated themselves from the predominantly blue and brown eyes and light brown and blond hair of the "natives." But no one in my circle of friends seemed to care.

There were few ethnic groups other than the Jews and the Colored People, as we were taught to call them. Non-diversity seemed to be a comfortable blanket over Princeton.

Chapter 5

PRINCETON HIGH SCHOOL desegregated while I was a sophomore. We had some drama: a walkout at the junior high; and a cross burning on the lawn of the high school, a photograph of which was in *Life* magazine. Mom and Dad didn't express any opinions at home. The colored kids began attending the formerly white junior high and high school instead of their "separate but equal" schools, and things seemed to calm down. The new students were courteous although reserved. We were surprised they dressed equally well and pretty much wore the same clothes as we did. After the initial events, it was a successful integration process. The colored kids came into the classes, made good grades, and overall probably were better behaved than the average white kid.

Rock and roll music was our thing. It was on AM radio, top-forty, hard-core. WKOY in Bluefield picked up early on the format. It became *the* station all of us listened to during the day. Their ratings went wild. They ran long strings of advertisements every two or three songs! Mom listened with me in the car when we were out together. She had unlimited patience. "They certainly have a lot of commercials," she said. But, other than that, she never complained.

At night, WKOY, only 10 miles away, faded out. Fortunately, Princeton's one and only radio station, WLOH (We Love Our Hills), had a request program at night when neither Princeton High School nor West Virginia University (WVU) had a ballgame. The "mighty fourteen-ninety's" studio, transmitter, and tower were all located on Radio Hill, the highest point in town. With the poor ground conductivity of the mountain terrain and only 250 watts, the signal made it at most 15 miles in the day, less at night.

Local radio selection was limited, but we quickly picked up on the big city AM rockers—50,000-watt powerhouse clear channel stations that pounded in at night: WABC in New York City, 660 AM with Cousin Brucie; and WLS, 890 AM in Chicago ("WLS, channel eighty-nine") with Dick Biondi were favorites.

I also had a deep connection with soul music, the R & B from black artists, which was the prime focus of WLAC in Nashville, on 1510 AM. WLAC also had a powerful signal. The king of their R & B program was the dulcet-voiced John R, aka John Richbourg. "This is John Aaaarrrrhh and this segment is brought to you by the Randy Record Shop in Gallatin, Tennessee," he intoned in a deep baritone that oozed out of the radio. The colored audience was the primary target of Royal Crown hair pomade, White Rose Petroleum Jelly, and other products on the show.

At night I would listen for distant stations. Those magic signals were a thrill, even with my small bedside radio, a low-end plastic Emerson. At times the Bahamas would skip in—it sounded like "Zed En Ess," the British pronunciation of the letters ZNS. These were completely different from the call letters of all the U.S. stations, which began with either a W or a K. The Canadian station's call sign was CKLW, also different. It was my first glimmer that other countries would have differences from the United States. Another example was Mexico, and I could tune the car radio, which had a much better receiver, to the top end of the AM band late on cold crisp winter nights in order to pull in the famous Wolfman Jack on XERF, across the border from Del Rio, Texas, in Ciudad Acuña. The Wolfman was a John R. type with an attitude.

It's a different accent. "Come on in, fellows."

Our scout leader has scheduled a visit with one of the ham radio operators in Princeton. Robert Emory lives a quarter mile from my parents' home. He's an imposing man, tall, stately, formally erect. He enunciates every syllable clearly, unlike the careless drawl of many locals. A few of his words sound like the old English that some still use on the eastern shore of Virginia. "Come on into the houuuse and ouuut of the damp air," he says at the door. We all troop in and go through the traditional living room, then down narrow stairs to the basement.

"Welcome to my station," Mr. Emory says, as he points to a gray metal chassis with multiple meters and a large off-on switch. "This is my transmitter. It's made by the Johnson Company in Minnesota. And this is my receiver." It's a large, impressive piece of equipment labeled SX-101. The switches make staccato metallic clicking sounds as the front panels come alive, and the equipment glows with a blue-gray aura in the dimly lit room. The atmosphere is electric, like being ushered into an inner sanctum in the Nautilus. He points to a large black cabinet, positioned on the floor behind the receiver and transmitter. "This is my amplifier," he continues in his precise manner. "Designed and built it myself. It's capable of a full kilowatt of power, a thousand watts, the legal maximum we amateur radio operators are allowed." The drone of electronic humming makes the atmosphere paranormal.

The amplifier stands at least six feet high. "Let's see what it can do," he says, reaching over and pushing a large red switch on the front of the black chassis. A deep groan commences, as if a subterranean electronic container is being filled. Something powerful stirs. Large meters spring to life. "We'll let the tubes warm up, and see if we can find someone to talk with."

By now my eyes are adjusting. Off to the side on another table, his workbench includes a soldering iron, voltmeter, and other technical-looking gadgets. It's clear that Mr. Emory is quite a radio man. He's also the manager of the local natural gas company, with no clear link between the radio hobby and his professional responsibilities. "That hum you boys hear is the power transformer for the amplifier," he continues. "It's a reassuring sound. Means all is well." The electronic throb adds to the seductive glow of the tubes, the cool dial lights on the meters, and the green lights on the amplifier.

He sits in his chair and pulls the desk microphone closer, then turns the main dial on the receiver. Crisp clear signals boom from the speaker. The signals are much stronger than I've ever heard from the radio stations on the little Emerson in my room.

"Calling CQ seventy-five meters." The cadence is slow, deliberate, and masculine. "This is W4JAV in Pikeville, Kentucky. Anyone around tonight?"

Mr. Emory is speaking into the microphone now. "W4JAV, this is W8GCZ, Whiskey Eight Golf Charlie Zulu calling. Over." He's called from his own station, right in front of my eyes. This is like AM radio except these ham operators have their own personal radio stations, along with a unique lingo. All of us are offered a turn at the microphone. It's clear the two men are enjoying the demonstration. "Don" over in Kentucky appears to know Mr. Emory, whom he calls Robert, and seems happy to show off his ham radio skills. It's strange that everyone goes by only their first name. But Mr. Emory assures us that's the norm.

"Hello, Don. My name is Jimmy. I'm a scout here in Troop Sixty-Six." In that basement room full of radio equipment, my Appalachian drawl sounds even more accented. I'm self-conscious and have to repeat my name.

It's magic . . . there's something very exciting about radio waves flying electronically and invisibly through the air. I'm hooked and want to be a radio man myself.

Our town consisted of four main residential areas, each one associated with an elementary school. One neighborhood lay in east Princeton, beyond the Thorn Street Bridge, separated by Brushy Creek. Another included the main housing sector to the south of Mercer Street, the heart of town and business sector.

The colored quarter was centered on High Street, which descriptively ran along a ridgeline, lending its name to the High Street Elementary School. The entire community, from educated (teachers, ministers and a few professionals were the aristocracy) to uneducated (domestics and laborers) lived here. I'd never been there. Where the colored areas abutted the white areas, things changed from all white to all black, from one alley to another with stark transition. Ironically, the minority area was located just beyond the nicest white residential area in Princeton in the oldest portion of town, where distinguished brick homes on leafy quiet streets housed the town's attorneys, physicians, and business owners. This peculiarity originated from time of the Civil War, when the two communities lived side by side, landed and non-landed.

That patrician area and other white residential areas on the north side of Mercer Street corresponded to Mercer Elementary School, a stately old building, located at the corner of Mercer Street, from whence it took its name, and Main Street. When Mom and Dad moved to Princeton, they bought a house on North Walker Street, in the Mercer School district.

Princeton High School has three social clubs. The sole boys' club is called Sigma Tau, and its members are mainly athletes and popular types. The jocks represent all three of the elementary residential areas, while the others are primarily from the Mercer School areas.

The single sheet, folded and stapled, is neatly handwritten with my name. I rip it open, keeping it low, in front of me, out of sight. A blue-inked typed mimeograph continues: "You are invited to attend a meeting for prospective members of the Sigma Tau social club. Come to a meeting in room 326 at 3:30 p.m. on Wednesday for additional information."

Wendie Johnston, by now solidly my best friend, and I are interested in Sigma Tau. So I hustle over to his locker, the now-smudged document in hand—actually hidden in my pants pocket, since it would be unseemly to flaunt that I am one of the chosen. Has he also gotten the same invitation?

He's smiling—that look—but retains the icy coolness he always displays. Wendie is tall and "cool" in the real, adult sense of the word. He's calm, reserved, assured. I'm more extemporaneous, trying harder on the surface to be popular. He's slender, a couple of inches taller than me, with fine, straight hair that's always combed in place, unless a gust of wind blows it around. His hair color matches his brown eyes. Wendie always wears slacks, what I call suit pants. I don't think he owns a pair of jeans.

"I see you got the letter as well. They must let just about anyone in these days." He says this with a demeanor that's warm in spite of the words. Translated: good for us both.

Time seems frozen until Wednesday. On that appointed day, the clock hands creep almost imperceptibly until classes end.

Finally, it's time. Wendie and I stand outside the room for a moment. I straighten my collar, take a deep breath, and open the door. Nearly 20 classmates are sitting around stiffly. The atmosphere is hushed. No one even whispers. A few class notes remain on the board—something about the annual coal output of the state. Jackson Taylor, well-known senior class president and starter on the basketball team, sits up in front with two others I don't recognize. After a minute or two he stands. He scans the room deliberately, seems to make eye contact with everyone, and begins with the confidence of an insider.

"Welcome, gentlemen. Congratulations. You're here because the Sigma Tau nominating committee has selected you as prospective members of our club. We think it's an honor and hope that, as you learn more about Sigma Tau, you'll feel that way as well. Our club represents things that are good about Princeton High School, and we're committed to maintaining the excellence of this school. Along the way, we'll give our members opportunities to serve, as well as to have some fellowship and fun." At that, he looks at one of his buddies, winks, and laughs a bit. "Service and fun. Key words." I recognize many of the people in the room from the Mercer School days. Donnie Davis is right in front of us. Taylor continues. I look at him with what I hope is proper respectful attention. "You'll need to memorize the Sigma Tau code of conduct and mission statement. You've got to know the entire Greek alphabet as well."

I glance at Wendie, next to me. This is really something. He keeps looking straight ahead.

"Ah, yes," Taylor continues, "There is the matter of the Sigma Tau paddle. All I can say now is that the paddle is a symbol of your dedication, since you'll have to do some woodworking and polishing to bring it up to fraternity standards. It will be part of the initiation exercise." A nervous murmur begins, then stops.

"Think about it, and if you want to proceed to become part of Sigma Tau, take a packet from the table." One of the Taylor's senior friends swivels in his chair and holds up the material. "It's all in the handout. Send in your application, along with the ten-dollar application fee, and you'll be issued all the material to learn, along with your paddle. That'll need to be smoothed out, painted, varnished, and completed before the final initiation and ceremony. That's it, gentlemen. Good luck and congratulations. I must leave now for a meeting." With a patrician flourish, he walks to the door of the classroom and leaves. The room remains silent until the door closes and then erupts in nervous conversation as we congratulate ourselves on our new honor and anticipated good fortune.

For weeks, every night is a late evening memorizing the information and working on the paddle. Sanding the edges to a nice rounded finish and making the surfaces glassy smooth is fun. Wendie doesn't seem to be taking it as seriously as I am.

The Sigma Tau initiation turned out to be a mostly harmless affair. We presented our "Greek" paddles, parroted the mission statement, and endured a little stupidity at an initiation party at the president's parents' prominent home just outside town on the site of their large Christmas tree farm. The club primarily seemed to exist to revel in the fact that it existed.

The girls had two social clubs: Sub Debs and Su Wans. Neither of them used Greek letters, and no one I knew could explain what "Su Wan" meant. Both of them were quite active, much more active than Sigma Tau, which wasn't hard. The Sub Debs and Su Wans waged a spirited competition for the attention of PHS's socially minded young women. The Sub Debs consisted mainly of the former Mercer School group, and the Su Wans included primarily, but not exclusively, the other white neighborhoods. Their prospective new members endured public harassment such as coming to school in hair curlers and out-of-date dresses. Apparently these were social badges of honor, including the initiates carrying books for the juniors and seniors. Wannabees gritted their teeth and pretended to ignore the anointed ones going through the process.

There usually was a dance at the Memorial Building after the Tigers' home football games, and the girls' two social clubs alternated sponsorship and decorating duties. The tradition at PHS dances included live bands, and the top choice was a group called the Blue Aces, legends in our area. In their twenties and thirties, the Blue Aces wore fancy brocaded jackets and pressed black slacks. They looked sharp. They *were* sharp. They not only knew the usual top-forty hits, but also the soul music and R & B on the Nashville station. There were six members: singer, lead guitar, keyboard, bass guitar, drummer, plus a sax player to provide the "horn" sound. The Blue Aces were the real deal and cut quite a picture with their fancy outfits and choreographed, synchronized movements: side, front, and back steps to the music.

The Memorial Building was an architectural jewel, one of those wonderful historic statements featuring a large rotunda that was open from the ground floor all the way up to the domed ceiling above the second floor. The formal entryway transitioned into symmetrical semicircular stairways rising dramatically up to the second floor, which consisted of a substantial open space around the staircase, the dance floor itself, and bathrooms on the opposite side of the stairs. The opening to the stairway at the top gave the room a grand sense of proportion, a sweeping aura for those inclined to be swept away by sweeping auras. People could walk outside the dance floor and stand around the banisters at the top, able to see and be seen. At one end of the dance floor was a stage, a raised section perfect for bands.

The protocol for these dances required you to buy a ticket from the Ma and Pa Club. Ensconced at a long table near the front door, the Ma and Pa folks would sell you one for a dollar. The admission requirements consisted of the payment of the dollar, being sober (or apparently so), and being white. At that time, there were only two racial classifications, as no Asians or Hispanics lived in Princeton. You were either white or colored.

In general, the white populations were descendants from the westward migration of the early 1850's into the Appalachians. So with the two broad racial selection categories, you could get into the dance if you paid your dollar, and you were a white person—or more accurately, not "colored." Sometimes the dollar was negotiable.

The team actually won that night, beating Hinton. Spirits were high, and it was a pleasant, dry evening. The sounds from the music carried all the way out to Courthouse Square, and Wendie and I could hear the beat as we neared the building.

I pay my dollar, walk up the steps drenched in hormones and adrenalin, and stand in the wide entranceway to the dance floor. The Su Wans, sponsors of tonight's dance, have fashioned a classic high school dance scene: crepe paper bunting and huge "Go Tigers" posters in blue and white all around the second floor. Many of our new high school classmates are milling around, and a few couples are dancing already. The players haven't arrived yet from the football field, so some of the studs are missing.

"You know, it floors me that some people can dance right away," I mention to Wendie.

"My friend, an adult beverage would help. But certainly that won't be available from the Su Wans," he comments dryly. "You might find it practical to have a little bourbon in a thin flask for such occasions."

"And of course you thought ahead for just such an occasion?"

"Unfortunately, not tonight," he says. This sort of talk is mostly bravado, but he's starting to experiment.

Wendie isn't much of a dancer, but he is a smooth talker and the girls seem to consider him handsome. He has one habit I can't stand: smoking—something that never interested me at all since Daddy puts out his cigarettes in his plate after meals, with the butt making a dying hiss in gravy. That, as well as the stench, leaves me completely cold on what appears to be a dirty and stupid habit.

The Blue Aces nail a terrific cover of "In the Still of the Night." More couples now are dancing, mostly juniors and seniors already going steady. The sophomore boys congregate in several groups at the dance, while the sophomore girls do the same in their separate clusters.

The football players are coming in now. Emerging from the staircase in small packs or, in the case of the star upperclassmen, accompanied by a cute girl, they meld into the crowd with pats on the back, handshakes, and other means of recognizing conquering heroes. A few of the girls dance among themselves. But most remain in their small nervous cliques casting furtive glances over at us, in our own separate anxious little groupings, matching their glimpses with guarded furtivity—if that's a word—of our own.

Several of the guys have been talking about a band they've formed. Buddy Lewis is a drummer in the high school band and lives and breaths music. He's a good dancer and mixes easily at social events. Buddy's nature is goofy, however you just can't help but like him. In addition, there's Carlton Gaskins, a blond James Dean look-alike with the unusual nickname of Slate. But who could call a James Dean type "Carlton?" Slate Gaskins is an end on the football team who taught himself to play the guitar. He and Buddy started jamming together at Buddy's house. After a while the word got around, and Lanny Woods, another self-taught musician, joined them. Lannie also is on the football team, an undersized, gritty little lineman who's a very good piano player. Unlike Buddy, the lovable wacky one, and leading-man type Slate, Lannie sports a perpetual dour appearance.

The three of them are headed our way. With Buddy, as always, it's all about the music. "Ain't them Blue Aces hot or what?" he says, with minor amounts vocal chords and major portions excited breath. "Jimmy, you know Slate Gaskins and Lannie Woods?"

"Sure." I leave out the Sigma Tau association. "Hi, guys. Good game." Slate played quite a bit, even though he is a sophomore. He caught several passes and made a crucial tackle near the end of the game to seal the win.

"Good defensive stop there at the end," Wendie says. With his ambition to be a sports journalist, he views the games differently than I do. For me it's root, root, root for the home team, for God and

Country—something along those lines. Wendie already looks at the games, which he calls "contests," as a strategic matter, and he's able to separate the strategy and the outcome from my straightforward and simple desire for the Princeton Tigers to win just because we're in Princeton. It *is* my school.

Lannie is quiet. He never says much at school, and tonight is no different. The demeanor matches his tight dark pants, pegged at the bottom, and his black shirt. As a 140 pound sophomore tackle, he hadn't played at all. It probably was for the best.

"You-all know we've started a band?" Buddy asks.

It's hard to hear. The Blue Aces are grooving, and "Mustang Sally" is the groove at the moment. "A band?" I ask.

"Yeah. We need a bass player. Either of you play bass guitar?"

"Yeah, sure. Just like that guy there," I say, motioning to the Aces' bass player.

"Jimmy's talent can be measured in thimblefuls, gentlemen," Wendie says. "But he can learn. Got a decade?"

Slate looked over at the band. "That's the stuff, all right," he said. "That's the stuff."

By the summer of 1958, the band started to take shape. Buddy, Slate, and Lannie recruited Ronald Blake as the bassist. Ronald was a class behind them. The word around was that he could play. As with many bass guitarists, he had a quiet personality. In fact, not only did he not talk a lot, he rarely ever changed his expression. His expression was so staid that he started being called "Peppy," a nickname that stuck with him his whole life. With the four main instruments in place and a lead guitar player who looked like a movie star, the band now called themselves the Roadsters. Over the summer, I started spending quite a bit of time with them as they practiced.

There was a problem, though. No one was an outstanding singer. Slate wowed the girls, and he could sing O.K. but not great—certainly not as great as he looked on stage. Both Buddy and Lannie did certain songs. But it became more and more clear that the band lacked a real singer, a true front man. At that point, Arcie Peterson's name came up.

"What about Arcie?" Slate said after a particularly bland session.

"Who?" Lannie mumbled through one of his scowls.

"He's one of the colored kids."

"Arcie Peterson," Buddy interjected. "He's in the band with me. Really good."

"He's in two of my classes. Nice guy," I added.

Slate continued. "I hear he can sing . . . really sing. Plays several instruments, too."

"Well, we've gotta do something," Buddy said. "All of us are doing O.K. with a few songs. But to be honest, we need some help."

"That's why I brought it up," Slate said. "Anyone got a problem with a colored kid?"

Surprisingly, Peppy spoke first. "Not me."

The others nodded. Decision made. Slate got the recruiting assignment.

He caught up with Arcie and me after our English class. "Are you sure?" Arcie asked. With Slate's friendly nod, they shook hands and the agreement was set.

Arcie proved to be a good fit. He was a dashing figure who could belt out the popular songs of the day, and he played every instrument in the band. His personality fit in well, and he was serious about both practicing and performing, as he had long-term plans for a music career.

The band usually practiced at Buddy's house. By now, my role had emerged as an official non-member member of the band who didn't play or sing, but was the cheerleader and suggested songs from an "expert" listening level of rock and roll and R & B on AM radio. I also offered one more advantage: I'd gotten my driver's license in the spring and was allowed to drive Mom's old Chevrolet. Since Arcie had no access to a car, I would drive him to and from practices.

For me, it was an easy summer: mowing lawns, goofing off, listening to great rock and roll, and hanging out with the band and Wendie Johnston.

Life was good.

Chapter 6

AFTER THE OUTING with the scout troop to Mr. Emory's incredible ham radio station in his basement, listening to shortwave broadcasts on the Magnavox AM-FM-Shortwave receiver in our living room became a fascinating new thing to explore. The Magnavox also had a record player, but I can't remember my parents ever playing a single record on it. All this electronic wonderment was in a massive wooden cabinet, which encased a large speaker. The knobs were heavy knurled plastic. They looked expensive, had heft. The three shortwave bands were shown on a wide linear scale, running from left to right. The radio portion and huge speaker produced wonderful full-bodied sounds. With only the unit's built-in antenna, the big international shortwave stations rolled in day and night with resonant voices and music.

Radio Moscow's stilted programming sounded robotic on their English broadcasts. But "Moscow Mailbag" departed from this unconvincing style. "This is Valery Kamarakov. It's nice to have you along on our North American transmission tonight. It's cool and dreary here in Moscow, at plus ten degrees. That's fifty on the Fahrenheit scale, and a chill is in the damp air this evening. Perhaps autumn will be early this year. It makes me wish I were making this broadcast from Havana, so I could warm up!" That seemed believable. Good English, too.

"Here's a letter from Mr. Charles Albright of Milwaukee, in the U.S. state of Wisconsin. Charles asks where I live and how my home compares with the average Russian's, and the average American's. Now that's a good question, so let me jump right in. My job here with Radio Moscow requires that I live in Moscow, so first of all, that means I live in a very large city, the largest in the Soviet Union. Most people here live in flats—or apartments as you Americans call them. Mine is on the fourth floor of a fairly average apartment building in the southwestern part of Moscow. It's too far to walk to the studios, and I don't own a car yet—maybe someday. But the public buses are good, and our subway is clean and reliable so I usually take the Metro to work. My flat is nice, about one hundred square meters. Oh yes. That's about a thousand square feet in your English measurement system. My wife and I have a kitchen, two bedrooms, a small dining area, and a small living room where we have a television and a phonograph player. It's probably about the same as Americans have if they live in a large city, like New York or Chicago. Russians who live in smaller towns or in the country on farms obviously have a different housing pattern, with land more available. But, all in all, I would think there are far more similarities than differences with Americans. One thing though—you Americans have many more cars than we Russians do. Your automotive industry developed more rapidly than ours has, and at this point cars still are quite expensive here. I will say, however, that our public transportation system in the Soviet Union is very good."

This guy sounded normal, not like their usual propaganda heads. He didn't seem to be parroting the party line like some of the crap from over there.

When the conditions were good, signals rolled in from Radio France, the BBC in London, and of course the Voice of America. Occasionally, I could pick up English-language programs from other broadcasters like Radio Bulgaria and Radio Cairo. The whole thing was mesmerizing.

Listening to the foreign broadcasters complemented my emerging interest in ham radio. Mom and Dad had mentioned my interest to Mr. Emory at church, and he gave me a copy of the License Manual Study Guide for hams. Other than scouting, it was the only thing I pursued with any real vigor, other than fitting in at school. Mr. Emory, much older, stern and formal, yet somehow clearly supportive, became my mentor and technical advisor for the Novice license.

"I've memorized everything in the manual," I tell Mr. Emory. "I think I'll do well if the test's like the questions here. But if it asks anything different from how the questions are laid out in the book . . . how electrical circuits really work . . . or if I have to interpret things . . . or if they make changes to the circuits and ask me to correct the problem . . . well, I'm sunk."

He furrows his brow, knowing I have no fundamental concept of electronics. "Well, Jimmy," he says, "you'll have no trouble with the rules and regulations, and overall I think you'll do just fine."

"I just want to get on the air," I say, looking down at the floor. "For me, it isn't about the electronics, the circuitry. It's about making contacts."

The Novice test must be administered by a licensed ham operator who has a "full capability" license, called a General Class license. Mr. Emory's call letters indicate he has this. I don't know it at the time, but he also has a First Class FCC Radiotelephone license and actually serves as the Chief Engineer at WLOH. He had written to the Federal Communications Commission and has all the paperwork for my exam.

On the evening of my exam, I'm absolutely tingling with excitement and adrenalin as I walk up Park Avenue, and then on to the top of the hill to his house. One of his antennas is visible from the street below, silhouetted against the sky in the fading light.

An old floor lamp creates a bright spot in the basement where he has a work-space laid out on a table next to his radio room. My hands quiver a bit as I open the test to the first page. It looks just like the license manual I've memorized until the pages are worn and ragged. All the questions about rules and regulations are a snap. They're multiple-choices, and I don't have to guess at a single one. Mr. Emory is sitting across the room reading the *Bluefield Daily Telegraph*, glancing over at me from time to time. I fill in these pages quickly, but the next section deals with electrical circuitry. That's going to be my downfall if it's not more or less exactly like the questions in the license manual. It's almost the same word for word! I feel like jumping up and cheering, but that wouldn't be called for, that's for sure. I read and reread the questions slowly . . . every one of them seems to be exactly the way the question was written in the study guide. I guess on only two questions. And on those, I have it down to one of two possibilities. So I look the whole thing over one last time, lay down my pencil with a bit of poorly concealed bravado, and look up. He lowers his newspaper.

"You finished, Jimmy?"

"I think so."

"Well, that was rather quick," he continues. "How did it go?"

"It was pretty much down the line like the license manual," I say. "Or I think it was."

"Yes, it was," he confirms. "Let me grade it. If you scored seventy or higher, we can move on to the code test."

"Grade it? Right here?" I stammer.

"That's right. Let me see. The answer key's right here somewhere." He walks into the radio room and picks up another envelope. "All right," he says, more relaxed than I've ever seen him. For the next few minutes, he reads over my answers, checking them off as correct. In fact, I miss only two: one is a silly error on a question I knew by heart, and the other is one of the two I had guessed on from the portion on electrical circuits. He puts the exam down with a flourish, the paperwork making a plopping sound as it hits the tabletop. "Well, Jimmy." He smiles broadly for the first time since I've been around him. "You not only passed your written Novice test, but you did it with a ninety-six percent score! Only two misses. Very good indeed."

The studying paid off. All that memorizing.

"That's great news. Thank you for the help." It isn't original, but it's the truth and it's from my heart.

"Hold your horses for a little while longer," he says. "There's still the Morse code test."

The Morse code test . . . that's going to be the easiest part of the test for me. We both know that. The few times he'd asked me to copy some code he sent, it was no problem.

The requirement for the Novice level is very slow, only five words per minute. In fact it takes forever to get your point across, and then to receive the other person's response. My code speed already is like a white-water stream compared to the drip-drip-drip of copying the code at five words per minute. Mr. Emory goes into the radio room, which he and every other ham call a shack, no matter if it *is* a shack or a fancy room full of the latest goodies. "Come on in here. Let's see if you're able to copy as well as you did last week or if suddenly you've forgotten what you knew." He lets out a chuckle. I stand up, practically float around the table into his shack, and sit down beside him.

"Over here, another pencil and paper," he says, motioning to a sheet of paper and sharpened pencil on the desktop. "Anytime you're ready." He rests his hand on the shiny brass telegraph key.

Feeling great relief after acing the written test, I confidently sit down, pick up the pencil, and take a deep breath. "All set."

He begins to send. For a second or two, everything is a jumble of sounds. My mind still is focused on the printed exam questions. Finally the slow sounds begin to have a clear form.

"The amateur radio operator must use good operating practice at all times." The code now is crisp. It translates in my head and comes out through my hand and the pencil like a stream of magic. Every letter is a crystal clear note of precision. He sends a final sentence and then has me read off my "copy."

"Perfect," he says. "Now, one last thing and you'll pass with flying colors." He pushes the telegraph key over to me. "Go to the end of what you've copied and send it back to me. In reverse order."

"Backward?"

"That's right. You wrote it all down. Just send it back to me in reverse order."

Right away, the trickiest part comes immediately. He ended his sending with a period! I'm very confident about all the letters and numbers, but the punctuation marks aren't used as often, and for some reason I blank out on what a period is in Morse code. I sit there staring at the telegraph key. It's a military surplus version, with the letters J-38 stamped clearly on the brass base section.

"Is there a problem?" Mr. Emory asks.

"No sir," I say. But all I can think of is the brass, which is polished. Then something in my mind goes *dit dah dit dah dit dah*, the code for a period in punctuation. Clear as a bell, just like that. I send the whole thing back, at least twice as fast as the required speed. The code flows out of my head, little soldiers marching out tappity-tap one after another.

"My goodness," he says. "That's plenty fast enough. You have nice spacing. Con-gratulations, young man. You passed your test with room to spare."

We walk up the narrow stairs into the hallway, past his wife who is reading in their quiet living room, and out onto the porch.

"I'll mail in your test paperwork first thing tomorrow. You're the first person around here to apply for a Novice in a while, so I'm not sure how long it will take to get your new ticket." A "ticket" is what hams call their license, for some reason.

"Thank you, sir. Thank you so much," I say, stepping off the porch steps into the amazing crispness of the evening.

After taking the Novice exam for the initial ham radio test, I waited and waited to get my license. Even though Mr. Emory had reviewed the results and assured me I'd passed with flying colors—nothing was official until the Federal Communications Commission said it was. The Feds! Can you believe that?

The actual letter arrived six long weeks later, on a Saturday. Mom brought in the mail and was leafing through the letters and bills when her expression suddenly changed. "Jimmy, this just might be that letter you were looking for!"

It was small—smaller than any normal-sized envelope. I was almost afraid to look at it. The letter had no regular three-cent stamp. In its place was an official looking designation stating "Federal Communications Commission, Official Business Only." My hands were unsteady as I opened the envelope and read my new call letters: KN8JPV. The "N" indicated the Novice, or entry-level, license. That would allow me to get on the air using Morse code, not voice, and talk to real amateur radio operators all over—at least as far as my transmitter and antenna would send a signal.

Chapter 7

EVERYONE'S BACK. IT'S the first week of our junior year and we're standing in front of the drugstore as a thunderous muffler exhaust, the "glass pack" sound, ricochets off the stone buildings on Mercer Street. A 1948 Mercury convertible pulls up in front. Mack Andrews guns it before turning off the engine. He leaves the radio on WKOY in Bluefield. "I had a girl. Donna was her name, dah dah dah daaah. Since I met her, I've never been the same."

Mack's always had a job working for his dad, the general manager of a construction company. But a buck an hour is good money. "I know it's not fancy to dig ditches and foundations," he says, "but I've always got spending money and can fill the car with premium gas." At thirty cents a gallon, that's a luxury. He slides casually over to the passenger side, his black DA glistening with Brylcreem. "Huh? Huh? Wha'da you think?" he asks, not expecting a response.

"Very cool." Eddie Jones takes the bait. Up to this point, Eddie is the only other one in the group who's bought his own car. "Where'd you get the work done?" Mack worked hard for some time to fix up the old Mercury. The original engine was in bad shape, and the faded blue paint was a goner.

"Tony Martin did the body work," Mack says, opening the door. "Over at his shop. I helped sand off the old paint job. Also buffed off the first two coats." A crowd now has gathered. The original pin-holed chrome and other battered ornaments, including the hood emblem, are gone. The car exudes a glossy-smooth midnight-purple finish. "Check out the hood. Totally shaved," he continues, running his hand over where the Mercury hood emblem would have been. "Smooth as silk. Pretty cool, huh?"

"The motor's a two hundred cubic inch V8 we found. Guy rebuilds the things. Lives out on the Oakvale Road. He has a little shop there. Performs magic with motors: new rings, oversized bore, four-barrel carb." With theatrical flourish, he walks around to the rear of the car. "And the rear end!" The Merc's bumper is noticeably lower than the front. "Chopped the sucker four inches." Leaning over, Mack points to two masculine exhaust pipes protruding out the rear—strapping things, practically shouting "don't mess with me." He glances around. Everyone is listening. "And great new glass packs. Listen to this!"

With that, he moseys back to the front, slides in behind the steering wheel, and starts the engine. It fires immediately and he gooses it. The new mufflers flat-out roar, flaring a full-throated sound that reverberates off the storefronts until people look in our direction. Satisfied, he backs off the gas, and the exhaust gurgles back into a pleasant idling rumble.

"You better watch it in that car. Carlotti'll get you," someone said. This comment coincided with the transfer of State Police Sergeant Tony Carlotti from northern West Virginia to the Princeton district. According to the *Daily Telegraph*, he's leading a campaign against prostitution and organized gambling crime activity over at Keystone. Carlotti's tough-guy capability already made the rounds when he single-handedly hauled in an entire family of white trash who ran an armed still operation over near Bramwell. The picture in the newspaper showed him holding a shotgun, wearing reflective sunglasses, looking like those tough southern chain gang prison guards in gritty movies.

In contrast, Cool Eddie Jones drives a flat black, totally stock '50 Ford. To his credit, it's a convertible, although the paint's faded and the engine is the original in-line six. Eddie's nickname is "Cool" because he is so non-cool. He wears his light brown hair in a severe flattop two inches high, like a row of hair sticks. Some guys can wear a flattop and look virile and tough, like Lannie Woods. Eddie looks like a choirboy. He's smart, a little withdrawn, and easy to be around. Eddie is another guy who's always had a job, and the car is one of the fruits of his labors.

Unlike Mack's grand entrances, Eddie's procedure at the drugstore is to play a game of Chicken with the meter maid who putters up and down Mercer Street checking the parking meters for expired time flags. "I don't see any good reason to give the City of Princeton my hard-earned money if I don't have to," he says. A risk taker, he sits in the end stool and maintains a constant vigil for the lady cop.

My car . . . actually Mom's car . . . is quite different, an older light-green 1950 Chevrolet, a six-cylinder four-door sedan with a straight-drive transmission on the steering column. We always were a General Motors family. The radio is an AM-only version like virtually all car radios. The Delco vacuum-tube model picks up WKOY in the day and WLS clearly at night. The Chevy has pretty fair get-up-and-go, too. But what it has in terms of practicality and dependability are offset by definite deficiencies in sex appeal, especially compared with Mack's hopped-up Merc. Even Cool Eddie Jones' old Ford convertible is spiffier. Mom and I name the faded green machine "The Bomb" to burnish its image.

Since Daddy is Sales Manager at Gibson's Motors, he has a new customer demonstrator model for his personal use, usually a top-of-the-line Buick sedan. "Large Buicks are comfortable, fine automobiles," he says. He favors the latest model Roadmaster, and never calls a car a car, always an automobile.

Wendie has a new job working for the *Bluefield Telegraph*'s Princeton office as a sportswriter and general go-fer, and although he keeps himself in cigarettes, he can't afford a car of his own. At least not yet. His dad died several years ago, and Wendie's mother works hard to keep the family going.

"I'm stuck with the family Chrysler," he says. "I like their products, so it ain't all that bad." Wendie uses perfect, even retro-formal English with one exception: He'll use "ain't" as an exclamation point to prove he's a with-it type of guy.

Chapter 8

FOOTBALL SEASON OPENS with optimism. For one thing, the Tigers have several promising players returning, including Donnie Davis and his cousin Henry Davis, who are back as halfback and quarterback, respectively. In addition, several huge linemen from Stumpy Bottom anchor the line. Since I realize I'd be football fodder and I'm never going to be able to make Princeton's high-powered basketball team, I decide to talk with Coach Ebert about being a football team manager. In fact, Wendie and I discuss it and decide to approach him as a package deal. With Wendie's desire to get into sports journalism, other than being out there on the field, being on the sidelines and in the clubhouse is the next best thing.

Just before our appointment at Coach Ebert's office, waiting nervously for the door to open, we're surprised when Perry Solomon comes out. They shake hands and the coach says, "I'll look forward to you helping out, Solomon. Welcome to Tiger football."

With that, Coach Ebert turns his attention to us. "Good afternoon, gentlemen. You fellows here to see me?"

"May we speak with you about helping out as managers?"

John L. Ebert is not renowned for the winningest football teams, but he *is* noted for his insistence on proper grammar in his English and literature classes. He turns to Wendie and answers. "You may indeed, and it's nice to hear you express yourself so well. Come on in, both of you." He leads the way into his cramped office, motioning to the two small metal seats, and drops heavily into the chair behind his desk. Rows of English literature books, as well as photos of former teams, line the shelves and walls. Nowhere is any sign of a league championship trophy.

With that compliment in hand, Wendie continues. "Coach, we're interested in helping out the team by working as managers." He looks over at me. "Both of us."

"We do need two more from the junior class," the coach says. "We take three from the junior and three from the senior class, and we only take on new people as juniors. As you saw, Perry Solomon was just here. He'll be one of the juniors. All three of the fellows who helped out last year are going to continue as seniors. So I have two spots left. It's a lot of work, but you would be right in the thick of things."

Inside the action! He couldn't have said anything more enticing. I could sense Wendie's excitement without ever looking his way.

Coach runs through all the requirements: Be there before practice starts and stay after it's over; lay out the clean jerseys and pants before practice; after practice, sort the containers with all the dirty and sweaty clothes so they can be picked up by a local laundry; and line the field before practices with powdered lime using a spreader. Various salves and balms must be on hand to alleviate bruises, scratches, or worse. One called analgesic balm is used as a general purpose remedy for anything short of a broken bone, and smells up a room so badly that everyone's sinuses get cleared out. Finally, we'd be go-fers for anything the coaches needed or forgot.

Coach Ebert runs through the entire drill. He pauses, gives us a serious look, and leans back in his chair. "Have I scared you away by now?"

I look over at Wendie. He's on a mission.

"It's a deal, if you'll take us both," Wendie says.

"Fine," the coach says, nodding. He seems pleased. I'm a little numb. *What did we just do?* "That settles it. You two plus Solomon are the three juniors for the season. I have some others looking to talk with me about this, but you gentlemen fill the bill." He stands up. Taking his cue, we do the same. "Check out the schedule, and be at the field thirty minutes early. You'll get all the details you need from Ronny Edwards, one of the seniors. Thanks. Let's have a good season." We shake hands.

It all happens so fast! Once we're out in the hall and some distance from Coach Ebert's office, I confess to some second thoughts. "It sounds like a lot of work."

"No sweat," Wendie says. He's set. "Just think of all the inside looks we're going to get about how the team is doing."

"You just see this as a story for the paper."

"I'll learn more about high school football this way than if I try to be a hundred-and-fifty-pound punching bag for some of those gargantuans."

So it begins. Every day after school we go out to the football field and straight into the cinderblock dressing room, located behind one of the end zones. No more cherry Cokes and hot cars down on Mercer Street. Wendie, Perry, and I sort jockstraps and other articles of clothing, learn the names of various balms and gels, and figure out how to work with Ace bandages as well as assorted other items formerly unknown to me. I become a good field liner. Practices go on daily. The team begins to take shape, as does our little group of six managers.

The game with Big Creek is our first one of the season—and a home game at that. A tough opponent at any time, Big Creek is a rural consolidated school in McDowell County that includes all the kids from the rough-and-tumble coal camps, farms, and tiny towns outside Welch, the county seat. Many of those guys live a rugged life and consider the Princeton game a chance to beat up on some soft city kids, which they usually do. The Owls are one of the toughest southern West Virginia high school football teams and usually grind down the Tigers before the night is over. But the season is young, it's a home game for us, and, hey, we have the guys from Stumpy Bottom.

The tension before the game is palpable. The players sit silently at their lockers, put on their pads, and get dressed in the brand-spanking-new uniforms. Finally, the team troops out to the field for pre-game stretches and walk-through practice plays. A small number of Big Creek fans have arrived early. They rise as one and hoist a sign that says "Proud of the Owls" in huge letters when their team comes out. After the on-field workout, Coach Ebert and the other coaches lead the team back into the dressing area, and I get to hear my first "coach's talk." Coach Ebert is not a shouter. He's an elegant-looking man, every hair always in place, well dressed. He seems confident and cool as he calmly states that the team is prepared, has the talent, and can defeat (that is his word, "defeat," not "beat" or "whip their asses" or whatever) Big Creek. He goes on to say the first game is an opportunity to demonstrate what the team has learned, and that we can win if we play "Tiger football." Everyone starts hollering and does a massive "touch the coach's hand." It's hard for us managers to get anywhere close to the magic center of this living, breathing, symbolic heart. But we press forward on the outer fringe and give it our best. The smell of sweat and analgesic balm permeates the mass of bodies.

The game starts well. We kick off, and the Owls don't make a first down. They punt. Our guys make two first downs, a quarterback keeper on an option by Henry Davis for one and a pass to Slate Gaskins, playing end, for the other. At that point the Big Creek coach calls a time-out. This is our big managerial opening and we hustle out towels and water. I'm all pumped up as we run onto the field. The center crown is much higher than the sidelines, two feet higher at least. The lights out here are brighter than on the sidelines, much brighter. The players are psyched. "We can take these guys," says Donnie. Another guy who has trouble putting five consecutive words together shouts, "Kick the shit out of 'em" over and over.

Midway through the first quarter, the stage is set. The Princeton Tigers are on the way to winning number one. However, someone fails to tell the other team. The next play, Donnie is tackled hard and fumbles. Big Creek goes on to score—they're up 7-0 with the point after. By the end of the half, it's 17-0, and they pull away to win 38-10.

As the junior managers, we're the last ones out of the dressing room, other than the coaches, since the seniors make us get the dirty uniforms ready for laundry pickup.

After the first home game, there's a Sadie Hawkins dance at the Memorial Building. At this point, Margie Rey Howland has entered the picture—Margie Rey, my first girlfriend. We're both juniors and have dated, sort of, since the school year began. She's cute and petite, no more than five feet tall, with a vivacious personality and a small but trim hourglass figure. Talking with her is easy. She seems to be interested in what I say and laughs a lot. She's a good dancer, a good student, and is involved in tons of school activities.

She's also out of town that weekend. "We'll be away visiting Aunt Martha in Huntington," she'd told me. "You be good because my spies will be watching."

After Wendie, Perry, and I finally get away from the locker room, I drive to the Memorial Building. We hear the bass as soon as I park The Bomb—those low-frequency notes could drive the worms right up out of the ground! The 50-degree weather is nice, usual for an early fall evening at 2,600-foot elevation.

"With Margie Rey away, the cat can play! Footloose and fancy-free. All that nonsense," Wendie offers with a smile.

Wendie isn't much of a dancer, although he enjoys the scene. He can slow dance, but he never learned the jitterbug or other fast dances. His manner of speech, using proper English with sly nuances, reflects his interest in writing as a future endeavor. In fact, his part-time position with the *Bluefield Daily Telegraph* has been expanded to cover football games for nearby Concord College on Saturdays. His experience "in the club-house," as he expresses it, is paying off.

"Is the man about to be unleashed upon the unwary damsels of the town?"

"Cute, Wendie, very cute. She said she'd have spies out everywhere. Besides that, I like her."

"Pity you. So many interesting fish in the sea." He shivers over his raised collar as we walk into the building, pass inspection by the Mas and Pas, pay our dollar, feel the pleasant warmth, and head up the stairs. The Sub Debs have decorated the building tonight, as part of their competition with the Su Wans.

Perry gravitates over to sit with Lawrence Kiefer and some of the chess club types and Jewish boys sitting on metal folding chairs positioned around the edge of the dance floor. "Hey, Borinsk!" I shout over the music at Lawrence, whose uncle is named Irving Borinsky. The family owns a high-end ladies' store in town.

The Aces segue into "At the Hop," a nice fast one. Effie Thompson, a girl from our class, walks over and asks me to dance. "Sadie Hawkins night," she says as she reaches for my hand.

"Nice going, Champ," Wendie comments.

Effie shoots him a nasty look as we move onto the floor. It's easy to feel the music, and when the song ends, she makes it clear she'd like to continue dancing. The band is good at moving quickly from one song to the next, so they minimize the awkward "stand around and think about it" time.

"Good song," I shout. Rock and roll is fun, but not great for making conversation. Effie is a good dancer, voluptuously attractive, a girl already in a woman's body. She lives over in Stumpy Bottom. Has a "forbidden fruit" reputation. Goes out with rough guys.

When the song ends, the Aces go right into a slow one, "Donna" by Richie Valens, one of the most popular songs of the year. Effie never lets go of my hand even the slightest and we begin to waltz. We start politely and a bit stiffly, keeping time to the music. She gently leans closer, and I reciprocate. Her cheek touches mine. I can sense the firmness of her breasts. Surely Margie Rey's spies will see us now.

Effie's fun to be around. Too much fun. I thank her and walk back to where Wendie is standing. Wendie makes a crack about the "little encounter," as he puts it.

As the evening nears its end, Perry walks back over. "How about a ride home? Lawrence and I don't have any wheels and it's chilly out there." Perry lives near me and Lawrence is in the Mercer area. It's easy.

"Button up lads. There's going to be frost on the pumpkins," says Wendie. The temperature is headed into the 40's.

The four of us head outside into the brisk air, over to The Bomb. "Take a look at the stars, guys," someone says. "It doesn't get much better than this." Perry and Lawrence get into the rear seat, and Wendie takes his usual seat in front.

"I'm hungry," I mention. "Anyone care to run up to Mooney's and see what's up?"

"Let's do it," says Wendie. A glance in the rearview mirror confirms the decision as I pull away from the parking lot. We pass the large hand-lettered "Go Tigers," and "Beat Big Creek" signs on the outside of the Memorial Building and can hear the Blue Aces wrapping up the last song as the lights come on upstairs.

From Courthouse Square, we pass by Mills Market and Gibson's Motors, and The Bomb makes a slight groan on the steep hill up to the drive-in. There's no doubt that Mooney's has the best hot dogs in the entire known world. The bun is steamed just right and the hot wiener is encased in steaming chili. Chilled coleslaw and minced onion are added in just the right proportions, and the whole thing comes out wrapped in thin waxed paper, warm to the touch. The combination provides a layered taste and temperature experience that has made Mooney's hot dogs the best-known teen food around.

Everyone is parked facing inward, toward the bright lights. Everyone except Mack Andrews and the purple-black customized 1948 Mercury, which is inside the ring, facing outward like an ebony panther in the lights.

"Jimmy, it's about time you got here along with your puke-green car," Mack hollers with a big grin on his face. "Oh my Lord. You've got Wendie and the guys. Too bad. I'd hoped you'd be sporting a babe since the word's out that Margie Rey is out of town." Mack can torture you but, at the same time his soft lilt and friendly grin make it good-natured.

"At least I know how to park a car."

"You have a point there. But with a beaut like this, you gotta be seen in the lights!" With that nugget of philosophy, he returns to his conversation with his girlfriend, Annie.

We're all hungry. Good healthy social tension like a dance will do that. After several rounds of hot dogs and Cokes, everyone's satisfied. We collectively tip the carhop 50 cents and I back out, squeezing between the closely packed cars.

"Let's take one quick run through town and then call it a night." Positive murmurs from my three passengers serve as approvals. We turn left and head back down the hill into town, displayed below in an orderly grid of lights.

Downtown cruising involves making loops on Mercer Street with the Court House circle at one end and the Thorn Street Bridge at the other. Cruisers repeat this as many times as it takes in order to see and be seen, until traffic grinds to a complete halt, or until they run out of time or gas. This procedure infuriates the local townspeople as well as the travelers on Route 460, the main link between Roanoke and Bluefield. Traffic is a hodgepodge of various comers and goers, heavy coal trucks, out-of-state cars, locals, and cruisers at certain times. Vibrant retail stores line both sides of the street.

The gas tank gauge catches my eye. Almost a quarter. That should be plenty.

"Wendie, turn on the radio. Get something good."

The dial lights come on immediately, but it takes 30 seconds or so to warm up. Harry Gentry's nightly call-in show is doing commercials on WLOH. We want music *now*. Chicago booms in at night. "Hit the middle button. That's WLS."

Dick Biondi's machine-gun tenor voice tattoos us with his fast northern DJ speech pattern. "Another back-to-back daily double on Channel Eighty-Nine!" He begins with Ricky Nelson's "Poor Little Fool." With WLS turned up loud, and sated with Mooney's best, we drive down Mercer Street feeling good about things in the world on a Friday night, even if the Tigers did lose. The dance, hot dogs, and companionship are "pretty fine," to use Wendie-speak. As we wait for a light to change, a car pulls to within inches.

"Wonder who's behind us," I say. "It's gotta be someone we know."

When the light finally turns green, the stream of cars slowly moves forward. At one point, a gap in the oncoming traffic opens and the headlights just behind us jump out and pass us. A VW quickly cuts back in front of us, just missing our front fender.

"Asshole." My word is spontaneous.

"New Jersey plates—it's a Concord car," says Wendie, who has been spending time on campus with his fledgling sports assignments. Concord's student body includes kids from both the local area and the Northeast. Four letterman jackets in the old VW completely fill up the small car. "Those dorks must be football players. I've got to cover their game tomorrow for the *Daily Telegraph*. They're gonna get their asses handed to them by Glenville State."

That last move got me all riled up, and now they appear to be slowing, holding us back. Suddenly the stream of traffic has a break. I floor it and pass them back, with a flourish that includes the same "cut back in" move they used on us a few minutes earlier. We're just about to reach the street for Lawrence's house when the VW edges up behind us and gives us a sharp tap on our bumper. It catches me off guard and I miss the turn. Now we're picking up speed, heading for the Thorn Street Bridge. They're just off our rear bumper.

"Tell you what." My voice has a quiver. "Let's put some space between us. These jerks will turn off at the Athens Road intersection and head back over to Concord. We can turn around and get back home. This is getting old."

We speed up but they don't drop back. We're both doing about 45 and the spacing is still close—really close. As we approach the Athens Road intersection, I check the rearview mirror hoping to see a turn signal indicating they're heading back to Athens. Nothing. The light is green, and we both head straight. Other than entering the Turnpike and heading north toward Beckley, that's the last major place to turn around before the edge of Princeton and the long road down Oakvale Mountain.

"Still behind us." Wendie's voice has a clear sense of urgency.

"I'm not sure exactly what to do." My throat's getting tight. "Can't do a U-turn out here. They're right on our tail." The gas gauge shows an eighth of a tank now. Toward the "E" end of the scale it drops fast. "We could get on the Turnpike, but honestly I don't think we have enough gas to make it to the first gas station." The music on WLS is an irritant now.

"Just keep going a bit," says Perry from the rear seat. "They'll back off."

"Sounds prudent," agrees Wendie. This settles the immediate course of action.

Our two-car caravan passes the Turnpike turnoff, the last real place to exit other than rural driveways and a few obscure little country hollows. We begin the long, winding descent down Oakvale Mountain, on the road clinging to the sides of the hills, headed toward the Virginia state line. At the first decent straight stretch—there are precious few—they accelerate, if that term can be used for an older VW overloaded with four huge guys in it, and pass us. They're going at least 60, and a bruiser on the front passenger side gives us the finger as they draw ahead.

"Good!" I say. "They're going on. What the hell was all that about!" Everyone gives a collective sigh of relief.

"There's a turn-off just ahead, around the curve" says Wendie. "You can turn around at Possum Hollow Road. Apparently people actually live out here in this godforsaken place."

"Let's do it." The gas gauge is falling, but The Bomb is running easily now as we approach the curve. It's warm inside and the atmosphere is easing. With the downhill grade, I'm braking a bit to maintain a conservative speed following the recent tension. As we round the curve, I can't believe my eyes! They've pulled the VW sideways across both lanes, blocking the whole center portion. One half of each lane is occupied by the car. Two of the guys are out of the car, one standing at each end.

They've got the road blocked! The Bomb is several hundred yards from the VW now. I'm slowing down, trying to figure out what to do. Check the rearview mirror—no headlights back there, it's completely dark. For the moment, we're the only cars around. No one says a word. Fear is etched on the faces of Perry and Lawrence in the backseat.

It's clear to me that I'm not going to stop the car on Oakvale Mountain, right below a big curve. It's bad enough having one car blocking part of Route 460. Two cars would be a disaster waiting to happen, and two cars stopped with Concord football players beating the shit out of four high school boys is unthinkable by any standard. Time switches to slow motion. We're now only 50 yards away, in the right hand lane doing 30 miles an hour. Their headlights are pointed away, making the hillside strangely light where a seep glistens. The driver looks directly into my headlights. I can't stop. It isn't an option. So I hit the accelerator and aim for the half lane that's clear on the right.

"Hang on!" I yell. "We're going around."

The VW actually starts to move back toward us—crazy. The space is closing. They're trying to force us to stop, which is now impossible, or else hit the guardrail.

"Watch out!" I can't help shouting. Everything is in slow motion, moving in strange directions. The big guy in the football jacket who was blocking the right side of the road is scrambling out of the way. The Bomb is up to 40, now 50, as I accelerate downhill. It's all or nothing. Time stands still as we shoot the gap, missing the rear bumper of the VW by a foot as the car barely misses the heavy metal strips separating us from the steep mountainside on the right.

We're through.

"Are they fucking crazy?" Wendie screams.

Our right two wheels now are on the berm and the wet ground is slippery. The rear of the car sliding to the right. Got to be careful. Got to ease it back. Too much correction and we'll spin out and roll over.

The Concord College boys are scrambling back into the VW. Headlights flash back into view. By now we have a good running start. We're doing almost 65 as we enter the next sweeping curve. The Bomb quivers a bit, then bites into the road. There is little traffic at midnight other than a few hoot-owl shift workers coming back from the Celanese chemical plant at Pearisburg and 18-wheelers on their way between Roanoke and Charleston. In the rearview mirror, the VW's lights flicker and ricochet through the barren trees. We round the curve with a good half-mile lead.

"Hold on!" There are seat belts only in the front, so Perry and Lawrence will get bounced around when I do the little end-a-round bit. "We're gonna do a U-ey. Get ready." I stand on the brakes. The Bomb goes sideways, slews 50 yards, and screeches to a stop in the middle of the road.

"Stupid transmission. Can't get reverse," I groan. There. I have it. The car shoots back 20 feet, tires squealing, into the burning smell of the brake shoes. Now into first. We accelerate back up the steep road. Oncoming headlights reflect off the black trees as the VW nears the curve separating us. I speed-shift through second, my foot never leaving the accelerator. The whole chassis twists and shudders from the torque. We're over in the right-hand lane, shifting into third gear, getting everything the car has to give when the VW skids around the curve into sight.

The world is in slow motion again. We pass a few feet apart going in different directions. We're clear!

We continue up the hill as the VW lurches to a stop and starts to turn around. "A confrontation would have been nasty, gentlemen. Unfortunate indeed," says Wendie.

"No shit, great philosopher." I check the rearview mirror and keep the accelerator floored. With a steep uphill grade, we're rapidly pulling away. But the gas gauge is nearly on top of the "E."

"They're turning around!" screams Perry as he looks out the rear window.

"I know," I say. "But that thing won't do anything uphill. They can't catch us and we're not stopping." After a minute or two I can't see their lights any longer, and for the first time we begin to relax.

"What a fuckin' road race."

For once, Wendie has no topper for my comment. The backseat boys, as white as ghosts, mutely agree. At the top of Oakvale Mountain, we flash past the Turnpike entrance and head back into Princeton. The light is green at the Athens Road intersection, and we roar through at 60, soon crossing over the Thorn Street Bridge. After taking Lawrence and Perry home, I finally park in our driveway, the gas gauge now to the left end of the "E."

Wendie and I sit on the front porch. After some silence, I say, "Damndest thing I ever saw. How did all that come to be?"

"Hell of a driving show as far as I'm concerned," he says, lighting up a cigarette. "Hell of a show."

I'm completely drained. Wendie shakes hands with me in a respectful formal manner and starts walking up toward his house.

Chapter 9

FOOTBALL SEASON FINALLY ended, thank heaven. The major time commitment to mysterious balms and hideously dirty athletic underwear was over. Wendie's work for the paper appeared to be gaining momentum.

"I've been writing a piece for the *Daily Telegraph* about the Concord basketball team," he said. "Deadline's tomorrow. Lots of midnight oil. Tons of the gooey stuff."

"So the sportswriter thing really is happening?" I asked.

"I suppose you could say that. The paper liked the football coverage on Saturdays, and I heard the school was pleased, too. That's surprising since they went two and eight. Of course I only did the home games and they were two and three, so I got to report on almost a break-even home season!"

"When you're a famous reporter for *The New York Times*, I can say I knew you back when you were covering Concord College Mountain Lion football."

"Of course I'll deny ever knowing you," he concluded with a wry smile, not even looking my way.

Daddy was home for supper that evening. "Uuh-ummph." His smoking caused mucous buildup, and he usually cleared his throat before starting a conversation or answering the telephone.

"Had a pretty good day today. A man from Matoka placed an order for a new Park Avenue. That's a beautiful automobile." With Daddy, "automobile," not "car," was the word. "In addition, we delivered the new Skylark to Mrs. Elkins here in town." Daddy never used an adult's first name, certainly not when talking to me. "The delivery went well."

It was nice to see him and Mom actually enjoying themselves.

I had a vague understanding that his income was based on the sale of cars. But I never knew if there was a salary component or if commission sales alone made up his earnings. There were two other salesmen, so there must have been some base salary—or at least some percentage of the business that others made. After all, Daddy was sales manager.

The title seemed important to him, with all the framed certificates lining his office at Gibson's stating he was a member of this-or-that sales managers' club, and that he had achieved various levels of accomplishment in the GM region. Daddy, to his credit, helped me get a part-time job at work. He always called it the dealership. "Mr. Gibson approved a nice job for you, Jimmy. It will pay fifty cents an hour," he announced one evening during a rare family supper together. It was clear he had gone to bat for me. That was good money. Daddy rarely showed much overt interest in any of my activities, so arranging it was a big deal.

I'd be helping the parts manager in the "parts cage," as the enclosure was called, every day after school and occasionally on Saturdays. It was clear Daddy was proud of the opportunity. He said several of the mechanics were pushing to get their sons the job since it was a traditional step on the ladder of becoming an automotive mechanic. Those were good jobs in Princeton.

"I'm not sure this is something I'll be able to do," I said, choosing my words carefully. "But thanks for going to bat for me. I know there are plenty of people who'd like it. I'll give it a try." I tried to send a message of gratitude and to recognize it had taken some political capital on his part to line it up. Many guys my age would have absolutely killed to have that experience, plus the money. As for me . . . if only it involved electronic components.

Mr. Harmon was a no-nonsense man who seemed to respect Daddy. He'd been the parts manager at Gibson's for years. He knew his stuff, and it must have been frustrating to have to explain the most rudimentary things. But he gave me the opportunity to get in there and learn right from the start. For a kid who hardly knew the difference between a brake shoe and a carburetor gasket, I tried to make a good effort.

After the first week, it was evident I had no interest in becoming a long-term helper in the parts cage and was clearly a drag on him. Mr. Harmon finally used me mainly as a runner, sending me over to the local parts distributor in the Gibson's pickup truck to bring back orders he phoned in. I also stopped and picked up hamburgers for everyone's lunch. It wasn't fair to him (or to me) to continue working there.

"I can't do this," I confessed to Mom five days into the job.

"Why don't you try another week or two," she suggested. "That way, you'll know you gave it a fair try. Then if it's not a good match, people will understand. I know Daddy was pleased when Mr. Harmon had the opening and Mr. Gibson approved the position for you."

The job lasted exactly two weeks. I submitted my oral "resignation" on Friday afternoon. "Mr. Harmon, I'm sorry. You've been more than fair, but I'm just not the right person for this sort of work. I hope I haven't let you down. You'll get someone who loves cars and wants the experience."

"That's O.K., Jimmy," he said. "I understand." He probably did, yet didn't. For a high school boy to turn down up to 10 bucks a week for a part-time job working with automotive parts, being in and around gearheads and real mechanics . . . it just didn't get any better than that. That's what he had to be thinking. But all he said was that he understood. I offered to stay on until he had a replacement, but he said that wasn't necessary. He probably had someone lined up. It was fine with me.

Daddy was out late. It was an Elks Club night. He got up as usual to go to work Saturday morning. His job was a six-day-a-week responsibility, and Saturday was the busiest day at the dealership. I got up and came down to breakfast to tell him about the decision. He knew already. Mr. Harmon probably had mentioned it to him after I left. He may have found out at the Elks Club. I thanked him for the opportunity and told him I was sorry it hadn't worked out. Daddy didn't chastise me. In fact, he said almost nothing at all.

He didn't make it home until well after midnight Saturday. Someone drove him home and parked his new demonstrator in the driveway. I heard the muffled voices out on the front porch. Then a car drove away.

Daddy stumbled through the living room, banging into furniture. The smoke from his Lucky Strikes drifted upstairs.

"Joe! Joe, set 'em up. A round for the house, Joe." He repeated this line again and again in the kitchen. I heard him pull out a chair. There was a loud noise. He must have fallen. Mom had to be awake. I went downstairs, wondering if he'd hurt himself. Mom came out of their bedroom at the same time and walked into the kitchen ahead of me. We helped him up. He was giddy and laughing. A new bottle of Four Roses was on the kitchen table. His voice, ringing in my ears, along with the acrid cigarette smoke wafting up through the open heating grate, were lasting signatures of the evening.

When I get up Sunday morning, Daddy is still in bed. The kitchen is cleaned up. Mom says he drank the entire bottle. She handled all that somehow. As we drive to church, the new demonstrator reeks from the overflowing ashtray. Mom's silence must mask a deep anger.

The First Methodist Church is a large stone structure located where both Park Avenue and Center Avenue join Mercer Street. Yes, the same crow's foot intersection where that crazy incident with the Concord football players began. I'd never mentioned that to her. We locate a spot in the parking area, which also serves as outdoor basketball courts, and head to our respective Sunday school classes. Donnie and Henry Davis both are active in my class, along with several of the Mercer School girls. They all seem extremely respectful of church traditions. The Methodists are generally stable—unlike the Baptists, who always are debating interpretations of the Bible, with people leaving because of disagreements.

Following Sunday school, I meander over to the main sanctuary for the regular worship service. The surroundings are sedate, comfortable, and soothing. A series of large stained-glass windows depict Jesus and the disciples, Jesus with a flock of birds, and other familiar scenes. The organ music is lovely. The choir is nuanced and full. The floors are richly carpeted, and in the pulpit there's always an experienced minister who is mature and well versed in the Bible. We don't get tongue-lashed or commanded to smell the "sulfur rising up from the fires of hell" in the First Methodist Church of Princeton, West Virginia. The message is traditional, comforting, and predictable.

Religion is changing for me, transitioning from an absolute given to something I no longer accept unconditionally. Wendie Johnston is the only person to whom I've confided my religious beliefs, or, more accurately, my questions. I just don't see how there can be so many billions of people on Earth, and somehow only our Christian forefathers got it right. Are all the Chinese, Hindus, Muslims and whoever else wrong? They're all going straight to hell? Do not pass go. Do not collect $200. Straight to the down elevator?

"It makes no sense to me that a divine Creator would somehow know every thought that every person ever had or ever will have," I tell Wendie. "When a person dies, do they see their family as if they were exactly the age and shape of that moment? What happens when little Johnny grows up and gets bald and fat? Does good old grandfather Jones ever get to see Johnny as he turns out later in life, as a low-life cheating husband, or always as sweet little Johnny? Are people preserved in all the various ages and weight categories to match all those who knew and remembered, and loved or hated them along the way?"

Wendie just looks at me.

I go on to try and explain my amateurish calculations regarding the Great Flood story in the Bible. "There are not enough water molecules in the atmosphere to produce even a fraction of the water necessary to cover the land mass. Besides that, why have the Japanese writers never mentioned their island was flooded?"

"Frankly, you make my head hurt," Wendie says.

Chapter 10

IT'S ALMOST FIVE o'clock and the band's practicing tonight. I've got to pick up Arcie and take him over to Buddy's house. Somehow it's still not entirely comfortable for me to turn off Low Gap Road and swing over one block to Arcie's small house. Being in the colored neighborhoods is different. Usually he comes right out, but not this time. Just as I'm ready to switch off the engine and go knock at the door, the front window curtains part. Mrs. Peterson waves and gestures, which translates to "He'll be right out." So I relax and let the heater do its thing. Arcie soon bounds out the door and trots to the car, puts his guitar on the rear seat, then gets in. He has an additional instrument with him, which he places gingerly between us on the front seat.

"Hey, man. Thanks for the lift."

By now, we've spent lots of casual time together. But the racial diversity part still feels a bit new.

"What's in the case?"

"You haven't seen my sax?"

"Sax?"

"Tonight's horn night!"

Buddy's mother answers the door, smiling warmly at me and more formally at Arcie. "You two go right on downstairs. Buddy will be down in a minute. The other boys are down there already. And be careful. The lighting isn't very good."

"Yes ma'am," I say. Arcie smiles but says nothing as we head down the narrow stairway to the basement, which is cozy and warm. The other guys have set up already. Slate's doing guitar riffs, and Peppy

Blake and Lannie Woods are sitting on the couch talking. Buddy is still upstairs, apparently negotiating a relaxation of the family's noise abatement rules for the evening.

Suddenly there's Buddy's familiar lilt. "Well, gollee. It's Jimmy. And, hey Arcie . . . my man. How're ya doing?"

"No complaints, "Arcie says, "I think I got all the new material."

The band uses four basic musical instruments: keyboard, lead guitar, bass guitar, and drums. They'd molded into a basic cover band even before Arcie joined. Now, with Arcie, they have a key piece that was missing. Slate gives them a handsome front man, and Lannie off to one side provides a scowling tough guy who's good on the keyboards. Buddy, with his ever-pleasant goofy smile, along with Peppy and his, "I'm asleep but my eyes are still open" appearance, are in the rear. Since some R & B music is crossing over into the mainstream, they're working on a horn sound. Arcie gives the band credibility in terms of soul.

I leaf through a *Life* magazine while they start. They run through "Sixteen Candles" by the Crests, to check Arcie's knowledge of the lyrics and also to make sure they're in the right key for his range, as well as "It's Only Make Believe," which is a terrific closer when the band wants to end the evening with a great slow song.

"O.K.," Slate says. "Let's try the sax. I've been thinking about some songs. Arcie, how about 'Poison Ivy?'"

"That would work," he says. "Got a sax in there for sure." Since they already know the words, it's a matter of working in the sax, and after several goes at it they have a good version.

"You're the man!" says Slate, as Arcie finishes. "Is there anything you can't do? I just don't have the right genes." He pats Arcie on his shoulder and laughs.

"You're right, brother," says Arcie. "Too much blonde hair."

It's a productive session and the two hours go by quickly. Mrs. Lewis brings down a tray of cookies and some Cokes. "You boys sound very good tonight," she says. "If I could understand the words, it would *really* be something."

We walk outside to the cars. Buddy recently bought a two-door 1950 white Cadillac. It's in good condition, with the standard V8 engine plus new glass pack dual exhausts he's added. In addition, the radio has a fancy automatic select capability—it stops on the next station—as well as an automatic light-detecting sensor that dims the bright headlights all by itself at night when an oncoming car approaches. Jaw droppers all.

Later that week, Slate calls me at home to tell me the band is booked Friday night over near Hinton. He's psyched, almost shouting. "JD's Roadhouse. We'll have a great crowd."

"You guys are getting a buzz."

"Can you bring Arcie?"

"Sure. No problem."

"This one will be for the door. You're the doorman!"

"Doorman?"

"The guy sits by the door and collects the money, a buck a head—that's the deal—from everyone who comes in. Anyone there already . . . you gotta be a charmer and ask 'em to support the band. The guy who owns the place says it's the house rule. No one has a problem with it. If someone wants to be an asshole, just let it go. We get the door, guy who owns the place sells more beer, locals get live music. Everyone wins."

"Got it. It's me against all those rednecks and miner types."

"Don't forget the guys who pull out truck motors with their bare hands."

"No sweat."

"We need to get there at seven for load-in and sound check. JD wants to start the music right at eight. There won't be many people there at seven, so it'll be easy to collect a buck and set up at the door. Let your folks know it'll be a late night."

"Late?"

"Late. Just tell 'em." It was as if he were winking over the phone.

"I'll get Arcie and pick him up at five-thirty. It'll take a good hour and a half from here."

"O.K. See you-all over there," he said. "We ought to make good money. You're in for a full share. Those miners don't know who the Roadsters are, but they're gonna find out."

"I can't wait till summer. You know, get some rays at the pool. Just can't seem to tan, no matter what I do." At that point it strikes me how foolish I must sound. Arcie can't be interested one whit in my tendency to burn.

He and I are on the way, cruising in The Bomb past the one traffic light in Athens. Only a few weeks remain in our junior year. I can't believe it—the hallowed senior year next year.

"Well, you see, I tan fairly easily," Arcie says. I blush and fumble.

"I suppose my comment was off base. Sorry." I try to recalibrate. It's embarrassing. The Bomb's tires keep slapping the spots on the highway where the tar bubbled up. For a moment, it's the only sound other than the drone of the motor.

"Jimmy, the whole swimming pool situation is a problem for us." It's clear who "us" is. Princeton has a stated rule. The pool is private. "No blacks. That's not fair."

I glance at him. He stares straight ahead.

Silence again. We're out of Athens now and driving faster past a rare straight stretch. To be honest, I hadn't thought about the pool and the Whites Only policy. It would be gallant to say I was a courageous defender of social equality and things moral, willing to take on the status quo. The segregation policy of the South more or less made the problem invisible. It was easy not to notice, not to worry about things and people we couldn't (or wouldn't) see. But here the two of us are. And one of us is someone my age, one of "them," more talented in his little toe than I am overall—certainly in the area of music—directly in the line of discrimination.

"I see your point," I mumble, unable to defend the undefendable. It's uncomfortable. How *did* such a private civic facility get financed? It must have been on a membership basis, although I have no recollection of Mom or Dad saying anything about dues.

"Where do you go swimming?" I blurt out. "Do you-all have a place?"

"Well, there are creeks. Some places available over at Bluestone Lake. You know, an area run by my people. And there's a pool in Bluefield. But it's kind of run-down."

A couple of minutes of silence pass as both of us process the subject. "You know, it doesn't seem fair," I meekly offer. "But, to be practical, could the Princeton Pool make it if it opened to everyone and then the white people boycotted it? I mean, would that work?" Not exactly the dynamic change agent. Rationalizing the wrong.

The motor noise and roadway tire whine fill the background. Nothing is said for a moment.

"I don't know," Arcie ventures. "I do know it isn't right."

He hesitates a few seconds, then continues. "You know, another thing that's not fair is the theater."

There are one or two theaters in Bluefield. But the Mercer Theater is the place in Princeton in terms of first run shows.

"What do you mean?" I ask, hesitantly. "Can't you go to the Mercer?"

"Go to the Mercer. I suppose you can call it that, but we've gotta sit upstairs. It's dirty 'cause they don't clean up that often. All that, and the seats are ripped. It's just not as nice as where you-all sit downstairs. I know. I've looked over the railing when the house lights come on. I'm tellin' you, it's better all around down where you are."

"Not as clean? What do you mean? They don't clean up the trash, the popcorn bags, all that stuff?" It dawns on me: Am I trying to argue that it would be O.K. for him to be required to sit upstairs if it were clean? What exactly is my point?

"No way!" For the first time, anger flashes. He raises his voice. "It's a mess up there. Mom and Dad won't go to the Mercer. They almost always go to the Paramount over in Bluefield. That's a black theater, and it's better than the crummy upstairs at the Mercer."

"I never thought about these things," I stammer and then retreat into another period of contemplation. By this time we're past Pipestem State Park and are nearing the Bluestone Lake area. "It doesn't seem right."

"Yeah. I wonder *when* and *if* it'll ever change." He says both words especially clearly. Both of us seem taken aback by the frank exchange.

The bright lights of JD's Route 20 Roadhouse come into view. In West Virginia-speak, a roadhouse is a beer joint out in the county, outside an incorporated area. JD's has a nice-sized parking area with a gravel base. It's decent, even in wet weather.

The large sign out in front is gaudy with lights.

Tonight
Roadsters Live Music

Slate and Lannie are there already. Lannie has his keyboard up and is running through chords. Buddy's Caddy isn't there yet.

"How's it going?" I ask. Lannie looks up with his trademark scowl.

"It's going."

"Damn Sam, Lannie, you look so happy!"

A slight grin crosses his face. All is well with the grumpster.

Just then there's the characteristic boom as the Caddy decelerates and the dual glass packs clear their throats. Soon the door opens and Buddy stumbles in, completely obscured by the panoply of percussion instrumentation. He looks like a peddler, his slight frame completely covered with drums and drum supports, as if he were unloading his goods from a frontier trading wagon.

"Uh, hello," he mutters, reaching for a deep breath. Peppy Blake is in tow, carrying his large bass guitar case in one hand and a snare drum in the other. "Sorry we're a bit late. Had to stop for gas." Buddy speaks with a rhythmic rise and fall of sound within a sentence.

"Dammit, Jimmy," he says as he sets up the drums, "I can't believe that sorry green car actually beat me here."

"Don't knock The Bomb," Arcie interjects. "It grows on you. Ran like a clock all the way over here."

"You're lucky. You took your life in your hands when you got in that thing. Gotta run out and get the rest of my stuff." With that, Buddy is out the door.

Following the sound check, Slate passes out the playlist. By this time, smatterings of people have drifted in and it's time to make my first rounds. The first couple sits in one of the vinyl booths. Her peroxided hair is all poofed up and combed back over her forehead. West Virginia-style big hair. Roots showing. The man, in his mid-thirties, wears a union jacket along with a blue and gold WVU cap. Big and barrel-chested, he looks like he could break my arm with his little finger.

"*Hi the Roadsters are playing tonight 'til midnight they're from Princeton they're really good the charge is one dollar per person for the music.*" There. I get it all out. The entire pitch non-stop just like I memorized it.

He doesn't look at me.

"Oh, great! Charles, pay the boy," Big Hair says.

"How much?"

It seems prudent not to mention I'd said a dollar in my nervous spiel. It was in there somewhere. "A dollar per person."

He reaches into his pocket, pulls out a wad of bills, and peels off two ones. They're new—make a snapping sound. Wordlessly he hands them to me, stuffs the money back into his jeans, and returns to his longneck Budweiser.

Only a handful of people are in JD's this early, so it takes only a few minutes to make the rounds. No one is unpleasant, and I get better at my little speech. In fact, there's never any trouble the entire night. The women all are eager to hear a live band. Besides, most of them aren't paying for it anyway. Sometimes a group of guys gets testy, but nothing serious. By seven forty-five, people are coming in non-stop, and at eight sharp the band kicks off the set list with "That'll Be the Day," the big Buddy Holly hit. It's a "white" hit and Slate sings it with Arcie also playing guitar and standing a half step behind him.

Cars keep pulling into the lot, and the crunching of the gravel continues as people approach the door. I repeat my little bit. Now it's smooth. By the time the guys end their third song, a slow one, the dance floor is packed and I'm scrambling to keep up with the line at the door.

By nine, the place is jammed. From my perch on a stool by the door, it's clear that JD is making money hand over fist. He catches my eye and pops the thumbs-up sign. Waitresses are rushing around. Between running the draught spigot and getting all those cold beer bottles out of the cooler, JD is a busy man, a happy man. At 50 cents each, business is good.

The neon light from the Black Label and Budweiser signs provides indirect lighting to the dance floor, while the club has several small spotlights trained on the band. A haze of cigarette smoke cloaks the dance floor, as well as the booth area on the periphery, and the tables farther away, between the dance area and the kitchen. A narrow aisle leads to the restroom area, which is illuminated by a large sign reminding us that Schlitz is the beer that made Milwaukee famous.

Things are "right." It's a happening scene. Burley men with caps stating "Consol Nr. 23," or "N&W Railroad" mill about in good spirits. Some dance, most drink and talk. Many are with dates. The women dance sometimes with other women, and with male partners when the gals can get them on the floor. I keep my seat by the door, and by nine-thirty most everyone who's coming is there already. So with a break now between new customers, I count the money, mostly in one-dollar bills, plus a handful of fives and tens. Over $200. Not bad at all! Realistically, we have to be violating the fire code, since you can hardly make your way through to the bathroom.

"Hi there, darlin'. People sure are havin' a big ol' time!" She looks to be 40, but the tight blouse and jeans fit right. "I'm Juanita, and what's your name, young feller?" She could pass for twenty-something from the neck down but her face indicates some tough years.

"Hi there yourself, Juanita." I'm stammering, even though I've given the same little speech over and over. "The music charge is a dollar. The band'll be on until midnight. They're from Princeton. Really good."

"You gonna make sweet little ol' me pay a whole dollar? Me and my girlfriend Carlene?" Only then I notice the other girl. She looks more or less the same, but with a harder look.

"You know, ladies, if I let you sweet things in, everyone else here, since they all paid their little old dollar, they'd be mad at me. And the band would get shorted. You wouldn't want that, would you?"

"Come on, Carlene, check it out," Juanita says, as she pushes two crumpled ones toward me. "O.K. young feller, we'll take your word. Look, there's Danny. See him over there?"

With that, they brush past me and perch on the edge of the dance floor, a sea of smoky gray-blue neon atmosphere and dim lighting cloaking moving bodies. Someone hollers over from the booth area, and the two of them are on their way to sit with friends. By the next song, both are on the dance floor.

By ten o'clock, people are feeling it. The band is completing the final part of "Lonely Teardrops." Arcie is the only one who can hit the high notes, and he does it in falsetto.

"Thank you for coming. We hope you-all are having as much fun as we are," Slate tells the crowd. "We're the Roadsters from Princeton. We'll be right back after a short pause for the cause." His voice echoes off the neon signs on the back walls as JD puts on some jukebox music.

We all gather outside in the parking lot. Everyone but me lights up as we stand in a circle in the pleasant cool air. Pickup trucks and cars sweep by on the busy highway between Hinton and Bluestone Lake.

"How's it going, Jimmy?" Slate asks. "Money-wise."

"Great. We're at two hundred and eight bucks. A lot of people."

"Golly, it seemed like they wouldn't stop coming in that door for a long while," says Buddy. "I love it! Makes me play better."

"I'm glad something makes you play better," mumbles Lannie, a hint of a smile softening his crinkly dourness.

"Thanks for that diplomatic contribution," Slate says. He turns to me. "First off, Jimmy, charge people fifty cents a head from now on, in case anyone else comes in. There might be a few stragglers yet."

"O.K."

"Second, Arcie and I have a little surprise for you-all. Turns out that our man Arcie here knows a guy who runs a club over in Hinton. R & B place, all colored. They need a late night band tonight and we're it. We go on at one—play 'til four." The collective silence from the guys is palpable. Only Slate and Arcie, with knowing grins, show any expression.

"We *start* at one o'clock?" asks Buddy.

"You got it. One fucking o'clock. It'll give us time to wrap it up here at midnight sharp. Can't go over. Tear down and load-in over in Hinton. Arcie made the deal, so he and Jimmy are the lead car. Be sure to stick close together so you don't get lost. Two hundred bucks for three hours. Overall tonight, we'll top four hundred. Good money for sure."

"Uh, what's this place called?" Buddy continues.

The words from Slate sound like Paradise Club. Then he breaks it into parts. "Pair-a-dice."

Chapter 11

THE BAND SOUNDS even better after the break. Slate tells everyone to cut out the booze since it's going to be a late night. But that doesn't stop some of the girls from slipping bourbon and Cokes to the guys. After all, it looks like a Coke and ice cubes with a little foam. JD's is a beer joint. But as long as people keep it discreet, and keep on ordering Cokes, no one seems worried. Cokes cost the same as beers—JD's no fool. The crowd loves us. I feel like a real part of the group. By the third set things thin out, making it easier to dance, show off some moves. You might think the rough-and-ready guys might not have the moves. You'd be right. But the girls with the gimmie-hat crowd definitely have them. I can vouch for that. Juanita, my friend from the front door, ends up doing some back-holler (that's West Virginia-speak for back-hollow) action and she and her side-kick Carlene end up best buds with a couple of the gimmies. The band ends up with $210. A great payday, or paynight, or half-paynight to be exact.

After we pack up and haul the gear back out to the cars, Arcie and I pull out of JD's and turn right toward Hinton, rather than back to Athens and Princeton. At twelve-thirty in the morning this feels strange.

"Jimmy, let me tell you about the Pair-a-Dice," Arcie begins as soon as we're out on Route 20. "My mother grew up in Hinton. Her cousin owns the club. It's pretty wild. I've never actually been there but I think I've got the skinny on it."

"Tell me."

"The stuff they do there is, well, a lot of it's illegal. I don't know exactly how they get away with it, but somehow they do. They have hard liquor. And there's part of the club where you can play cards and throw dice . . . you know, for money. Gambling stuff."

The story sounds right out of the Prohibition era. Al Capone and Chicago, but in little old Hinton. We reach town at about a quarter till one, our little caravan of three cars: The Bomb, followed by Slate and Lannie in Slate's dad's late-model Chevrolet, then Buddy and Peppy in the white Caddy. The streets are coal black, wet from dew. Halos from the streetlights punctuate the darkness like indistinct megaphones of light, revealing the dampness of the asphalt below. The town feels isolated, detached, and empty.

"Turn here," Arcie says, motioning to the left. We leave Main Street, into which Route 20 has morphed, and drive up a hill past old churches and aged brick homes. No lights shine in any windows. Only a few porch lights are visible. Blackness becomes pervasive as the neighborhood changes into smaller houses and a less well-kept area, then transitions into a warehouse district.

"Pull up over there," he says, and points to a single streetlight that illuminates the corner. There are no additional signs of life.

"People park a block away. You won't see any cars right here," says Arcie as he opens the door. The other two cars pull in.

"Tell me again. Where the hell are we?" Buddy asks, stretching in the early morning air. "Where's the action, man?"

"Right there, Buddy. Right there" Arcie walks toward a single door, illuminated by a single bulb. "Gentlemen, welcome to the Pair-a-Dice club!"

He knocks three times. A peephole clicks open, just like in the Speakeasy joints in old movies. A big black eyeball glares at us.

"Yeah?"

"It's Arcie Peterson and the band from Princeton."

"Hold on." The eyeball vanishes as the peephole closes with a snap. A short time later, the door swings open and a large colored man—and I mean large—motions us in.

"Quick. In here."

Arcie's cousin, Jug, runs the Pair-a-Dice. His instructions are simple and direct. "Glad you-all are here. No one talks about what happens in this place. O.K.?"

We all nod furiously.

"Two hundred bucks. Play to four. Take one break when you need to. You guys play. You don't see nothin', you don't say nothin'. Things are cool. Understand?"

More intense nodding. No one says a word.

"Good. Go bring in your stuff. Hookups are over there, in that corner. Give it hell!"

We go back outside to unload the cars and set up. I have nothing to do in terms of doorman work, so once the equipment has been lugged in and plugged in, I'm off duty. The guys run their cords and audio cables, and within ten minutes the Roadsters, now the late night Roadsters, are ready.

"What'll you-all have?" the man behind the first eyeball asks. "Beer, bourbon, gin, rum. Name it." Here, there's no age limit.

Slate and Arcie cross out most of the white teenager puff songs. That cuts off nearly everything you wouldn't hear on John R.'s program on WLAC. Jerry Lee Lewis and a few others make the cut, plus the R & B stuff. Arcie will be playing the sax on quite a few and singing on almost every one. Arcie is best when he's belting. He's a better rocker than a crooner.

They start with the old standby "Let the Good Times Roll," from '56, and the good times do roll. Indeed. Never in my life have I seen such dancing, such moves. The crowd is well dressed, nothing like the jeans, heavy boots, and gimmie-hat crowd at JD's, or the khakis and button-down shirt crowd at the Memorial Building. This is one resplendent group. The men wear expensive sweaters, woolen trousers with pleats, and shiny leather shoes, often with elevated heels. Lots of pendants and gold jewelry. The women have on tight skirts, really tight, and equally revealing tops. Most have the Royal Crown Hair Pomade look—heavily oiled and pressed, straightened black hair.

Following the initial Shirley and Lee tune, the band does Jerry Lee Lewis' "Great Balls of Fire," one of the few planned songs by a white singer. But the Killer crosses over to R & B easily. The third song is the Diamonds' "Little Darlin," with no downtime at all. The place throbs. Jug flashes Arcie a nod through the sweaty haze and cigarette smoke.

The Pair-a-Dice fills a medium-sized cinderblock building, invisible to the world as a club from the outside, with few frills inside. The dance floor is made of wood: smooth, worn. It's been there a while. The band area is at a wall, elevated just a tad. Small spotlights illuminate the microphones. Tables are scattered around the periphery of the dance floor, with enough seating for at least 100 people. The bar is set up all along one wall, with plenty of room for people, mostly men, to stand around. The women appear to stay in the table and chairs area. On the table area side, away from the dance floor, several brightly lit areas become clearer as my eyes adjust to the lighting and the haze. Two large circular tables are animated with card games. Beyond the card game area, there's some sort of area that, as far as I can tell, involves tossing dice up against a wall. Both areas are going strong. The card tables seem to be male-only, but women as well as men are throwing dice. Large piles of bills are visible on the card tables. The dancers and the gamblers clearly are having a great time.

What would I say if the cops busted this place right now? "But officer, I'm only the doorman with the band!" Crazy.

One of Slate's best songs in terms of his guitar playing is "Johnny Be Good" by Chuck Berry, so it's no surprise when he starts the famous riff to lead it off. He and Arcie, who has no saxophone part to play, sing together with a cool harmony. One particularly attractive girl is really into the music, putting on a show as her low-cut white blouse stretches tight and exposes a silky tan brassiere. She's got plenty there.

Her partner, about 30, is the alpha male, based on the way other men defer to him. The band is glued to her. Buddy's working the drums with a special flourish as she does her stuff with Mr. Alpha on the dance floor.

Suddenly a blurred image streaks toward the flashy couple. Another woman, somewhat older, tackles the sexpot right in the middle of some of her hottest moves. Both go down. What follows lasts only a minute, but I'll remember it my entire life. The room is filled with shrieking and screaming as the two women roll over and over on the floor. The music ends abruptly. Mesmerized, the band members stand there, in place, gawking. As the older woman gains control and jerks the younger woman by her hair, Mr. Alpha and others separate them. Wanna-be-Ms.-Alpha's blouse is ripped, her sensuous lingerie fully exposed. She starts crying. Large portions of make-up are smeared across her face.

The attacker is literally spitting-angry. "You little bitch. You just can't come in here and act like this. You stay away from him. I told you before!"

"He don't love you," screams the young woman, heaving her bosom between deep gasps for air.

"No way! We been together for three years. I got two young'uns at home. Now get your sorry black ass outta here and outta my sight!" With that definitive statement, the older woman straightens out her dress, now covered with dust from the floor.

Another woman appears out of the crowd and puts her arm around the young woman. "Come on, Christine. Let's get you cleaned up, honey," she says, and guides her, sniffling and sobbing, in the direction of the ladies' bathroom.

"Curtis, I don't like this at all," the attacker shouts, now turning her attention to the man. "What d'you want me to tell little Arthur and Lillyann at home? Tell 'em their daddy making a fool of himself over at the club? That what you want?"

Alpha male, now with a name, puts his arm around her. "It's O.K., Rosey, it's all right. Let's sit down, talk this over." With that, they go all the way back to the very last table, in the darkest portion of the seating area. It's the last I see of them.

Everything else remains calm the rest of the evening—or I should say, the morning. One of the younger girls obviously flirts with Slate. "Gorgeous blond dude," she keeps hollering. Given the surroundings and the previous altercation, he just smiles and keeps playing. The guys take a break around two-thirty. Slate keeps to himself. After that, the atmosphere is mellower and the band does more slow songs.

On the way back to Princeton, Arcie and I talk about the experience. "You know something. I've never been in a place like that."

"Neither have I," he says. "But all in all, it's cool. The women . . . they're something!"

"That's for sure," I say, not mentioning the fight. "You know the weirdest thing? I felt completely . . ." The word finally comes. ". . . like a minority." There, that's the word. "Every which way. The color of my skin. The way I'm dressed. The way I talk. The whole deal."

Arcie's look is long, knowing.

"It was strange, man. Strange," I continue, simplistically expecting some type of verbal response.

After some thought, he says, "Yeah, I could see the same reaction from the other guys. Being a minority is a different experience."

"I felt like I had no control," I say. "No say. A 'nobody gives a shit' kind of person. The first time in my whole life."

Soon he's asleep. The only sound is the hum of the motor and the occasional whap-whap-whap of the tires against the road sections.

We pull up in front of his house at five-thirty. Arcie wakes up just in time to stretch and reach for his saxophone and guitar case in the rear seat. "See you later," he mumbles, as he taps me on the shoulder. "Thanks a lot for the ride . . . and the conversation. You'll be O.K."

Chapter 12

MOM WENT BACK to work before Susie started at WVU in Morgantown in order to pay our college tuitions and expenses. It was understood that we would go to college. Every one of Dad's brothers and sisters had gone to college, with Dad himself the only one with fewer than four years. Mom's family grew up in the shadow of Centre College and the medical field was the default career path at the University of Louisville.

My sister's original plan was to follow Mom into nursing with an RN degree. But with more biology and chemistry courses and additional practical training, it became clear to her that she lacked an inner calling for the healthcare field. Susie always liked English literature and enjoyed the classroom scene, so she decided to switch to education.

"Mom." Susie stopped—there seemed to be some awkwardness. "I met a girl I like, and we want to room together this year. She's from Clarksburg."

Mom sensed something. "I thought you would room with Becky Roberts again this year. You two got along well last year."

"That's true, but Becky's going to continue in nursing. We both felt it would be better to room with someone who has the same major. You know, same classes. Help each other with homework, that sort of thing. Becky's going to room with another nursing student, a girl from Pennsylvania."

Mom puttered around at the sink.

"Layotis Smith and I are taking the same courses. She'll also major in education, with English as her primary area."

"Layotis. That's an unusual name isn't it?"

The question was ignored. "She's from a nice family. Her mother is a schoolteacher in Clarksburg. I'm not sure what her dad does. She has several brothers and sisters." With that, the phone rang. Susie got most of the calls when she was home.

Mom and Dad were consistently polite and reserved when it came to race. When Mom first went back to work she'd hired a cleaning lady who came over once a week. But the woman was—to put it bluntly—undependable. Mom found out she had a boyfriend that came over when I was at school and Mom and Dad were at work. Stuff like that quickly got around. The neighbors noticed things. Mom had "let her go," which was the expression we used instead of firing.

The word "nigger" was never used in our house. I feel certain I never heard either of my parents ever say the word. To me, it was ugly. Yet social exchange between whites and blacks was a sensitive matter. Anything that might bring a white girl into an interaction of any sort with a colored boy would signal unease with our parents . . . probably even with most of my own peers.

After she finished her phone call, Susie walked through the kitchen without a word and joined me on the front porch. The morning was cool and pleasant. My sister and I didn't talk often. Three years is a major difference. We circulated in our little universes in different orbits. The look on her face was dead-serious.

"I need to tell you something." She's whispering, accented in that earnest Princeton cadence. "It's about Layotis. The girl I plan to room with this year."

"I heard you talking with Mom."

A car horn interrupts us. Wendie Johnston waves as he drives up the hill. He bought a Chrysler convertible with his money from writing for the *Daily Telegraph*. The car is some version of metallic red, only three years old, and is covered with chrome. The top's down. We both wave.

"Layotis is black," she says.

Black. Susie doesn't use the word colored.

"We got to know each other last year when she was in my English class. She's so sweet."

I try not to show any emotion.

"Mom doesn't have any problem with the band and you giving Arcie Peterson a ride," she says. "What do you think?"

"I don't know," I finally say, after a pause. "I really don't know. Do *they* know Layotis is . . ." Words rotate in my mind. ". . . black?"

"I haven't told Mom that. She probably picked up on her name."

"You need to get it resolved. You certainly don't want Mom and Dad to be helping you carry your stuff into a dorm room and have a big surprise. Know what I mean?"

"I realize that."

We sit there for a minute or two, my older sister and I. Finally Susie says, "Keep all this stuff about Layotis to yourself for now. I'll deal with it somehow."

A week later, Susie comes downstairs and motions me to the front porch. Mom and Dad vetoed Layotis as her roommate. They were polite but firm.

"They want me to have a white roommate. Mom said it's not that Layotis isn't a good person—she said she's sure she is. But it would be too much of a cultural change for me. They phrased it, 'We're doing this for you, to prevent you from going through difficulties.' When I questioned that, Daddy was more direct. He put his foot down, and when I pushed him on it, he said that if I insisted, I'd have to pay my own college expenses. I can't do that."

I stand there, trying to absorb both her sense of the changing world as well as my own timidity. Talking with Arcie on the way to and from band gigs is one thing. But actually living with a person of another race in a college dorm room. . . . the whole issue challenges my simple routine, my prior sense of order. Real diversity hasn't occurred to me, I suppose. I'm a person who, for the most part, is still trying to figure what life is about. Dealing with another culture is outside my ability to cope at this time.

I'm not able to offer anything more meaningful than to let Susie sniffle and vent.

Chapter 13

ONE OF THE benefits of having Mr. Emory as my ham radio mentor was that he was the chief engineer at WLOH. It was a part-time job, his "fun job," as he said, in addition to managing the natural gas company in Princeton. He kept the equipment certified (he might have been the only person who *could* do this since he'd built the transmitter in his basement) and was in a position to recommend me when a Sunday announcer slot opened up. One person opened the station and signed on the air at six, another took over at three and had it until sign-off at midnight. I would be the only one there Sunday mornings once I proved myself.

Sunday was the most unusual day of the week. In-studio religious programs dominated the early morning, followed by the worship service from the First Methodist Church, carried live using special gadgets Mr. Emory had designed and built to pick up the microphone outputs and match them to the phone lines. While Sunday morning was very busy and challenging, the afternoon and evening were laid back with music that was to be "relaxing," the official word.

John Shelton, one of the regular weekend announcers, would be at the station to give me the low down. The man they'd been using as a Sunday morning announcer was leaving to go back to Virginia Tech. John kept repeating to me that this was a good opportunity. After the parts cage job at Gibson's and standing with a reversible "stop" and "slow" sign while the road crew repaved streets, there was no doubt about that.

First light was just cracking the horizon as I drove up the steep road to Radio Hill. The building was totally dark, the indistinct shape of the tower barely visible heading up into the mist. Finally a set of headlights flickered around the curve, pointed up the hill, transitioned into a car's shape, and pulled into the parking lot. I got out so he didn't have to wait for me.

"Hope you're a morning person," he says, saluting me with a thermos. "I'm John Shelton." We shake hands. "Come on in. Let's get the beast turned on." When we get to the front door, he fiddles with the key in the dark. "That should be better," he says as he switches on the lights.

The door opens to the main hallway, comprised of hard floor tiles that accentuate the sounds as we quickly pass the control room and continue into a short and dimly lighted passageway toward the rear of the building. A small sign indicates "Transmitter Room." The electronic creation inside looks at first glance just like the big ham radio amplifier I'd seen when our scout troop visited Mr. Emory's station.

"The heart of the mighty fourteen-ninety. It's not a standard commercial transmitter. Robert Emory built it. An amazing man."

I don't mention the other transmitter I saw at his home.

"WLOH is licensed for two hundred and fifty watts, day and night. WHIS in Bluefield runs five KW. But we do OK."

He gives the large black cabinet a little pat. "Putting the station on the air is straightforward. First, turn on the main power supply. It's right here." He points to a large toggle switch labeled "Filament Supply" in bold letters. "Let it warm up for five minutes. Five minutes is important—the tubes need to come up to temperature. Go ahead."

I push the metal toggle switch to the "On" position. Immediately a green light comes on above the filament supply switch and sound of a slight electrical hum fills the small room. Through perforated holes in the metal chassis, the vacuum tubes glow orange and blue.

"Good. Now let's go to the control room."

The sanctum beckons through glassed partitions, an enclosed bright beacon of turntables, tape decks, and precision clocks, whose second hands move in exaggerated, crisp little steps. A large microphone drops down from the overhead ceiling panels on extended flexible metallic tubing. He sits between two of the turntables and puts on a set of earphones. Three turntables and two tape decks are situated within arm's length. In what seems like seconds, he describes the set-up. It's all a blur. He glances at the clock.

"OK. Five 'til. Time to put the carrier on."

I'm right behind him as he hurries out of the control room, back to the transmitter room.

"Go ahead. Throw the plate switch." He points to the other large toggle switch, with the "Plate Supply" label. "I know. It's a bit overwhelming at six in the morning the first time." The heavy switch makes a metallic snapping sound when I push it up to the "On" position. Immediately the needles bounce up into the middle of the illuminated glass meters and a throbbing emanates from the rear portion of the black chassis. It catches me by surprise. John senses it. "That's the transformer." The power supply's handling the full load. Now the station's on. If you were listening, you'd hear a signal with no modulation. Just a blank carrier."

All I can imagine is Dick Biondi in a large room full of meters and electronic power. Fifty-thousand watts! My hero, an Oz-like figure, surrounded by a gigantic, glowing, all-powerful transmitter.

"I'll stay with you until noon or so. Once you feel comfortable, you can take it all by yourself until three when Lonnie Blanchett comes in for the rest of the day. Sunday mornings are really busy. We have several live groups who go on the air from Studio A."

"Studio A?"

"Right there, next to the control room. In addition, we run the First Methodist Church service at eleven o'clock with the phone line pickup. That should end at noon. They usually go over a bit but we need to read the news. There will be some commercials on the hour and the half hour, but all these live programs are moneymakers since they pay to get on the air. If there's no live programming, read the AP news on the hour, along with the temperature and time. Oh, and don't forget Miss Mabel's Gospel Hour."

"Miss Mabel?"

"An old gal who lives over in Tazewell. Sends in a tape each week. It runs a half hour."

"A half-hour Gospel Hour?"

"Yeah. Only Miss Mabel can make thirty minutes become an hour. But that's what she calls it. Then it's middle-of-the-road music all afternoon and evening. The owner wants Sundays to be when people can tune in and relax after church."

Back in the control room, we have a clear view through the large plate glass windows into the live performance studio. The lights are off, and only the dim outline of a piano, music stands, chairs, and several large stand-up microphones is visible.

"It's almost six. Get the tape of the national anthem. Over there," John says, pointing to small wooden filing spaces, each with a tape inside. One label says "National Anthem Sign-On."

"Put it into tape drive number one, right there, then go into the newsroom and tear off the current news summary. It oughta be typing out now," he says, not appearing nervous at all even though the second hand on the clock has only 15 little clicks to go.

Paper is spooled out all over the floor. The printer ferociously spits away all the while. The national anthem comes over the speaker, followed by a deep recorded voice stating the station's power, frequency, and location. I rip off what appears to be the morning's headlines from the AP, hoping it's what John wants, and hustle it to him. He looks it over just as the sign-on tape is ending and flips the microphone switch to "On-Air."

"Good morning, ladies and gentlemen. This is John Shelton with a brief summary of world and West Virginia news." Without a hitch, he reads the copy, gives the time and temperature, and then starts turntable number one, which holds a 33 RPM album titled, appropriately, "Sunday Morning Melodies."

He turns to me. "O.K. Good so far. This'll take us up to six-fifteen, when we have the first commercial. Look here. The station log shows precisely each one to be run. Some are on tape, but most are typed out, like this one—we read these on the air. It's important to get them on time because business owners do listen. They want them at specific times to target specific audiences."

"Who's listening at six Sunday morning?"

"A lot of people," John answers quickly. "Some are early risers, others are in a car on their way to work. Folks will start fixing breakfast and they'll turn on the radio in the kitchen. You'd be amazed. Now, when you read a commercial or play the tape, you've got to initial it in the station log. That's critical. It's our confirmation that the station put it on the air. The same goes for PSAs—public service announcements. Freebies as far as money is concerned. Important for what's called the public interest."

So many new things all at once.

"It gets routine," he says, picking up on my overload. "The fun stuff starts when we get live shows in there." He points over to the still dark Studio A. "Holy Rollers. Wait 'til you hear 'em."

"What do you mean?"

"They get all worked up and at some point start hollering, all in jibber jabber—you know, speaking in tongues."

"Tongues?"

"There's something in the Bible about speaking in tongues when the spirit is in you, when you feel the presence of the Lord."

"It doesn't sound like the usual fare at the First Methodist Church."

"That's for sure. But it just might liven up your day when you see it up close and personal!"

It all seemed overwhelming at first. But gradually began to make sense. My instruction started and stopped abruptly as he continued on the air, playing records and inserting occasional commercial breaks between songs. It seemed surreal to me, sitting one foot from John as he ended a comment to me, then pushed a button and spoke into the microphone to who knows how many hundreds or thousands of people.

He did most everything by himself until eight, when he had me read the news and commercials. He showed me how to cue the records on the turntables. I wore headphones and could position the records, with the "cue" position "off-air." There had to be just the right amount of start-up time as the turntable came up to speed before the needle reached the first audible portion and went out over the air.

The first live show on the program schedule was The Brother Bozart Hour. A little after eight-thirty, four men—presumably the Brother and three others—walked into the station. They went directly to Studio A, where they turned on the lights and took off their jackets and hats, putting them on a table. Clearly they knew the routine. They spent several minutes tuning a fiddle and guitar to the piano and then sat around. John walked over to see if everything was ready. We adjusted the microphone audio levels so they would be good from the get-go. I returned to the control room, cued the next record, and read the next commercial, all by myself.

At nine, John gave the station ID and the time, and said it was clear and 53 degrees. He introduced The Brother Bozart Hour and pointed his finger over to Studio A. The "On Air" sign flashed red, the good brother struck the first chord of "Nearer My God to Thee," and they were live with a format one-third authentic mountain gospel music, one-third "sermon," and one-third on-going request for money.

"Help me build this ministry. Get out the word of our dear Savior Jesus (he pronounced it 'Chee-Zus') to this part of the two Virginias, some day to the whole world, where sinners have yet to learn the truth through the cleansing waters of the one and only authentic Word," Brother Bozart intoned. His cadence rose and fell in rhythm, gathering strength and vigor. At nine forty-five, the front door opened once more and the men and women who would do the Upper Room Hour at ten o'clock filed in. The timing was tricky. While the Bozarts had had plenty of time to set up and get prepared, the studio was busy now. The Upper Room people took seats in the hall while the Bozart Hour wound down.

His final plea for money ended the program. "Only five dollars, brothers and sisters, *your* five dollars will allow us to continue this ministry. Send in your love gift to Brother Lonnie Bozart, that's B-O-Z-A-R-T, at Post Office Box one-sixty-one, Elgood, West Virginia. We'll not only keep coming over here to Princeton every Sunday morning to do the work of God, we'll get the word out on other stations as well. Thank you from the bottom of my heart, and until next week, be well, live right, and may the Lord Chee-Zus bless each and every one of you."

When two live programs were booked back to back, it was the station's policy to read the news at the hour so there was a five-minute break. It wasn't much, but enough to let the first group unhook, unplug, and put their instruments away, while the incoming people could come in quickly and position themselves. For the following live program, the instruments once again included the studio piano, but this time there was a guitar, a large upright bass, and a tambourine. In addition, two women formed a mini-choir. The Upper Room group had their own services Sunday evenings in a rented hall in Princeton, on the second story—hence the name Upper Room.

The leader was a serious, gaunt-looking man of about 50 who wore a suit and tie, one of those wide ties, like the one Huey Long wore. It had a large green and blue pattern on it and covered the entire front of his white shirt. He introduced himself as Reverend Blevins. He didn't play a musical instrument, but the key element of the program was his unique speaking ability.

"And now, ladies and gentlemen, WLOH is pleased to bring you Reverend Cecil Blevins and the Upper Room Hour." John announced it formally, following the news and weather. With that, the second live studio program of the morning was on the air.

"Watch this group. They really get going," he said to me as energetic music filled the studio. "Sometimes they shout, so you gotta be quick on the trigger and keep the mic volumes adjusted. It happens fast."

Unlike the Bozarts, the Upper Room people only mentioned money twice, once in the middle of the program, and once at the very end. The most unusual aspect of his delivery was the progression at times into babbles of words. They gushed out and were picked up by the others in the group: fast-clipped utterances. Speaking in tongues to the true believers. God was very real to them. It was clear to me, separated both by the glass of the control room, as well as my own doubts, that religion meant something entirely different to Reverend Blevins.

Religion for me, before I'd begun distancing myself, always had been a quiet subject, accepted as a matter of fact under the watchful eye of a handsome, bearded Jesus depicted in a clean, flowing garment with outstretched arms—the extensive panorama unfolding in the impressive, stained glass windows in the sanctuary of the First Methodist Church, while an organ played.

John's voice interrupted my thoughts. "Amazing what fifty bucks can buy in radio time, isn't it?"

After 55 minutes, Reverend Blevins signed off for another week, and at eleven o'clock a clear transition in programming content occurred when John allowed me to give the time and station call letters, and to announce, "This morning's church service is brought to you today, as every Sunday, by the First Methodist Church of Princeton, West Virginia." He threw the switch to patch in the remote broadcast over the telephone line. Mr. Emory's little electronic gadget connected one phone line to another and rich organ music, along with muffled sounds of people coughing and moving about in the large sanctuary, filled the airwaves. The final live religious broadcast of the day had begun.

After the hymns and sermon, the subtle but unmistakable indication of the collection process began. Muted organ music continued in the background, along with sounds of the elders as they moved about the pews passing the collection plates. Finally, the benediction brought the service to an end. John let me switch off the remote feed at one minute past noon, since he tried to include all of the minister's final remarks, but he said we could give Dr. Martin only one, maybe two minutes leeway. I read the noon AP news summary, started the LP that I'd cued previously, and WLOH began a block of mostly records and commercials for the afternoon.

There was one exception.

"You're all set, Jimmy," John told me. "The rest of the day is standard, with only Miss Mabel's tape at two. Do a news summary along with the time and temperature every hour on the hour. Be sure to fill in the logbook as you run every commercial or PSA. You're on your own. You've got my home phone number if you have any trouble. Lonnie will be here at three."

"Got it." My whole body was tingling.

"All right, buddy."

With that he gave me a pat on the shoulder. I watched as he walked down the hall. It was hard to believe. I was alone, at the helm of the ship plowing the proverbial airwaves from Radio Hill, the highest point in Princeton.

I found 45's on the "soft hit" list in the record library. They were, at least in my opinion, middle-of-the-road material. Many of the musical cuts were instrumental and played back-to-back, which allowed time to catch up on the logbook and check for more material. At one o'clock, the phone rang. It was John.

"The modulation sounds high. You might want to drop it a bit."

I had increased it to 80 percent, up from 50 percent where he'd had it earlier. I didn't mention that detail.

"I'll take care of it," I told him, and moved the knob until it decreased to 65 percent. With only 250 watts WLOH needed all the oomph it could get! Biondi and John R. clearly had plenty of punch with their big stations.

At two o'clock, I read the news and announced Miss Mabel's Gospel Hour, then started the tape. A spindly voice was heard, accompanied by piano playing—apparently Miss Mabel herself. She paid, I learned later, $30 for each program, mailing the tape every week from a Bluefield, Virginia address.

I initialed the station log to confirm the tape indeed had been played. I'm sure I put it back in a slot in the tape shelf. But somehow, it disappeared. To this day, I can't figure out what happened. When the station couldn't mail the tape back to her, it brought down the wrath of Miss Mabel, who apparently could become quite wrathful.

The final segment ran smoothly. Wendie Johnston called.

"Don't sound like a hick," he advised. "Be sure and pronounce the *g* at the end of words."

I thanked him sarcastically for his support. He finally acknowledged that the programming sounded smooth and that "you haven't destroyed the radio station yet." Lonnie came in for his three o'clock shift and immediately reached over and adjusted the modulation back to 50 percent. John must have called him.

When I got home, Daddy was asleep in the chair, surrounded by a blue haze. Mom was in the kitchen.

"I heard you on the radio," she said. "You sounded just fine!"

"Thanks, Mom. It was fun.

"The station sounded louder than normal."

Chapter 14

THE YEAR 1959 ushered in our senior year. Everyone's step seemed quicker. The Tiger football team once again was undefeated, at least until the initial game, and we managers, now the king rats as seniors, bossed the lowly juniors around as we toiled in the last warm days to get ready for the opener.

A pleasant surprise for me was being selected as a reporter for *Tiger Review*, the one-hour program on WLOH every Saturday morning. It was a big deal for incoming seniors, and two girls and I were picked. We'd submitted applications back in May, and I'd forgotten about it until Miss Gentry, a speech and English teacher, asked me if I still was interested. It seemed like a milestone on the roadmap to the big-time radio announcer hall of fame.

Wendie gave me the usual hard time. "What's the matter? They running dry on people who can enunciate the English language?" He was an editor on *The Tiger*, the annual yearbook, and continued to cover the Concord College football games for the *Bluefield Daily Telegraph*. "Is it that hard to pronounce words and maintain some semblance of the manner in which they are described in a dictionary?"

"Whimpy, er, um, Wendie—I'm sorry I didn't enunciate your name properly. The people at dear old PHS clearly can tell talent. Unlike some newspaper types I know."

"Good grief. I suppose your emergence as an incipient radioman contaminated their thought processes. Oh, by the way. I saw what's-her-name and her mother yesterday. She's back from her summer trip to God knows where, somewhere out West. She asked if you were around. I told her you had moved to Puente Arenas to become a monk, but somehow she didn't believe me."

Margie Rey had been away all summer. Every year she went to Utah to spend the summer with her aunt on a ranch. She said she'd be going to Brigham Young for college. BYU could have been on Mars as far as I knew. In the first few hectic days at school I saw her, of course. But we really hadn't reconnected after the absence, which had *not* made the parting sweeter. I decided to call her. While the Howlands' number was ringing, I dragged the long tangled green cord and stepped out on the back sun porch.

"Howland residence."

"Hello. It's Jimmy." *Why don't I have a more original line?*

"Hi. We haven't had a chance to talk."

"I know. Things are so busy the first few days." I pause. "How was your summer?"

"Oh, it was fine. Daddy's sister and her family live in the country, outside Salt Lake City. I spent almost the entire summer with my cousins. Now I can remember their names." She's laughing.

"What's the weather like out there?" Try to make conversation.

"Hot in the day, but it cools off at night. They live in a valley. There are really tall mountains around one side, to the east, thousands of feet higher than the valley floor. They have super skiing in the winter. It's much drier than here. I missed the green," she concludes, giggling a bit. "Salt Lake City is huge! And the temple is gorgeous . . . Oh . . . and everyone kids me about my accent."

"What accent?" I drawl, sounding like a hillbilly. We both laugh. "And, you said . . . Temple?"

"The LDS Temple," she adds. "A huge cathedral—like you see in story books. Spires and all that."

If I were more glib and slick like Wendie, I'd say something about gargoyles and ask about gnomes and hunchbacks. Her family attends the Mormon Church over in Pearisburg, Virginia, the only one in the area. From snippets of conversation I've overheard, Mom and Dad consider the church a somewhat irregular religious group. *Latter Day Saints* mean nothing to me. At least *Saints* sounds like it belongs in a church's name. The issue doesn't register with me. Conversation languishes.

Margie Rey's cute figure leaps into my mind. "How about going to a movie this weekend?" I ask.

"I'd love that."

"It'll have to be Saturday night. I'm a football manager again this year, and the team plays at Mullens." Anything but cool and smooth. I feel like the most inept communicator on earth.

She ends with sweet-little-girl speak. "I've got to run. But listen to the request show. There just might be a request for little ol' you." A hundred pinprick emotions dance, exciting little testosterone-fueled stick-men all in a row. Together, we bring the phone back into the kitchen, its cord all kinked up and twisted.

"Was that Margie Rey?" Mom asks, while she mixes up some concoction. "How was their trip to Utah?"

"Yes, and good," I answer absentmindedly. "We're going to the movie Saturday. It's O.K. to use The Bomb, isn't it?"

"That's fine." Mom likes Margie Rey. Her mother does Mom's hair at Ellen's Beauty Salon.

"Thanks. I'm going up to my room. Daddy not home?"

"Not yet."

It will be another late night. With Susie back at WVU, Mom and I are the home team. I walk up the stairs, turn on the little Emerson radio on my desk, and lounge on the bed. It's a comfortable evening, even upstairs where the temperature always is warmer than downstairs. Harry Gentry is playing the nightly requests on his call-in show, and at about a quarter past nine, his familiar voice announces, "And now, a special request—and she has a nice voice on the phone. 'To Know Him Is to Love Him' by The Teddy Bears, dedicated to Jimmy."

The little testosterone guys stir. At nine-thirty, I walk over into the tiny nook (the word "room" definitely connotes too much room) next to the chimney bricks. The space houses Mom's old Singer sewing machine and sewing supplies, as well as the small table that's the home of K8JPV, my grand (I use that term sarcastically) ham radio station. I've upgraded to the regular license, allowing me to drop the "N," which signifies the end to my novice license status.

Soon the familiar sounds of Morse code pop into my earphones. At night, the 40-meter band is alive, and signals from most of the eastern United States and Canada come in. My Hallicrafters S-38D receiver is a low-end, inexpensive model, and since the frequency drifts, I continually have to re-tune the stations. Finally it settles down and becomes more or less stable. One of my radio friends from Oak Ridge, Tennessee, is calling CQ—shorthand for "I'm seeking a contact." Maybe CQ means "seek you." When Don, whose call is K4PUZ, finishes, I answer him. We're the same age and share the same interest in the magic of short-wave radio. The distance between Princeton and eastern Tennessee is such that the "skip," or the distance the signal covers as it bounces off the sky, is good for both nights and days.

Mom comes upstairs about ten. Daddy still isn't home. "It's time for bed. Better wrap it up now." The timing is good. Don and I have just signed off.

"How's Susie doing at WVU?" I ask her.

"Oh, she's fine. She likes it in Education." Not a hint of the roommate issue.

Right then, a commotion of some sort erupts: sounds of scuffing shoes, talking, laughing, someone coughing. It's coming from the front porch. One of the voices is Daddy's. He's giggling.

"Take it easy, Jim. Slow down!" someone shouts.

More giggling.

"Shush! Be quiet," another voice says.

Daddy is laughing, whispering loudly in an exaggerated manner. "O.K., O.K. I'll be quiet." His words are slurred.

Footsteps retreat. An engine starts and a car pulls away. Men from the Elks Club often drive him home. They parked his Buick demonstrator outside on North Walker and drove back in one of their own cars. Daddy shuffles in. The door slams.

"I'm home." Almost theatrically staged, it's an attempt to sound as if it's five-thirty and the man of the house has returned from work.

"I'm upstairs with Jimmy. Supper is on the stove," Mom says loudly. "Be down in a minute." That is the end of our conversation. "Good night," she says, and gives me a little peck on my forehead. She seems resigned.

"It must be hard," I say.

"Yes, it is, honey." She leaves my room and heads down the stairs.

Now they're talking, sort of. I can't hear it all. Mom must be putting Daddy's food out for him. Their bedroom door closes. She's gone to bed. His distinctive cigarette smoke is drifting upstairs through the heat vent in the hallway. Daddy makes quite a bit of noise as he moves around the kitchen. Cabinet doors open and close. He bumps into the kitchen table. After a period of relative quiet the familiar one-way conversation begins. Daddy must be mixing Four Roses and Coke. There is no "stop" button.

"What'd you say, Joe?"

"Come on, Joe. Set 'em up."

The rhythm of school on Friday had a cadence of its own. Since the football team had its first game at Mullens, the bus would leave the field in Princeton at three. It was a two-hour drive and Coach Ebert wanted us to arrive at least two hours before game time so there'd be plenty of time to have a snack, dress, and warm up.

Each player was responsible for putting all his equipment in a duffle bag and carrying it to the rear end of the bus where we manager types would stack them. During the trip we'd lie on them, and do something creative like count the number of white dashed lines on the road as we looked out the rear window. Everyone was nervous. Conversations between the players were hushed.

We called the first time-out about halfway through the first quarter. While Wendie and I were passing around the water, guys shouted, "We can take these guys. We can take these guys!" We couldn't. We didn't. We lost 42 to 20. Mullens scored the final two touchdowns in the fourth quarter. Our guys ran out of gas.

After the bus ride back to the locker room in Princeton, we managers—both juniors and seniors—did the dirty laundry duty. I finally got home at one in the morning.

Not even six hours later, thunder, lightning, and a pouring rain waked me. I dragged myself out of bed at seven for some breakfast through both the physical and the metaphorical storms. What a day to have our first *Tiger Review*! Since I would be with the team all season, one of my assignments was to summarize every game—an insider's view along with Rebecca Eastland, who was a cheerleader. Becky and I had agreed to write our individual accounts and meet at the station at eight-fifteen to combine them into something coherent from the two perspectives. Hopefully, the resulting report would be a good way to cover every game in a unique fashion.

"How was the game last night? It sounds like it was exciting." Mom always put a positive slant on things. She'd already read the account in the *Daily Telegraph*. After my late night, I had newfound respect for the sports reporter who'd traveled over to the game. I didn't know how he'd managed to get his write-up back to the paper, since he couldn't have gotten back before midnight himself.

"Tough way to start the season," I said. "How's Daddy?" Saturday was always an important business day at Gibson's.

"He's getting ready. He was home early last night. He's fine."

"Good." I had nothing more to add. "Mom, I've gotta meet Becky Eastland at the radio station at a quarter past eight. We're doing the game report, and I need to pull my notes together."

"I understand," she said. "Here are some eggs and country ham from Aunt Mollie's farm. All very good. Be sure to drink all your orange juice."

At that moment, Daddy walked into the room and cleared his throat. The sounds scraped the inside of my ears.

It was impressive how professional and nice he looked when he went to work. "Where are you off to in such a big hurry? How was the game last night?" he asked.

"We lost forty-two to twenty. But the team played pretty well. Mullens is supposed to be strong." Hope springs eternal.

"That's good," he said. Daddy would check the scores of both the Princeton and Bluefield games so he could make small talk at Gibson's. He was able to carry on those peripheral conversations and could feign interest in what others are saying. I don't think the subject mattered one way or the other to him. But he always said, "You can't sell an automobile to someone if he dislikes you or thinks you don't care about him."

"I'm about ready to drive up to the radio station. Today's the first *Tiger Review* program."

"Well," he said, clearing his throat again, "have a good time." He probably had no idea what I was talking about. "I'm off to the dealership."

"Jim, are you sure you don't want me to fix you some breakfast?" Mom asked.

"That's all right, Sara," he answered and headed out through the TV room toward the front door. There was no apparent bitterness between them. Nor was there any overt affection.

It took me 10 minutes to jot down my notes. Nervousness started up as the time approached.

"I'll be back after ten. Bye, Mom."

"Break a leg," she said as I walked out the front door . . . that theatrical flare.

The Bomb started right away. It always did. I backed out of our driveway and let the car idle as it rolled down to the stop sign at Park Avenue. The radio warmed up, and there was John Shelton giving the news headlines, then saying, "Stay tuned for more Saturday morning music. Then at nine, we'll have our first *Tiger Review* program of the new school year. *Tiger Review* is the weekly update from Princeton High School."

"All right!" I yelled to myself.

Park Avenue climbed in a gentle and steady fashion, past older homes on large leafy lots. It ended abruptly at the intersection with Low Gap Road, a dangerous, narrow two-lane road that wound around behind Radio Hill. The two miles of roller-coaster ups and downs were punctuated by nasty S-curves, even tricky at 25 miles an hour. Finally I turned sharply onto a small street with no name—we called it Radio Drive. It climbed up to the very tip-top, ending in the gravel parking lot in front of the station. The radio station was a Deco-style: vertical opaque glass pane sections, one on each side of the front door, giving it the impression of a diner. The building itself appeared even smaller because it was dwarfed by the gigantic steel radio tower immediately behind it. The tower stood on a massive square base, at least 20 feet on a side, and jutted 150 feet high into the sky from the highest point of the hill. A radio station was supposed to look like this.

Fantasy alert: High school student is discovered on local program. Signed to a nationwide rock and roll show, alternating between WLS and WLAC on Saturday nights!

"Ye-ah!" Two syllables from the future radio king's accent.

Becky was there already. She had driven her father's late-model Buick that Mr. Eastland had purchased from Dad. I parked next the big car, grabbed my hastily scribbled notes, and headed for the front door. As I reached the entrance hallway, my thoughts flipped back to that Sunday morning. I still can't figure out what happened to Miss Mabel's Gospel Hour tape.

"Hi, Jimmy. Good morning."

Snap back to the present. "Good morning, Becky. All set?"

The lights in Studio A are on and stools are assembled around two stand-up microphones. Just like Sunday mornings. Becky, as usual, is dressed like she's at a fashion show. Perfect for any occasion. Always had been since our seventh grade days at Mercer School.

"Here are my notes," she says. "Look them over while I go over yours."

Her notes are typed on high-end note cards, the engraved types you'd send out to thank someone for a special gift, fancy ones with an embedded watermark. Her comments are a pep talk—as if you'd seen a defeat from afar and wanted to console the losers. She noted the crowd noise from the Princeton fans that had traveled to the game. The third quarter touchdown that closed the deficit to 28-20 was a moral victory.

That's all right with me. We include her material verbatim. My notes, random and messy on little three-by-five index cards, deal with what I consider inside stuff: the pre-game and post-game comments from Coach Ebert, and the half-time speech that our co-captains gave in the locker room. I have some team stats from the press box, too. The two reports are complementary.

"You know, this is pretty good," she says. She's right.

Meena Gordon walks in at quarter to nine. The three of us are together for the first time as the *Tiger Review* staff. She's tall, with extroverted self-confidence, dramatic dark features, and a strong speaking voice—seems right at home. She's all over the social scene and gossip, and that includes some humorous comments about the Sub Debs and Su Wans and their competition with each other. She has a few little ditties such as "Did you see who Lou Ann Spencer was talking to at her locker Tuesday afternoon? Lorena better pay attention." Between her report and our game summary we've got time for a couple of popular songs, which we select in advance so John Shelton has them set to go. The show goes off well.

"Good report on the game," Meena says afterward. But I know it's the gossip section that's sure to become the talk of the school.

"Hey, big shot. Where did you get all that social dirt?" I ask her.

"None of your beeswax," she says. "And you'd better be careful. I've got my spies checking, and I hear the name Margie Rey floating around. So you just never know." She shoots me a knowing wink and heads out.

The Bomb is clean and as spiffy as its fading green color can be. I've vacuumed out the interior and even used Windex to make sure the glass is spotless inside and outside.

Margie Rey lives out of town in a new brick home with large metal awnings, each with the letter "H." They look like eyebrows over the windows.

She opens the door before I can reach for the doorbell and motions me in. Her parents are in the family room, where Mr. Howland has his stereo equipment. Wooden speakers, large ones as well as strange little conical-shaped things, dominate the room. He goes into an animated discussion of audio equipment. It's amazing to me that a single pickup needle rotating around a groove in a record can somehow produce two separate channels of sound. How do they do that?

Mrs. Howland redirects the conversation. "Jimmy, how are your parents?"

I know from Mom that her name is Ellen and that she and my mother talk at her beauty shop, a tidy little three-seater located on Mercer Street.

"Just fine, Mrs. Howland," I answer, with a little pause as I mentally delete Ellen and insert Mrs. Howland. "How was your trip out West?" Nice move. Get them talking!

"It was just wonderful," Mrs. Howland answers. "Bill's sister lives in Utah. It's so different from here."

I try to think of a clever response or a probing question. *Tell me about the mountains that ring the Great Salt Lake to the east. What's it like to walk on Temple Square?*

I'm just sitting there—some sort of response is called for.

What does your daughter look like in her bra and panties?

Hold that for sure.

"It sounds so far away." It's all I can muster. *I'm an idiot!*

Margie Rey rescues me. "We'd better get going. The show starts in fifteen minutes."

She has on a sleeveless blouse made from sleek and sheer material. It's hard to appear to look at her mother and father yet maintain a peripheral view of her bosom.

Her voice is chirpy. "I'll be home no later than ten-thirty," she says as she stands.

"That's fine, honey. You both have fun," Mrs. Howland says. Mr. Howland is silent, with a knowing father's look in my direction. I glance at him just long enough to let him know I understand.

The Mercer Theater is filling up fast. We go in through the lobby with its thick but traffic-worn carpet. "Popcorn? Something to drink?" She declines, her light brown hair shifting smoothly from side to side.

There it is. A sign that says "Colored Seating" and an arrow pointing upstairs to the balcony.

I'd never noticed it before. My thoughts shift to late night discussions with Arcie. The main (white) entrance for the lower-level seats is straight ahead, unmarked. A young colored couple walks by and heads to the right and up the stairs. We proceed on straight. For the first time, I'm aware—acutely aware. There *is* a system in place. A system that treats people differently. It's right in front of me.

The lower level is about half full. We find two seats with a vacant one on either side. Margie Rey carries a sweater to wear over her tantalizingly sheer sleeveless blouse. We put it and my windbreaker on the two crucial empty seats to stake out a claim. It should remain open unless the theater gets crowded.

By the time the feature starts, I'm consumed with the elbow and forearm proximity move, culminating with some combination of holding hands or putting my arm around her shoulder. I sense she's leaning toward me, a successful beginning. Our arms are touching, even though it's a back-of-the-arm to a back-of-the-arm closeness. I can feel her warmth. The palm of my hand sweats from my nerves. After clumsily attempting a clandestine hand-drying movement, I tippy-toe my fingers across her wrist. She turns her palm up to meet my now only moderately damp hand. If she notices any residual moisture, she keeps it to herself. These complex moves require the first 30 minutes of the movie. We spend the next hour or so working our way through various hand-holding positions. The simple light touch. The "clasp," where my fingers alternate with her fingers. The stroking move where one of us gently moves a hand and caresses the other's. These all are proper and aboveboard, apart from the nefarious techniques where one person rubs the inside of the other's palm, indicating "I want you." The thought of that makes me blush and starts my hand sweating again. Those little testosterone soldiers are on the march again.

At nine forty-five, the movie ends. I'm emotionally exhausted. People from the balcony come down the stairs and join the stream proceeding into the main lobby area and out to the street. I scan their faces. What are they thinking?

Mooney's is its usual Saturday night happening place, so full I have to park off to one side. Wendie's chrome-mobile Chrysler convertible isn't there, but Mack Andrews is parked in his usual central position. A crowd draws us over.

"Jimmy, you actually got a date," Mack says and looks at Margie Rey. His glance lingers a bit long. "Congratulations for getting him out of his radio room for a change. Maybe you can help him understand there *is* a thing called female companionship!"

I blush. She seems confident. "Don't worry about it, Mack. If he needs tutoring, I can take care of it."

"He just might be salvageable," Mack replies, his black DA glistening in the neon lights.

The whole interaction is embarrassing. I say something, no doubt nerd-like, and lead her back to the bland green sanctuary of The Bomb. She slides across the seat to the middle.

Following something to eat, the sensation of her body next to mine brings out the little hormonal stickmen as we drive back. "Thanks for that request the other night," I mention.

"You heard it?" She seems pleased.

I slow down, carefully turn in, and switch off the motor. The driveway is beside the house where the front porch lights don't reach. There in the dark, she makes no effort to move toward the passenger door.

"Thanks for the movie," she says and turns—she's looking up at me. I lean over and kiss her. Her lips quiver just a bit, a tantalizingly tiny bit, as she leans toward me in response. After a few seconds, she slowly withdraws and puts her head on my shoulder. "I'd better get in now."

We hold hands as we walk to the front door and into the bright light.

"Good night," she says, opening the door. "I had fun."

The door closes with a well-insulated sound. As soon as I round the corner and am safely outside the cone of the lights, I sprint, running on air.

Chapter 15

THE PROCESS OF class officer selection took place at the start of every school year. Unknown (to us) teachers picked two students to run for each office, and somehow they nominated me for class treasurer. To be selected was an honor. That was the good news. The bad news was my opponent. She was so pretty it was hard to look her in the eye. Prior to the election, it must have been completely beyond any practical possibilities that she ever would have known, or cared, who I was.

Patti Moreland had a full figure. Not a blemish marred her smooth skin. And if that wasn't enough, she was nice to everyone. She never dated anyone from PHS. We heard she dated an older boy who'd graduated already from another high school.

The two candidates for each office were required to make a short campaign speech on the loudspeaker system at some point. Our guidance, much too gentle a word, from Miss Gentry included that we must say "if I be elected." Not "if I am," not "if I were to be," not "if you vote me in." "If I be elected!" None of us ever would be caught dead speaking that way, but that's what we all said. I actually got the opportunity to sit right next to the gorgeous Patti Moreland and we both said those exact words as we read our little two-minute speeches. The public address microphone, the broadcasting medium to the entire high school universe, was tucked away in a tiny anteroom—more of a cubby hole—next to the principal's office. The scene reminded me of the Wizard of Oz. We crouched behind a shabby curtain and talked into a microphone while magically, our voices boomed ethereally through the clouds, er, the classrooms. My speech, to misuse that word, stated that it was an honor to be considered and I would discharge the duties of class treasurer in an honest and credible manner. Of course I hadn't the slightest idea what the duties were. There had to be some connection with money. But no one ever explained to me in advance what a class treasurer did.

On Election Day, paper ballots were passed out in each senior home room. It was strange seeing my name printed right there on the ballot. I marked my X. At least I would get one vote. Wendie, who sat next to me, gave me the finger and smiled.

The results were announced the next day, and it came as no surprise that Patti had been elected. What was surprising was when Arcie Peterson stopped me in the hall.

"Jimmy, sorry you didn't make it. You know. Treasurer."

"No problem. I never expected to beat Patti."

"I thought for sure you'd win. Every one of my friends voted for you."

"Really? Are you kidding?"

"I'm telling you. And no one told them to," he said. "You're popular with my people. You're always polite. And you never give us any signs we aren't welcome."

"Well, thank you. But she's also nice."

"It's more than that. You're my man! You put up with me with all the band stuff. We talk. All that."

"You got a point there. Do I get extra credit for that?" He's right. We do talk. "Hey, class is starting. Catch you later."

"Take care."

History class emphasized details and facts, including memorizing the words to "The West Virginia Hills" ("how majestic and how grand"). But we didn't cover the more substantial economic and cultural drivers that led to separation from Virginia during the Civil War. Even though the U.S. Constitution clearly states that no state can be admitted to the

Union either as a part of another state or as a combination of two or more other states, President Lincoln decided to admit West Virginia, even as his own cabinet was split on it. And as a slave state at that! That wasn't taught at all.

What was presented was a barrage of dates and rote memory exercises. We had to know all 55 counties and their county seats. That's not history, that's a memory exercise. There could be a prize for that, like a spelling bee. Memorize, memorize, memorize. Why did I think this would not help me in 20 years? There's no way anyone will remember this. Forget years. How about 20 months for these details.

The first two verses of "The West Virginia Hills" . . . gotta memorize them.

After school, Mom asks about the election.

"Patti Moreland won, like I expected. But Arcie Peterson told me the colored kids all voted for me. That was interesting."

"How nice," Mom says. "That's something you can be proud of. It means you're treating them as you'd like to be treated."

I nodded and wondered if treating people with respect included having them as a roommate at WVU. It wasn't my fight. I hadn't taken sides in it. Was that cowardly?

"I'd better call Wendie," I tell Mom. "See if he's driving to school tomorrow." I drag the green phone to the back porch.

"Hello." His voice is measured.

"This is the Federal Bureau of Investigation. We're looking for Wendell Johnston." My best attempt at a serious voice.

"Is this J. Edgar himself? W. Johnston here, reporting for duty." Wendie doesn't miss a beat. Not a pause, nary a hitch.

"It's *Mr.* J. Edgar to low level newspaper guys."

"That's *Mr.* Newspaper Guy."

"O.K., Mr. Newspaper Guy. Any chance the chrome-mobile has a vacancy tomorrow morning?"

"You mean Mr. Future Pulitzer Prize Winner?"

"For the penetrating series on Concord College football?"

"That's correct, Mr. DJ. You got it. At least I'm not the Sunday announcer and sometimes disk jockey at a radio station in the boondocks."

That one hurts.

"Biondi got his start somewhere. Give me a break."

"O.K." He's easing up. "Quarter to eight."

Mom is sitting in a rocking chair, still watching television.

"Wendie's giving me a ride to school tomorrow," I offer, before she can ask.

"That's nice."

"I'm going up and listen on the ham radio for a while."

"Don't stay up too late. And remember your homework."

Soon the mystical sounds of Morse code flood into my earphones. "CQ BSA DE K4RDD K." K4RDD is calling CQ BSA. He lives near Atlanta, and I've contacted him before. Atlanta is a nice "skip" from Princeton at night. His call is shorthand for "I'm seeking a contact in the Boy Scouts of America contest." It's a radio contest sponsored by *Boys' Life* magazine.

The BSA contest, which runs for two full weeks, has just started, and the radio frequencies are full of teenage hams like me, sending their scouting rank along with name and location, as well as adult hams who had been scouts.

"K4RDD DE K8JPV," I tap out on my military surplus J-38 key.

Nothing.

"CQ BSA DE K4RDD K"

There he is again. Nice strong signal, too. He should be able to hear me.

"K4RDD K4RDD DE K8JPV K8JPV BSA K"

There, that's a good long call.

"K8JPV DE K4RDD R TNX FOR THE CALL UR SIGS 579 NR ATLANTA, GA MY NAME IS MARK. STAR BSA. HOW COPY? K8JPV DE K4RDD K"

The "K" means "end of transmission," or simply "over." I got him, my first contact in the contest. I'm pumped up. My time to respond.

K4RDD DE K8JPV R ("R" means "Roger," or "O.K.") TNX MARK UR SIGS 589 HR IN PRINCETON WVA MY NAME IS JIMMY. EAGLE BSA. 73 K4RDD DE K8JPV"

Just as I send the final portion of my call letters, the sound of the front door opening sneaks into my earphones. Then, "I'm home." Daddy sounds artificial. "I suppose I've missed supper by a little," he continues, apparently impressed by his enhanced sense of joviality.

"K8JPV DE K4RDD" Mark's signal breaks back into the present. "TNX JIMMY FOR THE . . ." At that moment, the front door shuts with a thud. Daddy begins singing.

"Carry me back to ol' Virginny, that's where the . . ."

His voice is louder in my ears than the radio signals. He pauses. He must see Mom by the television. I can hear Mark again. "AND 73. GL IN THE BSA CONTEST K8JPV DE K4RDD." The term "73" is radio lingo for "best wishes," and "GL" means "good luck." He got it all O.K.

Daddy moves a chair away from the kitchen table, making a loud scraping sound. Any sense of normalcy ends. Home like this, he'll smoke, eat, and drink until he slumps over or falls off the chair.

"Sara, is there anything to eat?" The sound follows the warm air up through the heater opening.

"Your plate is in the refrigerator. Do you want me to warm it up for you?"

"Thank you. That'd be nice." His words are way too smooth.

The chair creaks as she gets up. TV audio continues from a station in Roanoke. Now the refrigerator opens, then closes. Another door shuts. It must be the oven.

"It will take ten minutes or so. We had a nice supper tonight. I'm going to bed now," she says.

"Why, that's mighty nice of you," Daddy says. Such a charmer. Mom turns off the television. Her door closes. The house is quiet.

"Why *yes*!" he shouts suddenly. "I do believe I will have another one. Thank you, my good sir."

Where am I? Listening to K4RDD calling CQ BSA again. It's after eleven. The schoolwork remains undone.

"Carry me back to ol' Virginny, that's where the cotton fields . . ."

Wendie drives to school the next morning. A cool, wet deposit covers the Dodge. The windshield wipers sweep away the moisture, only to have it immediately reform. It takes the entire five-minute drive to school for the heater to dry off the windshield and make the chilly interior of the car tolerable.

With my early study hall, I should be able to get all the stuff done that I didn't do the night before. Publius and Furianus, the two main characters in my Latin textbook, are up to their usual hi-jinks in Rome. I take care of that reading before Miss Kane has the chance to catch me red-handed and humiliate me in Latin.

We're nudged through the intricacies of trigonometry in Mr. Johnson's class. He's a mild mannered-man who is pleasant and quiet in class—thus the nickname "Jolly Jack." So far, all that radioing last night hasn't done me in.

The lunch bell rings, and I set out on a mad dash through the crowded corridors to stash my books and papers. Donnie Davis and Marnie Bowland are flirting at his locker, one down from mine. Marnie is cute, but she smokes and seems a little "fast" somehow. She's wearing her Su Wan jacket. It goes with his letterman's jacket.

"Jimmy, you gonna take that test?" Donnie asks.

"What test?"

"Some sort of test . . . National Merit Scholarship," he says. "Mrs. Dunfee told me about it. She wants me to take it."

"Don't know a thing about it. When is it?"

"Pretty sure it's Saturday."

"Thanks for the info." That's interesting.

"Come on. Let's go eat," Donnie says to Marnie. She takes his arm, looking sexy and pouty. He points over to the table where the teachers gather to eat. "Go check it out, Jimmy."

I walk over and politely wait for them to look my way.

"Mrs. Dunfee, Donnie Davis just mentioned a test. Some sort of scholarship test. Could you give me some information?"

She looks at me and pauses. It's a bit disconcerting. Is this a secret?

She seems to collect herself. "Yes, Jimmy. It's the initial examination for the merit scholarships. They're available on a national scale."

Mr. Fletcher, the principal and a friend of our family from the First Methodist Church, sits across from her. "You should take it, Jimmy," he interjects. There is no doubt in his response. "Room three forty-one at nine. Saturday morning. Sign up there."

"Thanks." I say with relief. "I will."

Why does Donnie know about this and I don't? He's a student leader, of course, and a good student. My grades are decent, but not "A"s. I'm not focused on them. Last night is a good example of my not prioritizing studying.

Taking the test means missing *Tiger Review* at the radio station. But I drive to the school and climb the stairs. The silence in the building is in marked contrast to the usual daily clamor. The 10 or 15 other seniors already there are the brains and leaders of our class. Donnie comes in just after I do.

"Glad you were able to make it, Jimmy." Mrs. Dunfee seems sincere. But if she's so glad, why didn't she tell me in advance? "There's a charge of one dollar."

I have 50 cents total.

"Donnie," I whisper, "Do you have a buck I can borrow?"

"You're in luck," he says, reaching for his wallet. "My last two. One for you and one for me."

"Thanks. Pay you back Monday."

Mrs. Dunfee signs us in and then addresses the room. "I think that's everyone. You're here because you've been invited. We believe you have the ability to excel in the National Merit Scholarship program. It's an opportunity to benefit yourself as well as to bring recognition to Princeton High School."

I slink down in the seat.

"Could you tell us a little more about this?" one of the girls asks. "What exactly is the National Merit Scholarship?"

"It's a standardized examination given to incoming seniors—a test to measure knowledge. It's not an IQ test, but checks to see what you know and how you reason with facts," Mrs. Dunfee says. "Money is donated, and scholarships are available strictly on a merit basis. In addition, certain corporations have special funds available for employees' children who qualify."

Fat chance of that. I wonder if Gibson's Motors donated any scholarship money. That absurdity makes me giggle.

"Jimmy, do you have a question?" Mrs. Dunfee asks pointedly.

"No ma'am," I say, looking down at the desk. My face feels hot.

"Then, if there are no further questions, let's proceed," she says.

We spread out so everyone is separated by at least one vacant desk. For some reason, I'm completely calm. Based on snippets of conversation, it's clear that some of the kids have been prepping. They were cramming while I was occupied with my dirty jockstrap duties for the football team, the Roadsters, *Tiger Review*, the job at the radio station, the Boy Scout contest on ham radio, and of course, Margie Rey. It's pathetic in one way, great in another.

Anyhow, I feel smart, even if others don't think so. Everything I know is locked in there. What happens, happens.

The test is thorough and difficult, but it seems to go well. I know most of the answers and work the math problems in the side margins, at least to the extent we've been exposed to them. Several questions are based on strange "S" symbols and other characters. I have no idea what they mean, and don't spend any time on them.

My mind is clear and I'm thinking quickly. With ten minutes left, I finish the last page. The math portion is correct, except for the weird ones. I go back over everything to make sure I haven't made any silly errors. It looks pretty good.

Donnie is sitting several desks away. He's working feverishly on the final page. At that moment, Mrs. Dunfee says, "O.K., students. Time's up. Put down your pencils and hand your test sheets to me." He puts his hands up and shoves the air away with a symbolic breast stroke.

As we leave, Donnie hands his exam to her and pantomimes a huge wiping of his supposedly sweaty brow. "What a test!"

"Why, Mr. Don Davis, I'm sure you did just fine," she says. "Good luck against Oak Hill next week."

And good luck there was. Oak Hill came into town with three wins and no losses, while we'd lost our first three games. But the football gods were with us. Our guys played well, and we won 20 to 14 after Donnie recovered a fumble and ran it back for a touchdown with one minute left.

Following the game, the dirty laundry patrol, now made up of the three juniors, got all the uniforms into duffle bags and swept up the locker room. Wendie and I finally left for the Memorial Building. The Blue Aces were playing, so the dance was a big deal.

At the Ma and Pa table, the two women and one man were friendly, almost too forthcoming. It was easy: just walk up, pay your dollar, and be white. Everyone smiled. It would be honorable to say I abhorred the whole system and wanted to demonstrate in front of the building carrying a sign, and then arrange a major boycott to effect social change. But it wouldn't be true. After all the long, sincere, and informative discussions with Arcie, I *was* beginning to recognize the fundamental inequalities and wrongs in the system. But I was still passive. We all were.

Wendie and I paid our money and walked through the granite lobby and up the grand circular stairway. I adopted my most confident high school posture as we stood by a wall, our eyes adjusting to the darkness.

"One more and we'll take a brief break," the lead singer said as the last strains of a fast song ended. "Here's a slow one to close out the first set." He segued immediately into "Donna," sounding a lot like Richie Valens.

Margie Rey's light touch was a pleasant surprise.

"Hi, Jimmy. Good game tonight."

"Thanks. It feels good to win one."

I did feel a part of it, even though my main contribution included running out to get the kicking tee after the second half kickoff, lugging water onto the field during time-outs, and supervising the juniors dealing with dirty uniforms.

The music surrounded us. We walked a few steps out into the dance floor, found an opening and slid into the movement. She nestled up close. I could feel her against me.

After the last dance, we walked out to the car. Wendie and Ann Murphy, his new girlfriend, were making out in the front seat. I tapped lightly on the side window. "Excuse me. Any way to get a ride home?"

They attempted to look composed. Ann leaned forward as we ducked down and got into the rear seat. It was a quick trip to Margie Rey's. She and I had a few moments together near the front door. The front light was on, of course. We kissed there in the light. I waited until she closed the door, then walked back to the car. Wendie circled around Courthouse Square and headed up North Walker Street. He and Ann dropped me off, then turned away from the direction to Ann's house.

Daddy's car was in the driveway, a positive sign. Yet when I walked in, he was slumped in a chair, his head on the kitchen table. Cigarettes were burning in two different ashtrays. Blue haze enveloped the room.

"Daddy. You all right?"

He stirred. "Jimmy . . . that you?" The words were slurred. He struggled to sit up. "Were you at a dance?"

"Yes. At the Memorial Building."

"Mother mentioned it. Have a good time?"

"It was fun. Wendie Johnston brought me home."

"That's good," he said. "I'd better get to bed. Must be late."

"It's about midnight."

Daddy rose unsteadily, crushed out one of the two cigarettes, and stumbled toward their bedroom. I put his dirty dishes away and stubbed out the remaining cigarette. Its warm softness felt strange and dirty in my hand. Finally, I turned off the light and went upstairs. It was smokier up there than downstairs.

The alarm pierced the morning. Sounds from the kitchen made it into my semiconscious haze: bacon frying on the stove and Mom's footfalls. The combination of the sizzling and aroma jolted me into the present. Pulling on jeans and a shirt, I jotted down some observations from the game for *Tiger Review* and walked stiffly down the stairs. Someone was in the bathroom. Daddy must be up.

"Good morning, Jimmy," Mom said. She seemed cheerful and peppy. "How was the dance? Did you see Margie Rey?"

"Margie Rey was there. Wendie drove her home after the dance, then brought me back."

"Get some orange juice from the refrigerator, please," Mom said. "Don't you have the *Tiger Review* program this morning?"

"Yes ma'am. I just wrote some notes up in my room, so I'm set for my game report. It'll be more fun this time."

"Daddy should be out soon, so you go ahead and start on your breakfast," Mom said. "You want to be on time."

At that moment, Daddy walked into the room. In his tweed sports jacket with the suede arm patches, he could have passed for a college professor. There were no signs of last night.

He cleared his throat like he always did. "Breakfast smells awfully good."

Mom handed him a cup of coffee and the *Daily Telegraph*, all twenty pages, still folded in its as-thrown form from the front porch.

"Good morning," I said.

"When did you get in last night?"

I didn't want to deal with that. "After you went to bed." A little white lie.

"Glad you got home O.K.," he continued. "We have a busy day at the dealership today. Two different people are taking delivery of new automobiles."

Suddenly he looked up. "Look at this."

A bold headline in the *Telegraph* stated, "Negroes Protest in Bluefield."

The black-and-white photograph on the front page showed people in suits and ties, all Negroes except for uniformed West Virginia State Police troopers, all white. The protesters carried signs, preprinted and hand-lettered. "End Movie Discrimination" one said. "Stop Segregation NOW" stated another.

The demonstrators marched in front of the theater, right on Commerce Street. And there in the middle was Arcie! I'd never seen him in a regular coat and tie before. He looked tense but determined.

"That's Arcie Peterson," I said, as Mom came over to look. He stood next to the president of the N.A.A.C.P. in Charleston. The article described the protest outside the Monarch Theater, the largest movie theater in the area.

Daddy read the article silently as I finished eating.

"The Bomb's full of gas," she said.

"Thanks, Mom. Daddy, have a good day at work."

I was sure he'd forgotten about last night and that he didn't know I'd be on the radio within an hour. His eyes never left the article.

As usual, Becky Eastland was there already.

"Hi, Jimmy," she said. "It's more fun after a win, isn't it?" She looked like she was ready for a Miss Junior America photo shoot.

"Good morning, Miss Sunshine. Did you make the scene at the dance last night? Or did I spend so much time supervising the dirty laundry after the game that you'd been there and left already?"

She handed me the engraved notecards.

"I was there for a while, but left early to do the write-up."

Her stuff is perfect. It always is. We agree to do our usual ping-pong style. She'll start with the view from the sidelines. I'll add comments about Coach Ebert's talk and Donnie's charge to the team. That's good stuff, and it leads into what happened in the second half.

We've just finished when Meena Gordon bursts in and teases us, says her bit on the social scene includes a blockbuster. "It'll be worth waiting for."

John's voice comes over the Studio A intercom. "One minute to go, kids. Ready in there?" We nod. "You go live right after station ID."

We scrunch in a bit closer to the stand-up microphones. Butterflies. Does Biondi feel this way?

In the background John is wrapping up the news and weather. "You're tuned to WLOH. It's nine o'clock on a beautiful fall Saturday, and time for Princeton High School's *Tiger Review* program."

The On-Air sign flashes a brilliant red.

"Good morning, everyone. This is Rebecca Eastland, along with Meena Gordon and Jimmy Jackson. We've got the news and views for Princeton High, including the terrific come-from-behind win last night over the Oak Hill Red Devils here in Princeton. We've got some good music, and Meena will have her social scene goings-on for all of us."

Becky covers the sideline from her standpoint as a cheerleader. "The stands were full. Everyone on the sidelines felt the support of the crowd." She continues about the pleasant fall weather and the pre-game warm-up activities of the two cheerleading squads. "And now here's Jimmy."

"The Red Devils came into town, three wins and no losses, big and bad, looking to crack the West Virginia Top Ten this week. But the Tigers, who trailed fourteen to thirteen at the half, held them scoreless in a gritty, defensive second half. With only one minute left in the game, Slate Gaskins put a nasty hit on Oak Hill's receiver as he caught a pass at our forty-yard line. He coughed up the ball, and Princeton co-captain Donnie Davis scooped it up in the air and ran it back untouched for the go-ahead score. The Tigers got the extra point and held on to win twenty to fourteen. It was the first victory of the year for the Tigers—and Oak Hill's first defeat." It's routine stuff. Wendie could write that in a coma.

I wanted the listeners to sense the atmosphere in the locker room.

What I *wanted* to say was that Coach Ebert, an erect, tall man, emotionally controlled at all times, reminded the guys they were "in the game" (one of his favorite expressions). "Pull together. Seniors, provide leadership. We're a better team than we've shown so far. You're playing for your home town, your families. We can and we will defeat" (not whip, not beat the shit out of) "Oak Hill. Believe in yourselves . . . make good decisions on the field, force some breaks . . . the intangibles. I want to see grit and spirit. It's fourteen to thirteen now. Anyone's game. Play solid defense, hold them. Win the second half . . . win the game."

That was "the speech."

He looked at Donnie Davis. "Now let's hear from one of our senior co-captains."

Wendie was next to me, in the back. He leaned over close and whispered, "This had better be good."

"Guys," Donnie started. "We've had good times and not-so-good times. When we gave it everything we had, busted our butts, we've been O.K. If not, we knew we didn't leave anything behind. Oak Hill thinks they're headed for an undefeated year. Not me. We shut them down, we beat them. Take the second half. Who's with me?"

Someone immediately shouted, "Kick some ass!"

The team roared and bolted for the door. Coach Ebert followed them, walking deliberately. It would have been dangerous to stay in front of them, they were so fired up.

The "break" that Coach Ebert mentioned at halftime happened right in front of our bench, with the sharp crack of the shoulder pads, sounds of the Oak Hill player gasping for breath. His mouthpiece flew out, followed by blood and spit. The speed, violence, and full force of the game don't project to the stands. The ball popped right out, five yards straight up in the air . . . seemed to hang there. Donnie closed at full speed. He timed it perfectly and took it the other way without breaking stride.

There's the real drama. That should have been my report.

But it wasn't.

Meena has what I consider both the dullest and the most interesting portions of the program, since she does the Bulletin Board and closes out the program with The Scene. "The Stroll" by the Diamonds separates the football game report from a short synopsis of the dance. It's time for the social goodies.

"This is Meena Gordon with the Is, the Was, and the Might-be of our wonderful school." She goes on about seeing several new couples holding hands in the hallways and ends up with her "blockbuster of the week," a good tease line. "My spies report that Mack Andrews and Annie Franklin were seen having quite a serious spat up at Mooney's the other night. Your scribe followed up. Is this couple headed for splitsville? Sorry to have to tell it like it is.

"And now, from your *Tiger Review* reporters, have a good weekend. Get all that homework done. We'll be back next Saturday morning. Same time, same station." The On-Air light goes dark. John Shelton's voice comes over the monitor, wrapping up with a station break and commercial.

"Meena, where did you hear about Mack and Annie?" Becky asks.

"My lips are sealed, but it came from two different people. I think it's over."

Mack hasn't said a word to me about it. Becky and Meena are still talking in the parking lot when I leave.

None of us has mentioned the newspaper article.

Chapter 16

MARGIE REY HAS a church meeting in Pearisburg, so I plan to get on the radio and make some additional contacts in the Boy Scouts of America contest. At night the signals will skip in from further away, and I haven't gotten many stations from out West.

But first I have to call Mack and check up on Meena's scoop.

"Andrews, what's up?"

"What do you mean?" he says. Then, "Oh, that stuff on *Tiger Review*."

"You didn't say anything about that."

He hesitates. A sure sign. "It's been a little rough lately. It happens. How are things with you?"

"Fine." I don't elaborate.

He sounds more serious than usual.

By Saturday afternoon the radio contest was in full swing. I wasn't good enough to make the football or basketball team. But I was determined to make as many contacts in the BSA contest as anyone else. Stations from the East Coast would come in as soon as the sun set, but the signals further west peaked later. Since I had to sign-on WLOH at six, my plan was to operate the contest from sunset until midnight, get some sleep for several hours, then get back on and look for the West Coast stations before I had to leave. Actually, I was glad there was no date that night.

It turned out to be one of my best radio evenings. Many contest stations were on from the Midwest and Northeast. Skip conditions were excellent, and since no storms were close at all, there were no static crashes. I could hear the proverbial pin drop in terms of radio signals all over the eastern half of the country. By midnight I'd made 10 additional contacts, with stations in New York, Michigan, Missouri, Alabama, and even one in Maine, which was a new state for me altogether. By this time my head was ringing with tiny snippets of Morse code. The night breeze was sending Morse code, the house itself seemed to settle and make creaking noises in Morse code. Excited, but tired, I set the clock for four, when I'd get up to try for those West Coast stations.

Something was buzzing. My alarm. Layers of subconsciousness peeled away gradually until the room, dark as it was, resumed its inky shape with familiar forms. Complete silence now. No sounds inside or outside. No wind, no cars, no birds. Nothing. I managed to pull on a sweatshirt and walked barefoot over to the radio room. The receiver and transmitter were still on from the earlier operation, and the vacuum tubes cast a suffused light out through the holes in the metal chassis, making eerie small dots up and down the walls. I sat there, trying to clarify my senses, earphones covering my ears, looking at the tiny patterns.

CQ BSA de KN7BPR BSA K

A seven. They're rare. The seventh area is out west—most western states except for California, which has its own number, a number six in the call-sign, due to the large population. He's calling CQ for the contest. My hand trembles.

KN7BPR de K8JPV BSA K

He hears me. On the first call, too.

K8JPV de KN7BPR R TNX FOR UR CALL. UR RST 569 HR IN SALT LAKE CITY UT. MY NAME IS RONNY. FIRST CLASS. HW COPY? K8JPV DE KN7BPR K

Utah. Another brand new state.

KN7BPR DE K8JPV R RONNY AND TNX UR RST 579 HR IN PRINCETON WVA NAME IS JIMMY. EAGLE. BSA OK? KN7BPR DE K8JPV K

He's probably as excited as I am. It's just past two-thirty there, so he's staying up late just as I'm getting up really early. That contact certainly is a good one, and I doubt many of the scouting hams around the East Coast will get Utah in the contest. Ronny probably is thrilled to get a West Virginia station on his end. There aren't many of us on the air either. It's a good contact both ways.

He goes back to CQing in the contest. I keep listening for additional stations and before long, connect with additional stations in Texas and California. My BSA log is starting to fill out and should include a solid total when the contest ends in one more week. I feel good about things, with new states in Maine and Utah for the night. It's nearly five-thirty and completely dark outside. I pull on jeans and shoes and creep quietly down into the kitchen for some cereal and orange juice. The clock ticks to five thirty-five as I pick up the keys.

Problem! Daddy pulled his car into the driveway, and it's blocking The Bomb in the garage. I knock as softly as possible on Mom's and Dad's bedroom door.

"Jimmy, what's the matter?" Mom asks faintly.

"I'm really sorry. But I've got to move Daddy's car. Where are his keys?" Sounds follow her as she gets out of bed and walks over to his chest of drawers.

The door opens a crack. "Here they are," she whispers. "We should have taken care of this last night."

"I'll park his car in front of the house and put the keys on the kitchen table."

"Do you have enough time?"

"It's O.K. but I need to hustle."

"Did you get something to eat?"

"Sure did." Tension shows in my voice. "Mom, I've gotta get going. Bye."

I dash outside, start the new Buick, back it up, and move it to the curb. The hill is so steep. I angle the front wheels at 45 degrees and push in the parking brake as far as I can. There's the new car smell, along with a Lucky Strike aroma. Now quickly back to the house and the kitchen to put the keys on the table. It's quarter till six.

The Bomb usually spends the night in our small garage, an anachronism from a time when cars were smaller. There's barely room for the car through the garage door opening. At least it'll be dry and I won't have to deal with dew and dampness on the windshield. I squeeze in, fumbling with the keys in the dark. Looking carefully through the rearview mirror, I back it past my parents' bedroom window and onto the street. After driving faster than I should around the backside of Radio Hill, I pull into the station's gravel parking lot with five minutes to go.

In the dark, the building looks ominous with the black smudge of the huge tower looming above it like a supernatural insect. At the front door, I insert the key, sprint past the control room to the transmitter room, and switch the filament voltage power supply on. The transmitter tubes are supposed to warm up for five minutes.

Five fifty-nine. Filaments on for three minutes—got to get the transmitter on the air. Holding my breath, I push the big, red plate voltage switch to the active position. The high-voltage relays clang into place with a "thunk" and a low groaning hum sounds as the power supply supports the full load. The high-voltage meter on the front panel pops up from zero to 2,000 volts, and the plate current meter immediately bounces up to 200 milliamperes, both where they should be. The throbbing of the transformer appears normal as Mr. Emory's black transmitter springs to life. Not a moment to spare!

Breathing a sigh of relief, I close the door to the transmitter room, jog into the control room, and flip on the light switch. Overhead fluorescent lights flicker on. I pluck out the sign-on tape and pop it into the cassette holder. The clock's second hand clicks the three final steps to the top as the national anthem starts.

Chapter 17

THE PROTEST IN Bluefield was all over the school Monday: the front page photograph, the head of the N.A.A.C.P. in Charleston, the ministers, the signs, Arcie Peterson. Every perspective could be heard. "Nice" whites expressed concern about outsiders in proper terms. Rednecks spewed racist slurs and threats. The Jewish kids were silent, with a clearly heightened sense of a minority. The colored students, now using the word "black," kept to themselves, appeared more united.

Arcie had the links to the band, to the band's doorman. Of course we had talked. Talked a lot. After that evening, or morning, at the Pair-A-Dice club, for the first time I could understand being part of an alien system, one where others made the rules. Keep quiet. Don't see nuthin'. Don't say nuthin'. Understand?

We talked again at school that day. Just the two of us.

"Jimmy, believe it or not, I got to thinking about things, really thinking about things. Remember that night on the way over to JD's? Talking about the Mercer Theater, the upstairs balcony and all that. The swimming pool, too. Our minister called the house last week. Was looking for people to come over, be a part of it, carry signs. I had to go."

"Were you worried? Scared?"

Arcie paused a moment. "Sure. More determined than afraid, I suppose. If there's a word combining scared and committed, then that's the one.

He looked at me. Then smiled, and said, "Scarmitted."

It broke the ice. We both laughed.

It's fun hanging out with the band, but other things are becoming a larger part of my life. The Merit Scholarship results from the initial session qualified me as a semifinalist. The confirming exam is held a month later at Bluefield High School, where we all sit at desks carefully placed apart on the floor of the basketball gym. Two girls from PHS also qualify after both tests, and all three of us get letters telling us we are official Merit Scholarship finalists. I'm not sure what that means, but letters and brochures start coming to the house from colleges I've never heard of, "highly selective small colleges" in their words. Mom is excited and starts collecting them in a scrapbook.

Mom and I talk about this school and that, but going away to school in Ohio or the Northeast is way beyond my comfort zone. One of our discussions is interrupted by the green kitchen phone.

"Jimmy. You available Friday night? The Fifty-Two Club. We need your magic. It's another gig for the door." Slate announces this, without even a hello.

The football team has an off-week in the schedule after the big Oak Hill win.

"Sounds good. Want me to pick up Arcie?"

"Great," he says quickly. "We pack 'em in and you collect the dough."

The distance from our house to Arcie's is modest, measured in linear distance. Yet a cultural chasm exists. Neighborhoods change racially with little to no transition. White to black: across an alley, one street to the next. The homes appear to have been built in stages. Additions sprout at odd intervals. Materials used on different add-ons don't match. Metal siding abuts wood. One paint shade changes to another. Appendages add to appendages.

Arcie's on the porch, guitar in hand.

"The R & B master of the famous Roadsters himself." It's my best radio-style voice. His hair is slicked in a pomade style. His purple shirt has a sheen, gaudy but perfect for a band. He's got the look, all right. "Cool threads."

"Gotta play to the people, Jimmy. Gotta give 'em the show," he says, lowering the guitar into the backseat. "How're you doing? Haven't seen you much at school."

Arcie is in the school band and circulates in musical circles. Real music.

"You know, I'm snowed. There's schoolwork and the *Tiger Review* program, plus the job up at WLOH on Sundays. The football team, too. Mr. Water Boy and Smelly Jockstraps, you know."

Arcie clears his throat, like he has something to say. "You and Mack Andrews. You two . . . pretty good friends?"

"Sure."

"My locker's close to Margie Rey's. Mack's been hanging around."

I haven't seen Mack much since he and Annie broke up. He's always working in construction. He used to come over to the house. But I like him—don't recall hearing him being negative about anyone, ever. Mom likes him too. Says he has a "nice badboy" image with the car and that longish hair always slicked back. Besides, Margie Rey's parents are sticklers for "nice boys" for their daughter, being good Mormons and all.

We pull into the parking area at the club. It's nearly dark. Slate's wearing sunglasses, walking toward the club carrying his guitar case.

Frankie's La Saluta is on the highway five miles north of Bluefield, an Italian restaurant with the adjoining Club Fifty-Two, which includes a large dance floor decked out in an Italian theme: fake marble columns; hanging bunches of glass grapes; heavy Roman motif wallpaper with untold layers of nicotine. Is this what New Jersey looks like?

The sunglasses speak, "You ready to rock and roll?"

"You bet, chief."

"Gonna be a good one," Slate says as the three of us go inside.

Lannie and Buddy are there already. Buddy is usually the first to arrive since he has all the drum paraphernalia and needs extra time to get it all together. "Well, ain't it the rock and roll all-stars themselves."

"Buddy, my man," Arcie says. "You ready?"

"Does a bear shit in the woods?"

That induces a groan from Lannie, who's fussing with his keyboard. That's usual. The scowler-in-chief says nothing, his fingers playing notes audible only to him.

Peppy Lewis, who rides with Buddy, walks in a few minutes later, with long, slow strides and that far-off appearance, his bass and the remaining drum gear in tow.

The night goes well. I take in $150 at the door, and a man in a leisure suit tips the band $20 to play "Donna." All of us get free beer (or Coke, for Arcie and Peppy) and pizza, plus make $30. Well, the band members do. I get 20 bucks plus food and beer, and bask in the glow.

Arcie and I talk on the way to his house. Layers of the curtain continue to lift. It's nearly one o'clock when I drop him off. At home, the new Buick is in the driveway. The house is still. Daddy isn't slumped over at the kitchen table. It's a good night.

The next morning we breeze through *Tiger Review*. With no game Friday we have time for more music and idle chatter. Meena's blockbuster of the week is that a senior is "fascinated" with someone new but is keeping it to himself since "she's dating another guy."

When I get back home, Mom calls out to me. "Jimmy, there's a letter for you. From *Boys' Life* magazine."

Boys' Life? Why would I be getting a letter from them? My subscription is up to date. The letter looks official. It's addressed to Mr. James Jackson, K8JPV.

"What does it say? Read it out loud."

My eyes race ahead. The letter includes the results of the Boy Scout amateur radio contest. The list of call signs is long, two whole pages. There it is—my own call sign, near the top on page one. Number five nationwide! I force myself back to the start and read aloud.

> Dear James. Enclosed are the results of the 1959 Boy Scouts of America Amateur Radio Contest. We are pleased to notify you that your entry for station K8JPV earned the fifth highest score in the United States! As a result you qualify for an award, a Johnson Adventurer CW transmitter kit, donated by the E. F. Johnson Company of Waseca, Minnesota. This award will be shipped to the address listed on your entry within two weeks. Thank you for your entry and support of the *Boys' Life* Amateur Radio Contest. Congratulations on your excellent results. We hope you enjoy your award.

"Can you believe this?" I'm almost out of breath from reading the letter nonstop.

"Well, you certainly worked hard at it," Mom says. "You must have done very well. I'm really proud of you!" It was as if Sir Galahad had presented his favorite sword to me in the royal court!

Besides this letter, there are brochures from Reed College in Oregon and Kenyon College in Ohio. Their photos show leafy campuses with crisscrossing walkways between ivy-covered quads. Each looks like a wonderful school with smart people and a pretty campus. Each would prepare me for medical school or law school or other things that don't click with me.

Mom wants me to consider a medical field since Uncle Carter is a doctor and she has several uncles who are either MDs or dentists in Kentucky. Medicine appears to be her family's career path. But I have no interest in biology or anatomy, and I feel uncomfortable being in close proximity to people. Doctors have to poke and probe, touch people all over.

None of the schools feels like a good fit because there are no plans to be fitted. Private colleges are a moot point since we probably can't afford it. Even though there's the possibility of a National Merit Scholarship, Mrs. Dunfee told me the number of "pure" scholarships is quite limited. Most students who receive full or partial awards get them from funds established by companies, specifically companies that employ their father. Daddy works for a local car dealership, so there's nothing there. Perhaps General Motors has something for their dealers' employees' kids.

"Maybe you should look at electrical engineering. You enjoy radio," Mom says. We're having one of our "what-do-I-want-to-study" talks.

Actually, what I like is hearing short-wave signals bounce off some ionized level way up in the thin-air portion of the atmosphere, and listening to those big fat signals from WLAC and WLS at night with the deep fades and strong resurgences. I like the magic of the control room at WLOH, and the blue-green tint of the front panel of my ham station. But that isn't engineering.

"Have you thought about Virginia Tech?" she asks. "It has a good reputation. And it's not too far."

Tech definitely has the strongest engineering reputation. Daddy went there for over a year, and an uncle on his side of the family graduated. So there *is* some family connection. But Virginia Tech is a military college.

"Mom, I don't want to be full-time in the corps of cadets there. It would be hard enough with the engineering."

"I hadn't thought about that," she says. "But you *are* good in math."

Chapter 18

MARGIE REY SLIDES into the passenger side, her coat parting just enough to show her trim skirt and white blouse. The blouse is sleek, soft, and feminine. She has a demure look, a bashful manner since she knows she's attracted my attention, just like she's planned.

I levitate back around the car.

"*Tiger Review* was good this morning," she says, opening the conversation. "Good music."

"Thanks. Today was my turn to pick the songs. Becky and Meena don't especially like rhythm and blues all that much. So I had a chance to get on some good stuff. Did you hear the Jimmy Reed song?"

"Was that the one where you can't understand a word?"

We round the curve by the cemetery and head into town. In the winter, the sky becomes a flinty background, with no sunshine for days. The clouds are imperceptible as discrete objects, instead forming bands of bleak grays and slate blues that stretch across the horizon like a thin outer shell.

We find a parking space at the Mercer Theater. Black couples are coming and going to and from the balcony. Following the movie, she puts her arm through mine as we walk to the car. The Bomb is as cold as the 40-degree evening when we pull back out onto Mercer Street. The sky matches the chill.

"On to Mooney's for a Coke and something to eat?"

"That's fine," she answers. Then, "But I need to go home right after that. We've got to leave early to drive to Pearisburg for church. Dad has to be there early for an elders' meeting."

For reasons I don't understand, the LDS church is over in Pearisburg, Virginia, even though it's a small town.

The Bomb has gotten warm again on the drive up the hill. Mooney's is jammed. The only open spot is off to one side. "Look," Margie Rey says. "Over there. Mack and Eddie Jones. Can you believe it? Mack has the top down!" Eddie is standing next to Mack's Mercury, the champion in the ring of neon lights. Eddie has a jacket on, but Mack, sitting alone in his car, wears only a sweater. "What a character!"

Yeah, what a character. We thread our way over to check out the scene. Mack's car is running, his heater enveloping the Mercury in a cozy hot-air cocoon. He looks completely comfortable. The car squats, its rear end lowered. Two masculine, heavy-chrome exhausts jut out. The midnight purple triple-gloss sheen is spotless. The Naugahyde seat covers are light cream, with floor panels and rear interior sides the same regal color as the exterior. White-walled tires with wire-spoke wheels deliver the finishing touch. The glass packs gurgle along with the motor's rhythm, and a light mist of condensing vapor swirls out from the tail pipes.

Mack and the Merc, the center of attention, in the glow of Teenage-Centrum.

"Why, it's Jimmy Jackson and the lovely Miss Howland. To what do we owe such good fortune? This is a pleasant surprise. Margie Rey, you certainly do brighten up a dark and dreary evening."

Eddie is usually the quiet one of the group, but he adopts a mischievous smile. "Been accompanying Miss Howland to a movie?" It's obvious he's impressed with Mack's faux formality.

"I have."

Miss Howland looks down, the gesture a lady makes when she's clearly the center of attraction.

Mack, ever gallant, says, "Margie Rey, come into my open-air parlor. The heater's on and it's not bad at all."

She glances at me. Do I make her stand there? So there we are. Eddie and I out in the cold beside Mack's open-top convertible, while Margie Rey sits in the front seat with Mack, who impersonates the cat who swallowed the canary.

"Nice move, Mack," I say. Both Mr. Andrews and Miss Howland laugh. She says something to Mack, who grins.

"How about meeting us back here later?" Eddie asks. "Got something to ask you."

"Let me take Margie Rey home. I'll be back."

We finish the best chili-slaw dogs ever created by mankind. Margie Rey deftly picks out two french fries, popping them one by one slowly into her mouth. Suggestive thoughts conjure up on a wave of hormones.

As we head down the hill, the city lights form a white band on the bottom of the low cloud deck. We don't say much. Come to think of it, we don't talk too much about anything. I slow down to make the left into her driveway and turn off the headlights. She sits there, separated from me by a good two feet, not sending me any easy signals.

Everything is amplified in the dark stillness.

"Thanks for the show," she says. "And for Mooney's. It was fun seeing Eddie and Mack there. Isn't Mack's car something? I'll bet he's spent a lot of time—"

"And money." I finish her sentence.

"It looks like a nice car," she continues. "It was a little much, though, to have the top down."

"That's Mack."

We're at the last spot in the shadows before the front of the house and the lights.

"Good night. See you at school," she says and gives me a peck on the lips. She walks to the door and goes inside immediately. The door closes and makes a solid plop that underscores a sense of finality. On any scale of progression, we are . . . not. If Margie Rey had been watching—and I doubt she was—she would have seen me standing there a bit too long.

Chapter 19

THE CROWD AT Mooney's has thinned when I return. The night is chillier. Donnie Davis has joined Mack and Eddie, standing alongside the Mercury, as I pull up and keep The Bomb's engine running. Mack gets into the front, Eddie and Donnie into the rear.

"Are you guys out of your minds?" I ask.

Eddie's teeth are chattering. "It's not bad once you get used to it." He lacks any sense of conviction.

"Donnie, you must be hard up for companionship tonight," I continue. "Where's Marnie?"

"She has a family thing. Her aunt's birthday. I got a free pass . . . was with some of the guys on the team. The heater in this thing is something! It's like the tropics in here."

"It's not the heater. It's the heat," Eddie says. "Jimmy just took Margie Rey home. That's the secret!"

Right.

Mack starts. "Here's the deal. Eddie and I have this little disagreement going on. He seems to be under the mistaken impression that his Ford piece of crap can run with my car. Ever heard of such nonsense?"

"I have no position here," I say, still thinking about the little peck that ended my evening. "Eddie, you secretly drop in a new engine, or are you simply a lunatic?"

"You gotta *pay* to *play*," Eddie says. "How will Mack *know* if we don't *go*?"

Mack continues. "Cute. Just too cool. How about a little run out on the road to Glenwood Park, out past our friend's sweetie-pie's house. I got ten bucks that says you can't stay with the horses over there under my hood. In fact, we can impress Margie Rey by laying on our horns while we drive by."

"Cut the horns," I say flatly. That's all I need.

Eddie and Mack get out and put up Mack's top. There's a smattering of sarcastic applause from the remaining cars. One little *beep-beep* as well. Donnie moves up to The Bomb's passenger seat. He and I will witness the start of the race.

With little traffic at that late hour, our mini-caravan passes Courthouse Square and makes the left turn. Mack leads the way. His parents' home is just prior to the curve, so he'll be a model driver at that point. As we pass the cemetery and near the Howland's, he accelerates and blows his horn just as we pass the house. Eddie lays on his horn as well. Last in line, I try to make The Bomb invisible.

New Hope Road is a well-paved, two-lane highway. It has only one good straight stretch, nearly a half mile long, a veritable forever bookmarked by long sweeping curves at both ends. Midnight drag racers gather late at night and run side by side over a quarter-mile course, indicated by wide painted white stripes marking start and finish lines. As you might expect, the local residents take a dim view of these proceedings and have pressured the State Police to patrol that stretch frequently to nab the offenders.

Someone just turns on the front door light! By the time the light fades into a dot in the rearview mirror, Eddie and I are closing in on Mack, who has slowed down. We're bumper to bumper to bumper as we round the initial curve.

Mack's Merc is the only V8 of the group, and the rebuilt motor shows its stuff. He's speeding up now, and the three of us sweep into the straight stretch under full acceleration. The Bomb's sure-footed and always corners well, even though it doesn't look nimble. I'm right on Eddie's bumper even as he's falling back a little from Mack.

Somehow, the planned two-car race changes. I'm right on Eddie's tail. The road now is straight, the center lines no longer solid. The left lane is open. Like electrical sparks with high voltage, little adrenalin lightning strikes bounce around inside my body. My foot is on the accelerator. Hard to the floor. We're over in the passing lane and move up, up, slowly up, alongside Eddie. Both of us are running around 80, still gaining speed. Now 85. The cars are pretty much even, but the green machine has more to go. Inch-by-inch I'm gaining on him. Only a quarter mile of straight stretch left. The speedometer's never been this high before.

The Mercury's faster, all right. Mack heads into the curve, his brake lights on now. Suddenly, something else. Other lights.

"Someone's coming," Donnie shouts.

The other car is passing Mack, heading in our direction. I have to either get around Eddie or back off and tuck in behind him. By now, my rear bumper is all the way up beside Eddie's front fender. Just a little more.

Eddie moves over toward the right. The Bomb's hitting 90 now . . . steering's loosey-goosey.

Just a few seconds. The oncoming car now is on the same straight stretch, the lights directly toward us. It starts veering off the road. The Bomb finally inches on ahead, and I swing back into the right lane just as we sweep past.

Donnie looks back. "Jimmy, a State Trooper!"

"Shit."

We're done for. I'm braking but we're still going too fast. It's hard to stay in our lane in the curve. The car slides a bit. I get it back. On ahead, Mack is well out of sight. Eddie falls back behind us. In back of him the State Police car makes a U-turn. The headlights swing around violently and seem to lock in on us. The "bubblegum" lights on top switch on. He's coming. Fast.

The police car roars up in the rearview mirror, quickly overtaking Eddie, and both sets of car lights pull off onto the grassy shoulder. An escape plan races through my mind. Find a driveway, sneak off the road into some dark background? Cop cars can do 130, so he'll catch me, no problem, if I stay on the road. For a second, I look around for any kind of a side road or someone's driveway.

Nothing. It was a long shot anyway. We're done for.

That becomes crystal clear as the lights snap sharply back onto the highway. He fishtails as he spins his tires coming after us, a quarter mile behind. I brake, pull off onto the grass shoulder, and wait. Just then my right leg starts to shake uncontrollably. The police car explodes around the curve and tires squeal as he brakes hard and skids in behind us. The top flasher is going round and round, making eerie strobes on the black trees. Weird pulsing lights in the front grill alternate like a demonic object. As we wait for the inevitable, neither Donnie nor I say a word. Footsteps approach. We exchange one last look. My door jerks open. A piercing glare hits my eyes. In one motion, an iron grip clenches my jacket.

"Get out, you stupid shit."

My seatbelt's still attached! I'm shaking all over, but manage to release it. Immediately he yanks me up and out from behind the steering wheel like a marionette. His flashlight never leaves my eyes. He shouts even louder than before.

"You could kill someone, you and your idiot friend back there. Are you crazy?" The voice is imperative. Definitely *not* a southern accent.

I hold my breath, look away, partially blinded.

"You are so goddamn stupid." With one fluid motion he shoves me to the rear of the car. As if I were a feather. "Asshole." His words seethe and hiss. He hits me a solid blow across the side of my face. Before I realize what's happened, he swings his hand back in the opposite direction and hits me again.

He bats me around, hitting me with five or six good licks. Loud smacking sounds seem to come from somewhere else but synchronize with flashes in my brain. I'm leaning back as far as I can against the rear of the car. My face stings in the chill. There's no traffic in either direction. When it appears he's through, I sneak a look behind him. Eddie's car is stopped back there, his headlights visible through the trees. My eyes refocus. The name badge is heavy with black ink embedded in the metal. The letters jump out. "Sgt. A. Carlotti."

I just ran Tony Carlotti off the road!

"You and your goddamned buddy back there—you know what you guys were doing?" He's still very angry, but at least now he isn't hitting me. "I can't fuckin' believe you guys," he continues. "Let me see your license." Shaking uncontrollably, I reach for my wallet and hand it to him. The intense beam moves away. "Well, Mr. James Jackson, let's get you and your idiot friend back there to town and into the law enforcement system." He shoves the laminated card into his chest pocket.

I'm still shuddering. "Sir, what about my car?" My voice is a fragile slice.

"I'll get your keys. Your car stays here." He grabs me by the scruff of my jacket and turns me around roughly. "Wait here." He opens the driver's side door to get the keys.

"Who the hell are *you*?" The powerful flashlight refocuses.

"Don Davis, sir," Donnie answers. His voice is steady and respectful.

"And what are *you* doing here?"

"Riding with Jimmy, sir."

Carlotti gives Donnie a searing once-over. "So there are two of you. Get out of the car. Come with me."

Donnie says, "Yes sir" and gets out. Sergeant Carlotti reaches in and takes the car keys, then hands them to me.

"Lock it up. You're lucky you didn't kill yourselves—or someone else." He takes the keys again and herds us over to the patrol car. "In the back."

The door slams hard. There are no handles or door openers on either side. A rigid metal mesh, like a cage, separates the rear from the front. My face is stinging. Carlotti looks back at us, then does a powerful U-ey on the road and heads back. As his headlights swing past the rear of The Bomb, he guns it. A deep roar throbs throughout the chassis as the powerful engine accelerates. It's a good thing I didn't try any funny business and attempt to hide when he pulled Eddie over. He brakes rapidly, sliding on the asphalt, and pulls in facing the front of the Ford. Eddie is standing in front of his car in the full glare of the headlights, looking drawn, scared. Carlotti gets out and opens the rear door of the patrol car. Eddie gets in. Donnie now is in the middle as Eddie and I exchange looks.

He calls in. "Two suspects on a thirteen-bravo." His voice now is crisp and controlled. The squelch on the radio breaks as he and the dispatcher go back and forth. At Courthouse Square, he drives around it in the usual counterclockwise fashion until he pulls in at the stark sign "Police Use Only." He gets out of the car and opens the rear door on my side. "Straight ahead."

We walk through a brightly lit room and are herded through a second door. "Over there," he says and goes to an officer sitting at a desk behind a glass partition. I can't hear what they're saying. The room is bare, with only rows of metal chairs. The door we just came through has no usual doorknob on it, only a massive combination lock with a keypad.

Sergeant Carlotti walks over to us. "You boys were out on a public highway at midnight doing dangerous things. You're lucky you didn't kill someone, and you're lucky I didn't . . ." His voice trails off, stops. "Damned fools."

He turns to Donnie. "You say your name is Davis?"

"Yes sir. Don Davis."

"You get out of here. You used bad judgment to be in that situation. An officer is waiting outside. He'll take you home. One more thing. I don't want to see you out like that again. You'll be in big trouble next time, even if you're not driving. You understand? I'll be watching for you."

"Yes sir, I understand." He catches my eye, then gets up.

"That way. Back through that door," Carlotti says, a clear edge to his voice.

Donnie glances at Eddie and me as he and Carlotti walk to the door. There's a sharp mechanical clanking sound as it unlocks and swings back. The other officer must have released it electronically. As they leave, the door closes with metallic sounds as the heavy locking system reengages. The polished concrete floor reflects the image of the overhead lights, which seem brighter than ever.

Eddie sits there, one bare metal chair between us. The chairs have no give to them—they're bolted to the floor. He looks straight ahead, then down at his belt. He's breathing deeply.

"James Jackson, come over here." It's the officer behind the glass.

I rise and walk over. "Yes sir," I say, my voice cracking.

The desk is an old style with a metal top. The policeman holds my car keys and driver's license.

"These are yours, right?"

"Yes sir."

"I'm going to have to keep these items. Do you have anything else on your person?"

"Just my wallet and some change. And my watch."

"Hand them all to me."

He puts all the items into a large packet and writes out a list: wallet with driver's license, eight dollars and 32 cents, set of keys, watch.

"Sign this. Your personal possessions. For your protection." He looks up. "There, at the bottom." He points to a line.

"Yes sir." I write my full name on the line and hand it back.

"That's all. Sit back down again." Then his voice booms, "Edward Jones."

"Yes sir," Eddie answers in a reedy voice. His words sound forced. Like mine.

"You come over here also."

Eddie takes a deep breath and pushes up out of the chair. He walks over slowly. It's then that the dark wetness shows in the front of his khaki pants.

The officer goes through the same procedure. Eddie sits down again, this time next to me.

Before either of us can say anything, the officer continues, "Both you boys come over here." We rise as one and walk to our fate. "You were arrested on multiple charges, including speeding and reckless endangerment. Do you want to call your parents?"

"Yes sir," we say at the same time.

The phone rings and rings and rings. *Which one will answer?* Finally, after what may be 10 rings, Daddy's sleepy voice comes on the line. "Harumpf . . . Hello."

He sounds O.K.

"Daddy, this is Jimmy. I . . ." I start, then pause. I'm standing in a corner of the room. The phone is mounted on a wall. The concrete walls and floor amplify the sound of my voice.

"Are you all right?" he asks.

"There's been some trouble. I'm all right, but I'm at the courthouse."

Daddy's voice becomes focused. "The courthouse?"

"We're at the police station at the courthouse. I, err, we . . . we were pulled over by the State Police."

"What happened?"

"Eddie Jones and I are here. We were arrested."

"For what?"

I pause. My right leg starts quivering again.

"Racing. Out on the New Hope Road."

There's a brief silence. Mom's voice is in the background. She's up now. They both are standing by the phone in the kitchen. He says, "I'll be there as soon as I can."

"Come to the side entrance." It's difficult to say the words. "The door on the side. It says Mercer County Sheriff."

"All right." He hangs up. His voice is steady.

Eddie takes the phone. From my seat, I can hear Mr. Jones' voice. He's upset. Eddie looks straight ahead at the wall. After a short exchange, he slowly puts the phone back and walks over.

"Not good?" I ask.

"Dad is pissed. I still can't believe we did that." The absurdity is starting to sink in. "What are they going to do?"

"I don't know."

About that time the heavy door opens. A Princeton policeman comes in, pushing ahead of him a rough-looking man. Disheveled. Blood on his face. His shirt ripped and dirty, his lip busted, his nose running. He reeks of tobacco and alcohol.

"I swan, it wasn't my fault," he keeps saying. He's handcuffed, hands behind his back. "Goddammit, why'd you take me in? I didn't start it."

"Shut up, Clarence. Just keep quiet," the policeman says. "Sit over there, by the corner. You give me more trouble you go to solitary. Just zip it!"

"I ain't mad at you," the man says. The rip in his shirt goes all the way to his belt. His chest is smeared with dirt and snot as he walks past us, all the way to the last chair.

The Princeton cop goes over to the officer behind the glass. They talk and the policeman fills out some forms. Before long, the big door opens and Daddy walks in. Eddie and I both stand. I can tell that Daddy notices his wet spot.

"What happened?"

I don't beat around the bush. "We did some dumb stuff. Eddie and I, we were road-racing. We got pulled over by the State Police." I leave out the part about being side by side and any mention of Mack.

"How fast were you going?"

I lower my voice. "Eighty, maybe eighty-five." I can't bear to say 90.

"Was there drinking involved?" he says quickly.

"No sir. None at all," Eddie and I both answer at once. That's true. One positive in a bad situation.

There's a brief pause while the other man, his hands behind his waist, keeps snorting snot back up his nose and whimpering under his breath.

Daddy sits down beside me and lowers his voice. "Was there an accident? Any damage?"

"No, no accident. We pulled over when the state trooper put on his flashers." I have to come clean. Or at least cleaner. "But . . ." and I hesitate. "Eddie and I were side by side and the State Police car was coming the other way. He had to drive off the road as we passed by." I take a deep breath. "Then he turned around and came after us." There. The whole story, more or less. But still with no Mack, and no mention of who was in the passing lane.

Daddy exhales a long breath. "Where are your cars?"

"Parked on the side of the highway. Out there where we pulled off."

"You're all right. That's the main thing. But you're in a big jam. Let me go and talk with the officer. Wait here." He slowly stands up and walks to the glass partition. I'm not able to hear much. Mr. Jones still hasn't arrived.

After several minutes, he motions me over. "Jimmy, you're charged with speeding, improper passing of another motor vehicle, and endangering a police officer. These are serious charges. The police are keeping your driver's license."

"Daddy, I need to tell you something," I whisper. "Over here."

We walk away from the partition window. "Sergeant Carlotti pulled us over." Now he focuses on me even more. He's heard of Carlotti. Everyone has. "You forced Sergeant Carlotti off the road?" He gives me his most severe look, possibly the most personal interchange we've ever had. "You were racing on the road at midnight, and forced the oncoming vehicle, a State Police cruiser, into a ditch or whatever!"

"When I pulled over, he grabbed me and took me back to the rear of The Bomb and he . . ."

"Well, what?"

"He hit me."

"Hit you?" Daddy looks carefully at my face. "Your face isn't cut. Your cheeks are red, but you don't have any blood or bruises on you. Are you sure?"

"He hit me at least five or six times."

I could see he was thinking about what I just said. It would be hard to prove—my word against a State Police sergeant.

"There's a witness," I say.

"Eddie?"

"No, Eddie's car was already pulled over. Donnie Davis."

"Donnie Davis? Was he with you?" His voice rises.

I lower mine. "Donnie was riding with me. Sergeant Carlotti didn't see him when he jerked me out of the car and pushed me back to the rear. He didn't see him until he came back to get the car keys."

Daddy sighs loudly enough that Eddie notices.

He goes back to the partition and says something to the officer, who hands him the manila folder with my things in it, then comes back over. "Mother is waiting at home. She and I will go out to get the Chevrolet. Then we can talk." With that, he walks to Eddie, who is looking despondent, and asks, "Is your dad coming to get you?"

Right then, the large metal door opens and Mr. Jones walks in. He face is red and his anger is apparent. When he sees Daddy, he relaxes a bit.

"Mr. Jackson. Sorry to see you like this. What's going on?" He hasn't said anything at all to Eddie yet.

"I'm sorry we have to meet in this situation. Eddie can tell you about it. I'm afraid the boys have gotten themselves into some trouble. But it will be all right. There were no accidents or injuries. No alcohol." With that, Daddy walks to the door. I follow meekly. As we approach it, the electronic bolt lock clanks loudly and the door swings open. We walk through the other room and then out into the early morning air to the Buick.

"Thanks for coming," I say quietly.

He drives home without a word. It's one o'clock when we pull into the driveway. The house lights are on and Mom is standing inside by the front door. I take a deep breath and walk to the porch steps. She opens the door and rushes out. "Jimmy, what happened? Are you all right?"

"I'm sorry Mom. Eddie Jones and I got pulled over for speeding, racing, out on the New Hope Road."

She puts her arms around me. "Oh my. Did anyone get hurt? Is everyone all right?"

Daddy interrupts. "Yes, everyone's all right. But we need to go out there and get the Chevrolet. It's parked on the side of the road where they were stopped."

"Do I need to go?" Mom asks.

"Yes. Jimmy's driver's license has been retained by the police until the charges are resolved. Jimmy didn't mention everything. Apparently he and Eddie were racing side by side and they forced an oncoming automobile off the road. That oncoming vehicle was Sergeant Carlotti in a State Police car.

Mom takes in this new information in a state of semi-shock. "Well," she says in her soft Kentucky manner, "you stay here and Daddy and I will go get the car. I need some time to let all this sink in."

With that, we go inside. I stay in the kitchen to contemplate my fate. Mom puts her coat over her housecoat and takes her purse and her car keys. They go back outside. The front door closes with the familiar sound. They're gone.

They aren't gone long. I tell them the almost-complete version, with only the top-end speed and Mack's involvement omitted. Daddy is angry at my lousy judgment, but both are relieved that we didn't wreck ourselves or anyone else. Daddy asks more questions about Sergeant Carlotti and how he jerked me out of the car and hit me. It's one-thirty and all of us are coming off adrenalin highs.

I have to sign on at the radio station at six, and Mom has breakfast ready when I come downstairs a few hours later.

We're the only car on the road when she takes me to the station in the Buick. She says only a few words. "At least you weren't hurt, and you didn't hurt anyone else." Her look makes her disappointment clear.

I open the station and sleepwalk through the Holy Rollers and Miss Mabel's Gospel Hour. It's a long day. When she comes back to take me home, neither of us says a word.

The first phone call comes at about four. It's Wendie. "Excuse me, but is this the residence of Richard Petty?"

"Go away," I say. Then, "We need to talk."

"Five minutes."

The Dodge chrome-mobile pulls up a few minutes later.

"Have you given up walking a whole block?" I ask.

"Oh, the joy and privilege of owning and operating an automotive machine," he says, "having the authority granted by the State." It actually is therapeutic talking to him. He's a good listener when he needs to be, with a strong serious side when it counts.

"This thing might have been a disaster, you know. You really are lucky it wasn't worse." He then reverts to the sardonic. "Too bad you didn't put up a better fight against Carlotti. I hear he's running around the mining camps bragging about how he laid out some high school shit from Princeton, and the kid didn't lay a glove on him."

We both laugh, but he's right. I'm lucky it wasn't worse and know it. As Wendie leaves, he says, "I suppose you'd better plan on riding to school with me for a while."

"Thanks. See you tomorrow morning."

He nods and goes out the front door without looking back.

The next day at school, of course the "big race" is all the news. By this time the story has become more lurid, having ricocheted off enough retelling. According to the buzz, after we ran him off the road, Sergeant Carlotti had to chase us down, and of course his manly submission of me was amplified. But since I'm at school and bear no obvious marks of combat, it's difficult for the more extreme versions of the tale to catch on.

Meena Gordon is waiting for me at my locker. "You know," She begins slowly. "You and Eddie are . . ." Each word is drawn out. "Going to be my headline story . . . little nuggets on *Tiger Review*. Should I just go with the rumors? We need to talk."

"Meena, give me a break. This whole thing really was a stupid deal and I don't want to publicize it." I fumble with my combination lock, which won't open.

"Jimmy, I won't mess around. Really, is the basic rumor true? You and Eddie were caught by Sergeant Carlotti? Did he really beat you up?"

"Dammit, Meena. Come on. We were speeding. We got pulled over. We messed up."

"O.K. I'll pull some notes together this week and show them to you. You decide whether to comment or not. But you've gotta know this is the talk of the school."

I suppose I should say it isn't exciting to be the center of attention, but it really is. Margie Rey and I have lunch together. I tell her what happened, at least the story I told Mom and Dad. She heard the horns.

"Three cars went by the house," she says. "Mack was with you and Eddie, wasn't he?"

I don't reply.

She continues, "You were going back up to Mooney's to meet them. I can put two and one together."

"He was there but he didn't get stopped." I have to say something. She knew all along. "It's important to keep Mack out of this," I say. "Promise?"

"O.K."

"The police haven't asked either Eddie or me about anyone else." I didn't have to lie.

Daddy calls Mom and tells her he's coming home early from work, something he never does. We're going to have a family meeting, something we never do. At five o'clock, he walks in the door with a concerned look. He goes to their bedroom to change, then comes into the kitchen.

"Jimmy," he says gravely. "You are very fortunate not to have run headlong into that car coming the other way. You, Eddie, Donnie Davis, and the people in the other car could have been injured, or worse. It's actually good that it was a State Trooper, someone trained as a driver and able to handle an emergency like that."

"I—"

He breaks in sternly. "You could be charged with some serious accusations. Reckless endangerment of a police officer is a felony criminal charge and carries a jail sentence with it. Speeding and reckless driving are serious as well. Reckless driving alone can result in suspension of your driver's license."

"Will I have to go to trial?"

"The fact that Sergeant Carlotti struck you several times is serious," he says. "I can't accept that, although it's understandable that he was upset." His voice is even, steady. It's like he's reading a news commentary on the radio.

"I went over to the State Police headquarters today and talked with the officer in charge of this district. He's an Elks Club member. In exchange for our dropping any charges concerning the officer's use of excessive force, Mother and I have agreed to suspend your driver's license for six months. In return, you won't face any charges. Nothing will show up on your record." With that, he stops.

Just like that. Matter of fact.

"There's quite a lesson here," he starts up again. Each word is slowly and clearly stated. "I hope you will never repeat what happened Saturday night. Ever." It's the first time for him to address me so completely.

"Thanks," I mumble. "I understand. What about Eddie?"

"Mr. Lewis and I have been in contact, together and with the police. We agreed that you both will receive the same punishment." He continues to look directly at me. "Mr. Lewis and I will keep your driver's licenses for six months. I was going to get to this. Between now and the end of April, neither of you will be allowed to drive. If you do, you'll have to face all the original charges. You don't want to do that, I assure you!"

"No driving for six months!" I can't help myself.

"It means exactly that."

That was the decision, the arrangement. Eddie's dad took away his license for the same six months. Sergeant Carlotti was assigned to the Princeton office of the West Virginia State Police for several more years. During this time he cleaned out moonshining in a several coal mining counties, and closed down several houses of ill repute over at Keystone. He also had an outsized impact on two reckless teenage drivers. The gossip never reached Mack's parents. He and the fast '48 Merc remained on the road.

Chapter 20

IN ADDITION TO the license suspension, I was grounded for 30 days. I didn't complain. Like Daddy said, it could have been so much worse. Fortunately, there was Wendie and the red chrome-mobile Dodge convertible. He was my way to and from school, and if and when my social life ever got reengaged, he offered to let me double date with him and Ann.

"Jimmy, let me count the ways you've messed up your life" was a favorite Wendie saying. His job at the *Bluefield Daily Telegraph* was working out well, and his sports reporting byline now was common. Even as a high school student, it was clear he was good at the craft.

During my house detainment, Margie Rey and I only saw each other at school. We talked on the phone, but not every night. Sometimes she seemed to be the same. Sometimes there was something missing.

Daddy was stopping more and more at the Elks Club. He came home later and later. Now that I was at home every night myself, it was more noticeable. Yet Mom never talked to me about it. She would ask about my day and I would ask about her nursing work for the county. Routine stuff. Late one evening, I was in bed when cars pulled up in front of the house. Soon, men were talking on the porch.

"Jim, you need to stand up now. Hear me?"

Another voice, huskier and more powerful . . ."Jim, you're home. Pull it together. You all right?"

Daddy is coughing. Suddenly, other sounds: "Ummmpf, arrrgh!" The sound of liquid hitting the front porch: *Spliisshh.*

The first man again: "Bernard, get a towel from my car."

Mom's footsteps pound hurriedly through the house. The front door opens.

"Mrs. Jackson, I'm sorry about this," the husky voice says.

"That's all right. Help him in. Let's take him to the bathroom. I'll get him cleaned off." Mom sounds matter-of-fact, like it's a clinical procedure.

I creep out of my bedroom and look down from the top of the steps.

"I'm all right, Sara," Daddy keeps saying. But he's not able to walk. The two men have to support him, and the three of them stumble through the living room. "Thank you, gentlemen. I appreciate your help." He starts giggling. "Tell Ernest I'll settle up tomorrow. My credit is good."

"Are you sure you can handle this?" the larger man asks Mom.

"Yes, I can do it. Our son is here. Did you-all bring his car home?"

"Yes ma'am. It's parked in the driveway. I'll put the keys on the table right by the TV set. I'm sorry about all this."

"I appreciate your bringing him home. He shouldn't be driving."

"No ma'am. Well, good night now."

The men walk out through the living room and close the door.

I come downstairs. "Mom, do you need some help?" I feel out of place.

Daddy is sitting on the closed commode lid. Mom's washing his face, cleaning up the vomit dregs that had spattered down his shirt. They're on his suitcoat and pants as well.

He looks up at me with what appears to be shame and anger. "I'm all right." The words are slurred. "You go on back to sleep."

Mom and I exchange looks. "Daddy will be O.K.," she says. "He can get to bed when he's cleaned up."

My father sits there, disheveled, with a dazed look. I turn back toward the living room, which is full of our proud family objects in the dim light.

The next morning, Daddy is sitting at the breakfast table. I don't know how he does it. There's little conversation. Mom says hello, as if nothing has happened. The splatter of his vomit on the front porch is gone. Either Mom cleaned it off, or the men from the Elks Club wiped it off before they left. He's reading the paper, sipping a cup of coffee.

"Are you all right?" I ask him.

"I'm fine." His tone indicates no further discussion.

"Yes sir," I say to the implied instruction. I reach for the sports section, wondering if one of Wendie's articles will be there.

Wendie comes by at seven-thirty. School happens. I come home, Daddy usually doesn't. My homework improves, and so do my grades.

The football season dragged on. We finished two and eight, losing 77-0 at Bluefield in the final game. It was embarrassing. The Beavers started the game with a long scoring drive. Our straight tee formation, with mostly runs and occasional passes to Slate Gaskins and our other end, produced only one first down at the half. The Bluefield backs were fast, and their quarterback knew how to run the option. He made all the right decisions about when to keep the ball and when to toss it. It seemed the first half would never end.

"Gentleman, I know this has been a long and difficult season," Coach Ebert said at halftime. It was 42-0. The game was out of hand. The Beavers already had over 300 rushing yards, had not punted a single time, and had one touchdown on a punt return from one of our many kicks. We'd be lucky to have 50 yards of total offense.

"Keep your heads up. Play with pride. Don't get baited into any silly fouls or penalties. Bluefield will win this game. But you men are going to play with class. We have two more quarters this season. For some of you, it will be your final game. Most of you will be back next year. We'll have a fresh start. We *will* make changes. It *will* be better. You have my word on it. Now let's get out there. Play hard, run our plays right, and end the game on a positive note. No cheap stuff. I won't have it. That's it. Be careful. Watch yourself. Be alert. Avoid injuries."

Wendie and I sat at the back of the room. I could read him, and he alternated between looking straight ahead at Coach Ebert and at the floor. He viewed situations in a different way. I was buying the argument: It *would* be better next year. Wendie wasn't. His expression said, "Only one more half and all of us can go on to something else. And not a minute too soon."

The second half actually started out better. We took the kickoff and on the first play Donnie ran behind a nice hole in the line for 15 yards. The team made a second first down on a pass to Slate, who battled the Beavers' defensive end for a "jump ball." Their man fell, grabbing at Slate's leg. He missed, and Slate ran another 20 yards for our longest gain of the game to their 30-yard line. Bluefield called time-out, so we managers scrambled out with the water. Our guys sensed something. Across the field, their coach was screaming like a madman. The officials blew their whistles, and we ran back to our sideline.

On the next play Henry Davis wheeled around to hand off to Donnie to run that same running play off the right side. A big Beaver lineman crashed right over our center and smashed headlong into Henry. The ball popped out to the ground and the same bruiser recovered it. On their first play, Bluefield ran the option. The quarterback tossed it to their little halfback at the last moment and he ran 70 yards for a touchdown. All the air drained out of our admittedly faint hopes.

That did it. The Beavers were unstoppable the rest of the game, and our guys made only one more first down. Bluefield added insult to a dominating win by running up the score. They scored the last two touchdowns on passes and fancy running plays with laterals and some loop-the-loop stuff when they could have wound down the clock. But that fed the rivalry. We couldn't wait until basketball season to pound them in that sport.

House detention was finally over. On my first date with Margie Rey, or I should say, on our first double date with Wendie and Ann, she seemed reserved. When we finally were alone, she dropped the bomb. "We both should see other people."

It really wasn't a surprise. Something had been missing. But who likes to be dumped? She tried to be nice . . . turned on her most sincere smile. Breaking up with class.

"Jimmy, I'm really sorry." You know I think you're a nice person."

Right. I'm a nice person.

Maybe sheer logic could be used. "Is this related to the racing problem?" I asked. "I think I've learned a lesson here." Could I use my rehabilitation as a comeback?

"No, that's not it." She didn't sound convincing at all.

I felt so defensive. It was a lousy feeling.

It soon became clear that the person *she* "should see" was Mack ('48-Mercury-still-out-there-on-the-roads) Andrews.

"Can you believe it?" I asked Wendie.

"What would Shakespeare say about this calamity?" Wendie asked theatrically. "O woe is me!—or is it woe is I?"

When I didn't laugh he got serious. "You're lucky to be sitting here. You could be finishing your senior year taking correspondence courses from jail. Or even worse, taking them from a hospital somewhere. Or, God forbid, you could be . . ."

He was right.

I turned inward. Often I walked to and from school so I could be alone. To have time to mull things over. For one thing, I hadn't sent out a single college application, not a single request for financial aid. The first half of my senior year was zooming by. At least I wouldn't have to list a criminal offense on the applications.

Weekends were better. Saturday meant *Tiger Review.* And there were my friends on ham radio, including several "regulars," as Mom referred to them. I'd never met any in person. Some preferred the microphone—I now had a transmitter that also did voice—while others were only on Morse code. Not only did I not know what the code group looked like, I didn't know what their voices sounded like. But we were unique buddies with a bond. On Sunday mornings before daybreak, Mom drove me up the hill to sign on at WLOH. After the morning religious programs, I had from noon to three to work some soft popular music into the afternoon list of standards and instrumentals.

It would be an understatement to say things weren't good at home. I had no idea how Daddy managed to avoid having a wreck or getting nabbed with a DWI. Some nights he'd come home earlier, even have supper with us. Later, he'd start with the bourbon. Soon he'd be stupefied. If he ran out of Four Roses, he'd get on the phone. Before long a cab driver would knock on the door and deliver a new bottle.

Mom didn't argue with him. Instead she became sullen. Occasionally, she'd throw a dish or a glass on the kitchen floor, hard enough to smash it to bits. It made a racket, a real mess. Daddy would try to calm her down, saying "Sara, please don't do that." Mom would storm out of the kitchen into their bedroom. Then Daddy would be in the kitchen, alone, drinking, becoming sillier by the minute as he talked to "Joe," getting more and more looped.

At school, I pretended not to notice Mack and Margie Rey. I tried to ignore Meena's catty little comments on *Tiger Review.* It was hard. Can you say "loser?" Wendie and I rode to the dances together. Mostly I stood around the periphery, trying to look cool, whatever that meant, enduring the embarrassment and sting of seeing them. Mack was a good dancer. They both were. She looked even cuter now.

Letters from colleges kept coming. The official letter from the National Merit Scholarship office had stated that, "Your score was exemplary and qualifies you as a National Merit Finalist Scholar. However, you did not achieve the necessary results for National Merit funding; therefore, subsequent awards must come from privately funded sources." I should have talked with our high school counselor, but I never got around to it. She certainly didn't seek me out either. More letters came. One was from Washington University in Saint Louis. I had no idea how prestigious some of these schools were . . . had never heard of most of them. There was no follow-up.

It's hard to explain. Maybe there was some logical reason for my lack of interest. I don't know.

We did write one letter. It was to the University of Virginia, since Granny Jackson, Aunt Margaret, and Uncle George lived right across from the campus on Jefferson Park Avenue. I could stay with them. UVA replied that while no full scholarship was available, I should apply for admission and seek financial aid. Somehow, though, UVA didn't feel right. It didn't seem like "me" for some reason. That's a strange statement considering I didn't know who "me" was. I never followed up. I suppose one reason was that I always thought we were "middle class" since we lived in a brick home in the Mercer School District of Princeton and Daddy drove a new demonstrator Buick. We had a portrait of W. W. Jackson in his Civil War officer's uniform on our wall. Financial assistance? That seemed uncomfortably close to begging. Does any of this make sense?

Recognition from the Merit Scholarships did result in changes at school, including abandonment of my previous "no-effort" attitude on homework. Being grounded for a month had been a good thing. Of course, it was followed by Margie Rey and Mack. I put in more time and effort at home on my academics.

Our Latin teacher, Miss Kathleen Kane, is in good form this morning. She's the picture-perfect characterization of a dour high school teacher: stout; a brooch on her bosom; gunmetal blue-black hair, streaked with gray, pulled back severely in a short bun. "The Killer," as she is known *sub rosa* to all, brooks no monkey business.

"Mr. Jackson, read the first page of our lesson and translate it for the class." Fortunately, my recent hermit-like existence has prepared me for such a challenge. Not only had I read the lesson, I'd actually written out the English translation. Teenagers Publius and Furianus are visiting the Forum to hear a speech by Marc Antony. It's a big day in Rome.

"They were impressed that they were able to sit in the visitors' gallery and see and hear the famous orator," I conclude, feeling impressed, and relieved, myself.

"Well done," the Killer comments. "The verb also indicates excitement, but you captured the reading well."

I glance around, seeking some feedback for my small victory. Meena Gordon smirks and winks. Since absolutely nothing escapes the Killer's attention, she says. "Miss Gordon, since you appear to have enjoyed the last reading so intensely, would you care to read and then translate the next section, *et sin* any extraneous humor please."

Meena blossoms beet red. Fortunately, she aces it. The Killer actually seems pleased. We're two for two.

The entire day seems to turn on this. Mr. Johnson's trig class goes well. Then it's time for English. Diagramming sentences is abhorrent to many students, but it fits well with my sense of order. Three down and three to go!

"Jimmy, how're you doing now, you know, after all that Carlotti stuff?" Donnie Davis asks me as we're walking to lunch.

"Donnie, if you hadn't seen the whole thing, I'd have an arrest on my record. Eddie too. We could have gotten some jail time."

"I'm glad I was there. To verify he hit you, I mean. But to be honest . . . when you were passing Eddie . . . those headlights up ahead, coming around that curve . . ."

"Don't remind me. You know I got grounded for a month?"

"I heard. I guess you're off house arrest now."

"Correct. But I can't drive for six months. Not till the end of April."

"Hang in there. You know what the Good Book says, 'There is a time for all seasons.'"

On the way back from lunch, Ann Murphy is standing by her locker. She flips her hair back in a sassy way. "I was all set for a lot of double dating," she says, "but it looks like you're an unattached guy. So how much longer do I have Wendie all to myself?"

It's fun to cut up a little. "I noticed you two didn't exactly take the shortest way back to your house after he dropped me off the last time."

She cuts me off. "I don't want to sound catty, but I believe that was the last time I saw you and MR together. Your social calendar isn't exactly packed these days."

"The real reason we stopped going out was to give you and Wendie more private time." Then, "Oh the pain!" I fake having an attack. At that moment, in the middle of my supposed spasm, Callie Carver walks up to her locker, next to Ann's. I know her only remotely by name. She's a junior like Ann. She says hello to Ann, then smiles at me. Her smile is contagious. It reminds me of the Cheshire cat's in *Alice in Wonderland*, a super-full smile, ear to ear.

"Gotta run. See you girls." A little tingling sensation starts in my face.

Later that afternoon, as Wendie and I are driving home, he says, "Callie Carver is one of Ann's best friends. And the word has come to me by various channels, well, one channel in particular, that she sort of thinks you're, um, O.K." He pauses. "I see no reason on earth why this girl has come to such a warped conclusion. But somehow she has."

My mind is segueing to create a mental picture. Callie lives over in East Princeton somewhere. She's cute and seems to be popular.

"Isn't she in the Su Wans with Ann?"

He nods. Wendie and Ann have been dating for over six months now, and although he doesn't talk much about it, they're a steady item at school.

Snowflakes are floating down from the gray sky when we stop at Park Avenue. "I've got to drive to Athens and interview the basketball coach at Concord," he says. "Do you think Grantland Rice started like this?"

"Who's Grantland Rice?" I ask, with a shrug.

"Good grief," Wendie says. "Tomorrow, same time, same station. Be here. And be sure you know who Mr. Rice is by then. You probably have never heard of Bronco Nagurski either!"

"Bronco who?"

The chome-mobile disappears up the hill into the snow, which is heavier now. It feels good to come into the living room from the chill outside. But as soon as I approach the kitchen, it's obvious something is wrong. Mom is sitting down, her head lowered.

"Are you all right?" I ask.

"Daddy has gotten into some trouble. I just got off the phone with Susie in Morgantown. She's upset, and I'm not sure what to do."

"What's wrong? Is Daddy O.K.?"

"He stayed home this morning, after you left for school. Said he owes a lot of money. I don't know much about it."

"Owes money? For what?"

"He said he lost it . . . some sort of gambling." She appears shocked, embarrassed, and frightened at the same time. She looks at the kitchen wall while she talks. Mechanically, I look over at the same wall. The paint is streaked with residue. The house looks old and dingy.

"How much does he owe?"

"Ten thousand dollars! Something about the Elks Club. I have an appointment with Hoffman Daley." Hoffman Daley is a respected attorney in town. The Daleys go to the First Methodist Church and he knows Mom and Dad to some degree from there.

"That sounds like a good idea," I say, adding little value. Daddy has gotten really bad about going to the Elks Club. These days he almost never comes home on time. I hear him at the table late at night with his 'Hey, Joe' stuff after men bring him home. "He's going to have a wreck."

Mom looks back at the wall.

Chapter 21

MOM AND I had some time together after Daddy left for work Saturday morning. "I met with Hoffman Daley yesterday. He was very helpful," she said.

"How do you feel about all this?"

"I'm worried. Mr. Daley recommended that I take a tough position. He's concerned we could lose the house. With the amount of Daddy's debts, it's possible someone could put a lien on the property or . . ." She looked away. ". . . threaten Daddy or hurt him."

We sat there at the too-small table. Mom nursed her cup of coffee.

"Mr. Daley recommends that I give Daddy an ultimatum. He thinks Daddy is sick and needs help. One way to do that is to send a very strong message, and at the same time protect you and Susie, as well as myself."

It was clear now that Mom didn't want my advice. She wanted to tell me what she was thinking. She appeared to draw on some inward strength. "He prepared some legal papers. I intend to have Daddy sign them."

"Will he?"

"I think so. Daddy has a problem, a serious one," she said. "I'm determined on this. I called my brother yesterday after I got back from the law office. He agrees strongly with me."

And then, for the first time, she said, "I'm prepared to leave Daddy if he doesn't get straightened out."

Actually, he would have to leave Mom. According to her, the agreement would transfer the house and all associated property and furnishings to her. She'd have 100-percent ownership. In addition, Daddy would need to remove his name from all savings and checking accounts—his assets would pretty much be limited to the clothes on his back and in his closet. His paychecks would be deposited directly into Mom's account and she would give him a cash allowance. That was it. Mr. Daley recommended that it be structured that way, with nothing in Daddy's name. That way, no one could sue him and gain legal access to anything.

For a family that didn't talk about our problems, what a torrent of new developments! Mom was tough when she needed to be. All these details were floating through my head when a car horn sounded, interrupting the most serious discussion of my life.

"That's Wendie. He's on the show today, our guest, and he's taking me to the station. Be sure to listen."

She smiles. "Sorry about all this. But it will be all right."

"I don't know what to say."

"Everything will work out. I know it will. Mr. Daley is a good lawyer. He's a good person to rely on."

With that, and a second beep from Wendie, I grab my coat and go outside. The brisk air hits me. A skiff of snow coating the gray-green wooden porch makes it dangerously slick.

"Ah, the aspiring young radio personality himself," he says. The car is warm inside. Wendie must have had the engine running for five minutes in his driveway since the heater's going and the front window is completely clear.

"Good morning." I'm not taking the bait for a waiting punch line.

He picks up on my mood and we ride to the radio station in silence. The Chrome-mobile masters the small curvy lane going up Radio Hill and we park in the gravel lot below the tower colossus.

"Wendie Johnston, welcome to *Tiger Review*. You're a senior at Princeton High School, is that right?"

"The last time I checked." Wendie-speak right from the start.

"Good for you." Big laugh all around, "Yes that's good. You're interested in journalism as a career—sports journalism, to be more specific. Tell us about it."

"I've been interested in sports for a while," he said, "ever since following the great Oklahoma teams of Bud Wilkerson. It seemed like a good thing to be able to make a living, getting paid for . . . for doing something I like in the first place."

"You currently work for the *Bluefield Daily Telegraph* covering football and basketball for Concord College?" *I'm conducting a real interview, which is so cool.*

"Yes, Concord College. The Mountain Lions to be exact." Droll Wendie-speak again.

We transition into experiences at school and courses he's taken, or is now taking, which have proven helpful. I also ask him about influences—his version of Dick Biondi. Wendie mentions Stubby Currence, the grizzled senior writer and sports editor at the *Telegraph*, as well as a writer for *Sports Illustrated*.

It's a good five-minute segment. He talks about what interests him, which turns out to be interviewing the coaches and players, and reporting on the games. He includes the importance of language skills and the fact that he plans to go to Concord and major in English. Of course in that scenario he could keep his current job at the paper, perhaps even expand it to Princeton and Athens High School sports reporting as well.

Becky has picked the songs. She's given the list to John Shelton, and her selections transition one portion of the program to another. I like them all, especially "Angel Baby" by Rosie and the Originals. It's the one-hit wonder that includes the absolutely worst saxophone solo in the history of hit music.

Wendie stays in Studio A as we wrap up the show, and then the four of us stand around for a few minutes in the parking lot and chat. The air is cold and the sky is overcast, but our spirits are good.

"Great interview," Becky says.

"Right. I'll bet that Miss Shumate will use you as an example of a student who is mastering the English language," Meena adds.

"Well, um, I just don't know, well, um, what to say," Wendie mumbles, using the silly shorthand he and I have developed over the years.

"Now we discover that the next great journalistic mind of PHS actually can't string an entire sentence together," she says.

"Well, Meena, I just don't, um, don't know," he continues.

"Cut it out. It was good," Becky concludes. "See you-all Monday."

"Thanks, ladies. It was a good experience." Wendie snaps back. As we walk the short distance to his car, the gravel crunches underfoot.

He looks over at me. "You all right?"

"Just some stuff at home."

We drive the rest of the way without comment.

Mom seems to be in a better mood. She's skittering around the kitchen and greets me with the announcement that she baked a batch of oatmeal-raisin cookies during the program.

"How was the interview?" I asked.

"I thought it was very good. Wendie just might have encouraged someone to go into journalism." With that, I direct my attention to the cookies.

"The mailman came, and you got two QSL cards today," Mom continues, handing them to me. These are similar to postcards, except for being printed with the ham radio call letters on one side. We hams exchange them to confirm our contacts.

"Look at this! Utah—a new state for me." I'd contacted him after getting up really early that one morning during the Boy Scout contest. The card has his call sign, KN7BPR, in large red letters, and spaces for his equipment and antenna information. For a moment, I'm in the world of ham radio and forget the problems at home.

"It says I'm his first West Virginia contact!"

Mom was correct in her assessment of Hoffman Daley. He was a very good person for her to rely on. She never did show me the paperwork. Daddy never said a word about it to Susie or me in any way, shape, or form. I don't know how he paid off his gambling debts, or even if he did. I do know that Mom stayed at her job working for Mercer County as a public health nurse. The stated reason, no doubt partially true, was that Susie was at WVU and Mom's salary was being used to pay for college expenses. Since I'd be going somewhere next year, they would have two kids in college.

Daddy quit going to the Elks Club for several months, but at home he still managed to get schnockered. After supper, he drank Coke and Four Roses bourbon at the kitchen table and bellowed at Joe. There was no "off" switch. At least he wasn't gambling.

The cold wintry days gradually changed, day by day, and March finally arrived. It wouldn't be long until the end of April and the return of my driver's license. My grades were better than ever. Getting a dose of humility, reality, and accountability will do that for you. I still wasn't dating—not at all. Actually it wasn't bad. There was less pressure, and it was amazing how often someone would mention something to me along the lines of "Sandra Bailey told me she thinks you're nice" or "My friend Julie Benson said to tell you hello." The six months' punishment period represented symbolic, as well as actual, transition in what was important.

My 18th birthday, March 31st, finally arrived. Daddy left work early. Wendie drove down the hill to join us. Our small kitchen table, crammed next to the wall by the back door, was filled for the first time since Susie went back to WVU. Mom had fixed my favorite foods: pot roast, corn on the cob, and mashed potatoes with her gravy. She also made corn dodgers and baked cottage cheese, her two family specialties. Corn dodgers were cornmeal mush that was dribbled onto a hot frying pan in little globs. She fried them to a crispy state, then put butter and salt on the top and let them melt to form a crunchy surface. The baked cottage cheese had a crisp, chewy, hardened top surface, and the inside was sweet since she added sugar and butter to the mixture. It just didn't get any better than that.

Following the meal, Daddy smoked as usual. Wendie didn't smoke in our house, or in his own for that matter. His mother wouldn't permit it. He knew I disliked it. I sat there, watching Daddy's blue smoke fill the air over the table, feeling the familiar burning sensation in my lungs.

In her most theatrical fashion, Mom brought out a chocolate cake with 18 candles. It was quite a scene—all those teensy flickering lights amid the haze. "And here's your favorite dessert. For my favorite son. My very favorite son."

Wendie chimed in, "To her favorite son!" He winked at me. The unstated part . . . competition is limited. My mind jumped to the unstated duty that went along with being the only son.

"A-yand," Mom continued, stretching the word into two and a half syllables, "To his very best friend, Wendell Johnston."

"Hear, hear!" Wendie said as he leaned back in his chair, at least to the degree possible in our cramped seating arrangement.

Daddy kept a placid expression. He stubbed out his Lucky Strike, which went *ssssstt* as it drowned in gravy while I blew out the forest of tiny trees ablaze at their tops. The still-hot candles, oozing hot wax down their sides, were stacked to the side as Mom cut large slices.

"Mrs. Jackson, everything is terrific," Wendie said. His fork held a final bit of her specialty. "But I'm not sure what this is, er, what this was."

"That's baked cottage cheese. It's a Jackson family recipe, from Broadford, the old family home place.

"Terrific. Never had it before," he said. "The corn dodgers, now they're always good." He and I sometimes warmed up corn dodgers and ate them in a buttery coating as a snack. They could be reheated. But the baked cottage cheese . . . that was a treat Mom made only on special occasions.

It was a good birthday. Wendie and I walked out through the living room. He paused in front of the large charcoal portrait of W. W. Jackson, who looked stern in his Confederate lieutenant's uniform, and said, "Betcha that guy liked baked cottage cheese too."

Chapter 22

FINALLY.

The end of April.

I was permitted to drive.

My first outing with The Bomb was on a Friday night, at the Spring Fling, which was the annual event to encourage warmer weather. Change was in the air. Crocuses and thin new grass hinted at the season change.

Wendie was taking Ann, so I went by myself; my best pegged pants, loafers, shirt with collar up in the back—all that. It felt strange, a good form of strange, to be driving once again. That little escapade had cost me the better part of my senior year in some respects. But my routine now was a snap: school, *Tiger Review* on Saturday, the Sunday slot at WLOH, homework, ham radio, and rock and roll on the radio.

My grades were terrific. I felt less harried. Compared with pre-Carlotti, my life was bordering on monastic dedication. Adjusting to the restoration of privileges, I reunited with my trusty steed and drove conservatively to the Memorial Building around seven.

The Roadsters were booked to play. I wanted to see the guys. The race had been a cold-turkey ending to that chapter. The microphones, amps, monitor speakers, and cables were in place, and I caught the very end of their sound check. The band was getting big, booked all over the area. Arcie was a prominent front man, now quite the showman: white sports coat, dark shirt and tie, white shoes, and all the moves. He wore his hair long, straightened and slicked down. I knew he still could play any of the instruments if needed. The band liked to have Slate get microphone time as well. His blond mane and the sullen James Dean look attracted the girls.

It seemed strange to watch them get ready. We'd had some good times together . . . interesting times. They kicked it off at about eight, and the usual group of people who dance the first song got up and took to the floor.

Margie Rey and Mack got there around eight-thirty. Seeing them together was less painful now. The hair cream sculpting Mack's DA gleamed in the lights.

Wendie was over at Concord interviewing one of the basketball coaches. He'd said to look for him around nine. Ann would meet him there. I was standing around, not really paying any attention, when she came into the room and headed my way. Callie Carver was with her. I dug my hands deeper into my pants pockets, trying to look nonchalant.

"Jimmy, is Wendie here yet?" Ann asks. She seems on edge.

"Not yet. He said something about nine."

"Oh, that's right."

"The Su Wans planning a confrontation with the Sub Debs?" My voice rises over the pulsing music. "Like *West Side Story* . . . big east side-west side rumble?"

The Sub Debs from the Mercer School district had a snarky line that the Su Wans were the girls who couldn't get into the Sub Debs. I'd heard my sister say that on the phone to her Sub Deb friends.

They laugh. "Read the signs. We both sponsored this."

Ann and Callie head for a cluster of girls.

It's pleasant to be here, especially with a car. I've been so dependent on favors from Wendie and others. *Jimmy, the gossip king, the recovering social outcast.* The band has gotten better since the summer nights out at the beer joints and clubs. That seems so long ago.

The long rides to and from gigs talking with Arcie pop back into my mind. Yet the Ma and Pa patrol at the door underscore the fact that some things haven't changed. Arcie is here because he's with the band, not because he's a student at Princeton High School. He's a black face in a sea of white people.

The style and arrangements still are familiar. Standard covers of the popular top 40 songs. Arcie's stretching a bit in the middle of Little Anthony and the Imperials' "Tears on My Pillow" when Wendie taps me on the shoulder.

"Sorry to interrupt your solitude. You doing all right? Since you're standing here all by your lonely, supporting a side wall of this building, I would surmise things aren't all that great."

"Thanks for the encouraging words," I say, returning my gaze to the dimly lit dance floor just in time to see Margie Rey and Mack glide by. She's facing my way but looks away. "Ann is here. At least she was. I think she ran off with Boozy Leonard."

"She has better judgment than that, and she's probably in a more positive frame of mind than some people I know." He shoots me his official penetrating look. The tears on Little Anthony's pillow have dried, and the band is between songs. He lowers his voice. "Think positive thoughts, dammit."

Things do improve. Donnie Davis and Marnie Bowland come over. Marnie's a card. It's hard to stay depressed with her clever "bad-girl" persona. Meena Gordon walks by my standing-around-looking-cool-supporting-the-wall position to remind me that we have *Tiger Review* tomorrow and it's my week to select the songs.

Soon I'm alone, or as alone as one can be in a room with 200 people and a band. So I decide to walk around and find Wendie and Ann somewhere in the dim sea of humanity. Callie Carver, who's dancing with one of the junior boys, comes into view. Ann leans over and says, "You should ask Callie to dance."

The song ends, and the band launches into "Stay" by Maurice Williams and the Zodiacs. Emboldened by one of my favorite songs, as well as Ann's sharp little elbow to my side, I walk over to Callie.

"May I have this dance?" It sounds formal, but that's exactly what I say. Recovering social black sheep are allowed to do such things. She nods and smiles shyly. "Stay" is in between slow and fast dancing, so we do lots of turning while waltzing, punctuated by occasionally twirling her around under my outstretched hand. She's a much better dancer than I am, smooth and natural. As we rotate toward the band, Slate gives me his little natch-nod: I'm doing all right both in terms of my partner and my dancing. Arcie does a thumbs-up.

Between the loud music and all the dance moves, we haven't spoken much. Finally there's a short break. She makes no motion to walk back to the side.

"Thanks for the dance, Callie," I say. "You're really good."

She beams that special smile.

"Thanks, Jimmy," she says. "Are you friends with the band? They seem to know you." At that moment, Arcie starts in with the opening words to "Mr. Blue," the Fleetwoods song. I extend my hand automatically and we start to waltz. My left hand cups her right hand. We begin in a friendly but polite way.

"We're all seniors at school. Well, everyone but Peppy. I know them pretty well."

"Didn't you used to be in the band?" she asks, as her brown hair moves from side to side. *Aha!* She's heard.

"Oh, that." I can't help but laugh. "Not really. I wasn't in the band—you know, as a musician. But I did help them out last year. I was . . ." What's the right word? ". . . I was the doorman."

"The what?"

"I helped out with driving to gigs, and at certain places, collected money at the door. Doorman—I guess that's where the word comes from."

It sounds so formal, like a real job. Ridiculous all of a sudden. But combined with all those practice sessions, and all the talks with Arcie, I *had* been a part of it.

"I see," she says. But her look implies a foreign concept.

"Mr. Blue" is ending. It seems like the song must have been only a few seconds long—we talked, hardly moved at all. When we join Wendie and Ann, they're involved in a serious discussion. Ann's voice is edgy and penetrates the crowd noise.

"If that's the way you feel about it, fine with me."

Ann reaches for Callie's hand. They head toward the bathroom area, on the other side of the grand balcony stairway. Callie glances back at me.

"What's going on?" I ask over the music.

Wendie motions me over to a group of unoccupied chairs and sits down like he's a tired old man. "I don't know."

Wendie and I have talked about a lot of things, but never about our respective love lives, or the lack of same. So it isn't a big surprise to me that what is happening is, to be exact, a big surprise to me. I sit down, a chair between us. One of the girls looks our way. He deflects her glance dismissively and lowers his eyes to the vacant seat.

"Nothing actually is wrong," he continues. "It's just that nothing is right. Does that make any sense?"

"I suppose so. Listen, Wendie, I'm no expert on girls." Just then the golden couple walk by, headed for the door. Mack has his arm around her. I nod at them. "Isn't that sweet."

"Things have sort of, gradually, well . . ." He lapses into our private cool-speak. ". . . I mean, they have, like, bit by bit, lost their, uh . . . luster. Or, maybe you could say, turned to, er . . . shit."

"Is turned-to-shit a specific term in the field of psychology?"

"That's right. A definitive descriptive term. You got it, Sherlock. That's like the actual term the Concord coach used to describe his basketball team." A smile appears. "But it was off the record. Just like this flask in my jacket pocket."

Callie suddenly interrupts our not-so-philosophical conversation. "Ann called her sister. She's waiting outside now. Needs to be alone. I know two people who need a *cooling-off* period."

Slate's voice breaks into our conversation. "Thank you-all for coming. On behalf of the Sub Debs, the Su Wans, and the Roadsters, we hope you've had a great time at the nineteen-sixty Spring Fling. Thank you for having us. Hopefully spring actually will appear, so keep your hopes up. Get your partner, 'cause this is the last dance."

The last dance is The Last Dance, or to be exact, "Save the Last Dance for Me" by The Drifters. Callie looks at me. Suddenly, Wendie disappears from view. I gently turn toward her, bow a bit. Corny. She smiles.

This time she rests her head lightly on my shoulder. By high school waltzing standards, we're still rather proper. But this proper is electric. Gradually she nestles softly. She feels warm and gentle. I move my right hand lightly on her back. She seems to move closer. We're alone.

The music ends. The Ma and Pa people, victorious in their defense against integration at school dances, come upstairs and switch on the overhead lights.

"Do you have a ride?" I ask. "I'd be glad to take you home."

"I was going to call Daddy to come get me," she says. "Let me check. If it's all right, you can run me home. It'll save him having to drive over here."

We walk down the grand stairway to the bank of pay phones. The wait seems like forever. Will she be allowed to drive with the school madman?

Finally, she's back. The Cheshire cat smiles. She's cleared.

"It's O.K., but I have to go straight home." With that, she turns to the coatrack.

"Here, let me help you," I offer. Mr. Gallant manages to hold the coat upside down. We both giggle. "There, that's better. This way you don't have to stand on your head to wear it." As she slips into the wrap, I can't help but notice her trim figure.

Halfway to the car, she takes my arm loosely. It feels natural. Already, a thin coating of rime has settled on the windshield. The Bomb, ever the reliable champ, starts right away, but also as usual, it takes a while to warm up.

The moonlight reflects off the frosty sheen, giving her face a gentle glow. By now, the radio, if not the heater, has warmed up. With the middle button, Dick Biondi's voice fills the car. Rat-a-Tat. "Channel Eighty-Nine, W-L-S." Rat-a-Tat-Tat.

Many of the other cars head to Mooney's, but she needs to go straight home. We drive slowly around the courthouse. "Thanks again for the ride," she says, still bracing against the cold. "It's nice of you."

"Oh, no trouble," I say. It goes without saying that it's been a while since I've had a date, or even been in the company of a girl.

On Mercer Street, we pass the five classic columns of the First Baptist Church, then the major intersection of Park and Center Streets at Mercer by the First Methodist Church, and then the Mercer Theater. Finally the heater starts to kick in. The car becomes tolerable, then pleasant, as we reach the Thorn Street Bridge, which spans the railroad tracks and Brushy Creek.

"I live on Prince Street," she says as we pass over the bridge. "You can turn left on Caperton Avenue, just ahead."

Homes in this part of town are smaller. There are fewer trees in the yards.

"There it is," she says, motioning to a house on the corner. A Buick Roadmaster is parked up on the grass, at an angle in the front yard. The porch light is on.

I pull up on the same side of the street as the house, facing what would be oncoming cars, if there were any oncoming traffic at that hour. The motor is still running and The Bomb's headlights are on. It's the right thing to do, since I'm bringing her home, but not from a date, a real date.

"Thanks again for the ride," she says.

"I'm glad I could help. Too bad about whatever is going on with Wendie and Ann." Then, and it just pops out, "Callie, I had a really good time tonight."

"Me too," she says. On a complete impulse, I lean toward her. She turns to me. We kiss. Our first kiss, of course, but the warmest, softest, most sensual kiss I've ever experienced. Two seconds at most pass. Almost embarrassed at how wonderful it is, I move away.

"Let me come around and help you out." If there's such a thing as levitation in this world, it's happening now. My feet aren't touching the ground as I fly behind the car and open her door.

We walk together up the sidewalk. Shivering a little as the night air envelops her, she smiles her wonderful smile and quickly goes to her front steps. With a glance back, she opens the door and goes inside.

Something special has happened.

Chapter 23

THE BUICK DEMONSTRATOR is in the driveway. The young woman anchor with the eleven o'clock news on Channel Six stands on a wet street somewhere, reporting on a fire. She's trying to sound Midwestern, pronouncing her words in a nasal voice with exaggerated clarity to hide her southern Appalachian accent. The television pictures have a jerky, flinty characteristic, glowing through a blue haze, as videos show a doublewide in ruins.

Daddy's asleep in his chair, a cigarette perched precariously on the outer edges of the heavy glass ashtray. A skinny, gray ash portion curves grotesquely, ready to break off and fall. The remaining portion could flip out altogether, add to the pockmarks previously singed into the fabric, or worse.

Mom is asleep on the couch.

Daddy stirs, clears his throat. "Jimmy, that you?" He seems all right.

"It's me. I'm home."

"Mother said you went to a dance tonight."

A sleepy groan comes from the couch. "That you, Jimmy?"

"Hi, Mom. I'm home."

"How was the dance?" she asks.

"Oh, fine."

The weather portion of the news is beginning. As usual, spring will be coming late to the mountains. Light snow is forecasted over the weekend.

"I met someone tonight."

Mom perks up. "Oh, who?"

"Callie Carver."

"That's nice."

With the name Carver, Daddy looks over. "A Mr. Jake Carver bought a new Buick Roadmaster last year."

"There was a Roadmaster parked by the house."

"She must be Mr. Carver's daughter. He works over at the Celanese plant at Narrows. Seemed like a nice fellow."

Mom adds to the conversation. "I think I know the family. They attend the First Christian Church."

That settles it. Any family who buys a new car from Daddy and attends the First Christian Church is O.K.

"G'night, honey," Mom says. "I'm glad you had a nice time at the dance."

The second floor seems to be separated from the Lucky Strikes cloudbank clinging to the ceilings of the downstairs rooms. WLOH signs off the air at midnight. I can envision Harry Gentry wrapping up the request show, walking out of the control room and through the narrow hallway back to the transmitter room. He's just thrown the plate voltage switch to the "off" position, waited a bit for the final power tubes to cool, and then turned off the remainder. Mr. Emory's black transmitter sits there in the dark until just before six when John Shelton will arrive Saturday morning and reverse the procedure to sign on.

When the alarm goes off at seven, I'm already awake. The glow of last night . . . what a feeling. The crackling sound and smell of frying bacon adds to how rich life can be.

Mom's chipper voice does as well. "Good morning. How are you today?"

"Mom, do you think it would be all right to call Callie Carver this morning and ask her to the movies tonight? Would that be too soon? I mean I just really . . ." Thoughts race ahead. "I've hardly ever even talked to her before last night."

"If you had a nice time at the dance, then call her today. See if she would like to go out. After all, the worst she can say is no."

"That's not a good example. I'll call her after I get back from the station. By the way, speaking of bad things, Wendie broke up with Ann Murphy last night. At least it sure sounded that way to me." Mom's silent maternal look suffices for any additional conversation.

Becky Eastland has scheduled an interview with the phys ed teacher. The lady is big into physical exercise and why that's important. She's also the advisor for the cheerleaders, and has an important hand in deciding who makes the cut when the girls try out each year. Apparently the competition is intense. Only two girls are selected from each class.

Meena's "social scene" surprises me.

"Who was that senior seen with a junior at the dance last night? The mystery couple danced the last dance and it's reported that he drove her home." She doesn't mention names, but looks directly at me, and it's clear who she has in mind. She also reports on a "spat" between another twosome, her word. "A little tiff," she concludes. She gets that one wrong.

On the way out following the program, John Shelton stops me. "Good picks on the music. All set for tomorrow?"

"Sure thing. I'll be here."

As soon as I get home, Mom gives me her knowing look.

"Was that comment about you? Did you drive her home? You didn't mention that."

"She needed a ride." That's technically right. "I dropped her off at her front door. Always the chivalrous gentleman, you know." It's my time to smile. "You need the phone for a while?"

"Go right ahead. I promise not to listen."

With the mangled cord in hand, I'm halfway out to the sunporch when it dawns on me that I don't know her number. Back to the kitchen to look in the small phone book. That has to be the one. The only Carver on that street.

Outside again. Ring. Ring. Two more rings. Are they home?

"Hello." It's not her voice.

"Is this the Carver residence?"

"Yes."

"May I speak with Callie, please?" My voice is cracking with nerves. "This is Jimmy Jackson." Her mother shouldn't have to ask who's calling her daughter.

A pause, then, "Good morning, Jimmy. This is Callie's mother. She's not home right now." Not home. Bad news. But before I can decide what to say, Mrs. Carver continues. "She's at Ann Murphy's house this morning. If you'd like to call her there, I have the number."

"Yes ma'am. That would be really nice."

I thank her and sit for a moment, rebuilding my courage.

"Hello."

Another adult voice. Ann's mother?

I tell her who I am and that I'm calling for Callie Carver. It seems strange to be calling someone at another house to ask for a date.

"She's here. Just a minute." Then, "Callie, it's for you."

Muffled voices echo in the background. "It's a boy!"

"She'll be right here."

"Thank you."

My voice sounds threadbare. A five-second wait follows before someone picks up the phone.

"Hello."

It's her.

"Callie, this is Jimmy. Jimmy Jackson." I'm nervous, my palms are sweaty. I feel like I've come through a labyrinth.

"Hi, Jimmy." Her voice sounds pleasant, relaxed. Opposite of the way I feel. "This is a surprise."

"I didn't call too early, did I?" A courtesy. It's ten-fifteen.

She laughs. It sounds pleasant, cute. "Oh, no. It's good to talk with you. Again."

"Yes, me too. I had fun last night."

"I did too," Callie says, lowering her voice.

"Would it be possible . . ." *Of course it would be possible.* I start again. "Would you be able to go to a movie with me tonight?" Another blown sentence . . . unless she's been incapacitated since I dropped her off, she would be *able*. I decide not to rephrase the question. *Let it go.*

There's a pause. It's as if she's letting me sort through my language limitations.

"That would be nice."

For some reason, I'm not sure if that is a yes. Is "nice" the same as "yes?"

My battle with my insecurities and the language rages on for, say, a millionth of a second.

"Yes, I'd like that."

That's a yes!

"That's great." I blurt it out. Mom looks at me through the window between the porch and the small kitchen. She knows.

"The paper says the show starts at seven. How about me coming over at six-thirty?"

"That sounds good," she says. "By the way, we listened to *Tiger Review* on the radio this morning."

"Oh, thanks. It's been a lot of fun all year, even if it means an early start on Saturday mornings." I'm more at ease now. "Did you catch Meena Gordon's gossip stuff?"

She pauses. "Yes. Ann heard it too."

"I'm sorry things blew up."

"I am, too. But things like that just don't happen overnight."

We're on the same page. "Well, I'm really happy you're able to go out tonight. See you around six-thirty."

There it is. The "able" thing again.

Let it go.

"Bye." The sound of her voice lingers.

The phone's still warm against my ear . . . now with a dial tone.

"Bye," I repeat, now to myself and the dial tone.

Mom smiles knowingly.

The drive takes 10 minutes at most, and that's with traffic. Just in case, I leave early. After all, I could circle around over there as much as I needed to. At six-ten, I put on my jacket and tell Mom goodbye.

When you're early, it's all easy. Five minutes later, I've crossed the Thorn Street Bridge into East Princeton. There it is, Caperton Avenue, just three blocks from her house. I can't go up there yet. It would be embarrassing to circle around her block like some creep, so I continue straight ahead and soon am out at the Athens Road intersection.

A few more minutes—how to kill them. I turn left and start on the Athens Road. Gritty machine shops and strings of poor little churches and small frame houses line the road. Ten minutes killed. Time to turn around. There's a place, a small grocery store with a decent gravel parking lot. The Bomb is pleasantly warm inside. The gas tank is nearly full. Almost time. Back to the intersection and onto Thorn Street, then a right again, up Caperton Avenue, past the Key Street Methodist Church.

The front light is on. The Buick is parked in front, not up in the yard. I stop across the street, take a deep breath, and turn off the motor. Six-thirty on the dot. I get out and walk across the street, passing in front of the big Roadmaster. Daddy's comment comes to mind. That must have been a nice commission. Up the steps. The small porch has a swing at the far end, as well as two chairs crowded together and some kind of plastic potted plant. Nervous in a good way, my body tingles and my mind races.

Here it goes. I can't just stand out here in front. Two knocks—loud enough but not obnoxious. A lacy curtain material covers the glass panes in the wooden door.

Someone's coming. It's her. She opens the door and smiles. The soft material of her sweater clings to her.

"Let me take your coat."

I slip it off. The brilliance of her unusually broad smile accentuates the moment.

She puts the jacket on a coatrack just inside the door. It's already so top-heavy with winter paraphernalia that it looks unsteady.

The house is warm inside, warmer than we keep our home, with a pungent smell of cooking—food aromas. Not the odor of Lucky Strikes. The TV is on, loud. An upright piano stands by the front wall, on the other side of the coats, with newspapers and magazines in piles all around. Someone must be a reader, or a packrat. A large copy of a painting of Jesus dominates the wall. He's surrounded by little children and has a pleasant smile. An aura encircles his head. His hand is raised.

"Jimmy, this is my Dad, Jake," Callie is saying. I look away from Jesus as a burly man rises from his TV chair. "Daddy, this is Jimmy Jackson." Mr. Carver turns to me and extends his hand.

"Nice to meet you," he says. I listen hard over a loud game show on TV. The audience is applauding. Someone has won something.

"Thank you, sir. Pleased to meet you," I respond formally.

When men shake hands, it's important to manage a balanced and firm, manly handshake. There's nothing worse than to miscenter the hand-shaking hand with three crushed fingers, your thumb misplaced. You've got to lock in. His huge hand completely envelops mine. It's almost twice as large. Or at least it seems that way. All this is going through my mind as I manage a credible handshake with this no-nonsense man of around 40. Mr. Carver immediately turns back around and sits down again, facing the noise and screen. Apparently that's the "father introduction."

"Come in and meet my mother," Callie says.

The audience applauds once more.

Jesus eyes me non-stop as I follow Callie through the living room behind Mr. Carver's chair. We pass over a floor furnace grate that streams massive amounts of hot air up into the room. She leads me through the dining room and into the small kitchen at the rear of the house.

"Mom, this is Jimmy Jackson."

"Hello, Mrs. Carver," I say, getting in the initial words.

She lightly takes my extended hand. "I'm glad to meet you. Your mother, Sara, is such a nice person."

"Thank you. Mom mentioned she knows you, as well as several of your sisters."

Mrs. Carver is a small woman, with a sparkling smile and alert eyes. Her shallow voice seems to strain from the back of her throat. A very few threads of gray highlight her naturally black hair. Oversized glasses give her an owlish appearance.

"Callie says you're a senior."

"Yes ma'am."

High school's nearly over. "Congratulations."

I hope she hasn't heard. Would her next question be, "Have you ever lost your driving license? Is my daughter safe with you?"

Callie saves me. "It's getting late. We'd better get going."

Our perfunctory introductions concluded, I tell Mrs. Carver how nice it is to meet her. It actually is. I like her.

"Have a good time," Mrs. Carver says, as she bustles behind us.

Callie gets both coats from the rack and I help her slip into hers, trying not to be too obvious—ah, that front view again.

"Bye," she says. As we leave, her dad nods, gives me a quick once-over, and turns back to the TV.

On the way to the theater, we talk, actually have things to discuss. It seems natural, like we've been together a long time. Holding her hand is comfortable, too. No sweaty palms, which amazes me. Our hands just come together naturally. After the movie she puts her hand gently inside my arm at the elbow as we walk to the car . . . her touch is so light.

Following a brief trip to Mooney's, the return drive amid the cruisers on Mercer Street dissolves into nothingness. There are only the two of us. We are in front of her house again. All too soon.

"I had a nice time," she says.

"I did, too. Thanks for . . ." As I'm saying this, she seems to lean a little toward me. Is it my imagination?

No. Her lips are smooth and soft.

As we walk across the street to the porch, she again takes my arm.

Again, that radiant smile.

"Good night, Jimmy."

She walks to the door, glances back, and goes inside.

Something is different, just like last night.

The Bomb drives itself back to the main part of town and pulls into the driveway at home. All by itself.

I swear it.

CHAPTER 24

EARLY SUNDAY MORNING. No need for an alarm this morning. I've been awake for a half hour. What a wonderful evening.

Up on Radio Hill, the crisp morning air is bracing as I crunch over the frosty gravel. Every footfall echoes off the Deco front of the radio station. The building is completely dark with the exception of eerie periodic red flashes piercing the pre-dawn mist from the strobe lighting at the top of the tower.

The door lock opens with what now is a familiar metallic disengaging sound. The lights flick on. By now it's routine to handle signing on by myself, even in the winter when it's cold and dark.

The control room is comfortable since the controls and tape decks need to be at a constant temperature. Tossing my coat over a chair, I walk back to the transmitter room and the six-foot-tall black chassis that transforms what takes place in this small building to a circle of reception 20 miles across—at least on a good day.

Click! The filament switch is on. Wait several minutes for the tubes to warm up . . . the procedure is down pat. Now the plate voltage switch, with the immediate sharp clack of relays and the transition to the familiar deep groan as the transmitter comes up to full power. Anyone with their radio tuned to WLOH would hear their radio go quiet, but as yet with no modulation, no music or sounds. O.K. so far. Now—a few minutes to open the logbook and read the schedule. All the public service announcements and commercials are typed out with the times for each. In the small room with the AP teletypewriter, paper is amassed on the floor. The most recent AP news lies at the top of the spool. Insert the national anthem tape. The second hand clicks its final five stiff little steps . . . six on the dot. Sunday morning programming at the "Mighty 1490" is underway.

Miss Mabel's Gospel Hour now runs from eight-thirty to nine, a time change. Always a hoot, she plays her piano and records her own "messages" over in Tazewell, Virginia. Finally, Miss Mabel warbles off-key through the final stanza of "Closer My God to Thee."

"Ladies and gentlemen, you have been listening to Miss Mabel Slater and Miss Mabel's Gospel Hour. Don't forget to write her at Post Office Box eighty-eight, Tazewell, Virginia. Send your contribution so Miss Mabel can continue to witness for the Lord." That exact announcement must be read at the end of every Miss Mabel tape.

"It's now nine o'clock. You're tuned to WLOH in Princeton, West Virginia."

At nine, The Reverend Cecil Cline Sunday Evangelical Hour begins. This is a new group, since Brother Lonnie Bozart's pleas for money apparently had fallen short. Reverend Cline weighs 300 pounds. He always wears a suit, and he features ties that are short and wide, with bold patterns of crosses, butterflies, and angels. Reverend Cline's signature is his fire-and-brimstone sermon. His approach to getting everyone to Heaven (or to hell) is threatening everlasting damnation and serious suffering. Unless, that is, unless we repent our sins and "get right with Jesus," or as he says it, "ga-it right wit' Chee-zus." Between the "Chee" and the "zus," every last bit of air vacates his lungs since Reverend Cline gasps out "zus" with a dramatic raspy whisper.

Powerful stuff.

Reverend Cline upgraded from an old Ford to a new Mercury last month. He must be right with Chee-zus.

"I'm telling you." He inhales a great gulp of air. "Ya gotta ga-it right wit' Gawd. Ya gotta ga-it right wit' Chee-zus. Brothers and Sisters, I tell ya what ya gonna have to deal wit'. What ya gonna face. If'n ya don't . . . ya gonna *burn* in, I say, ya gonna *burrrn* in hell. I can *smell* it . . . I can *see* . . . *see* them poor souls who live in eternal, yes . . . eee-ternal *con-dem-na-shun*."

He pauses and wipes the sweat from his face with his handkerchief.

"Brothers and Sisters, hear the word of God while you still have time, while . . ." One final huge breath ". . . you can still *saaave* your soul!"

Then in a whisper, "Let us pray."

I make the formal segue. "Ladies and gentlemen, you have been listening to the Reverend Cecil Cline Sunday Evangelical Hour. Remember to send in your cards and letters to Reverend Cline, care of Post Office Box fourteen-fifty, Princeton, West Virginia. Help Reverend Cline spread the word of God. Thank you. It's now ten o'clock and you're listening to WLOH in Princeton, West Virginia."

The Upper Room Hour follows from ten to eleven, when the live Sunday morning service from the First Methodist Church begins.

It seems to me that there are a variety of ways to get right with Jesus—from Miss Mabel to Reverend Cline, to the Upper Room, and everyone in between, including the refined intonations of Dr. Robert L. Martin at the First Methodist Church.

Plenty of good DJ work presents itself between noon and three o'clock. Aside from the commercials—some on tape and some printed, which I read from the script—as well as the news on the hour, I'm free to play music until Lonnie Blancett comes in and takes over.

Callie and I were inseparable the rest of the year. For the first time, it really mattered. Of course there were major decisions to make. The letters from colleges were tailing off. Virginia Tech discontinued the mandatory full-time military requirement for the first time and made it optional.

Off I would go for my freshman year . . . and electrical engineering.

As Mom said, "You seem to enjoy radio."

The campus in Blacksburg was only 60 miles away. Being that close to Callie sealed the deal.

Part 3

Doylestown, Pennsylvania

"I am a part of all I have met;
Yet all experience is an arch wherethrough
Gleams that untraveled world . . ."

Alfred Lord Tennyson
Ulysses

Chapter 25

March, 1977

THERE ARE FIVE of us now. Callie and I have brought Katie, Kenny, and Joey into the world.

Kenny is outside. His long blond hair is below his ears, streaked with dirt. He's more and more distant. Callie and I are becoming regulars at his school for matters involving misbehavior. He's defiant, the black sheep with beautiful but hard blue eyes. Our relationship has gone from what I thought was good, to brittle and unfeeling.

"Come on in, Kenny. You need to get ready for supper." I call out. No response. "Come on." Louder this time. "Hurry."

Kenny appears around the barn—a dawdling, sullen 11-year old. He needs a bath, but I don't argue. Instead I go up the narrow steps to Callie's and my bedroom. The old farmhouse could have been featured in one of those country living magazines—long on character and charm: thick walls, original plank boards in the floors, early American fireplaces. But way too short on space. Only one bathroom.

Joey's room is an unheated add-on pillbox at the rear of the second floor. The seven year old never complains, he's the low maintenance kid. Sometimes I'm concerned we overlook him in the family dynamics.

Kenny's room and my ham radio room share the third floor at the top of the steep stairs. The ham radio shack is to the left behind a swinging door, formerly a loft storage area. His room is to the right. He has no privacy.

"Katie, are you ready?" I say, rounding the second floor landing of the stairwell. "Mom asked me to check." Nothing. Her door is closed.

"Katie?" There's a muffled sob. "Are you all right?" I'm directly outside her door. "May I come in?"

She's lying on her bed, her face in her pillow.

"What's the matter, honey?" It's my best fatherly voice.

"Everything," she sobs.

"I'm sorry. Do you want to talk about it?"

"The usual shit. Kenny is horrible. School is awful. I hate it here."

We had moved to Doylestown, Pennsylvania, a year before so I could take a job as general manager of a small high-tech semiconductor company. The job seemed perfect for the fast career track, worth the move from our home in Arizona. The culture is different here, unlike our Southern hometown and the cosmopolitan Phoenix area, where the young engineers are mostly Midwesterners and Californians. My boss is a brilliant Jewish man who grew up in New York City. He's an MIT graduate, but he lacks understanding of semiconductor technology—so his management style involves endless questions in continuing reviews, in which data pile upon detail, statistics upon minutia. Just the two of us in those dreaded "one-on-ones." I don't have the maturity and self-confidence to develop a relationship with him other than the formal reporting structure at work.

My frustrations at work overflow onto my family. The stress of being in this kind of situation is like being in a foreign land. I don't fully understand the nuances.

"I hate it here," she says again, tears streaking her cheeks.

"It'll be all right, I promise." I sit down on her bed and, even though she's only 14, I smooth her hair as if she's only five. Her crying is muffled, softer than before. "Dry your tears. Here's a tissue. Supper's ready."

It's a hopeful plea. With that, I leave her door ajar and go into our bedroom, another charming room that is too small by half. Sitting on a tiny chair, I take off the work clothes and slip on jeans and tennis shoes. That's better.

Back to the kitchen, "Kenny hasn't come in yet," Callie says without looking up. "There were problems at school today. Mr. Rickman called me this morning."

"Who?"

"You know. Mr. Rickman, the assistant principal for discipline. I still can't believe I called him Mr. Bird at that last meeting we had. It was the most embarrassing thing!"

Mr. Rickman, "Big Bird" as the kids call him, is tall with long arms. He's all wingspan.

I could see the room—the Bird, Kenny, my wife, and myself. Kenny had thrown an orange from lunch at the wall in the boys' bathroom. It splattered and made a real mess. He was suspended for two days. When Callie said "Mr. Bird," the conversation stopped. Dead silence. I had to look down at my shoes.

"He does sort of look like Big Bird on Sesame Street, you know," I say, trying to help in some pitiful way.

"Please go find Kenny and get him ready." The look on her face is one of being completely up to "there," whatever that is. "Is Katie all right?"

"She's crying in her room. I tried to get her calmed down."

How did we get into this crummy situation?

The barn is 40 yards or so behind the farmhouse, which was built in 1758. The original part of the house was built from stones plowed up in the fields. The stones are small and uneven, which means that the original builder wasn't affluent since he used fieldstones turned up by his plow as materials. The old walls are almost two feet thick. Add-ons have appeared as ensuing families could afford them. The barn is in surprisingly good shape: 30 years old at most, no rot, good rugged lumber, and no roof leaks.

The rear kitchen door closes behind me. I raise my voice. "Kenny! Supper's ready. Come on in."

A weak voice comes from behind the barn. "All right." He walks slowly, holding some sort of stick. His hands are filthy.

"Come on, you're going to need to wash up."

"Don't want to do that," he mutters. His hair is streaked with sweat. "Won't do that," he says louder.

He trudges ahead of me.

"Straight to the bathroom now." I try to touch his shoulder with some sort of caring motion.

"Leave me alone," he says, pulling away.

Chapter 26

WE GOT BACK to Princeton every year, at least once. Somehow that remained in our DNA. Mom was Mee-Maw to the kids, lovable and wonderfully, creatively ditzy. Kenny adored her. The two of them played the ukulele and sang "She'll Be Coming 'Round the Mountain" and "My Old Kentucky Home."

The kids slept upstairs: Kenny in my old room, Katie in Susie's old room, and Joey, only seven years old, on a cot in what used to be the radio nook—now exclusively used by Mee-Maw for her sewing. They would get up early and Callie would take them over to her parents for breakfast.

The house never changed. Mom's formal china cabinet sat in the same corner of the living room. The two Gibson girl paintings and the Kentucky cardinal watercolor hung on the same nails, dominating the walls in the cluttered living room in which no one ever sat. The house smelled like Lucky Strikes.

Mom was out on the sunporch working on the family tree. She now was in her mid-60's. Dad was nearly 70. Both were retired. "Daddy got some additional information from your Uncle Win," she said softly.

Uncle Win, short for Winfield, was Dad's oldest brother. He'd earned a chemistry degree at Emory and Henry College and then worked at the Oak Ridge National Laboratories. No one in the family knew much about what he did.

Mr. Johnson, my geometry teacher, once had mentioned Oak Ridge Labs. He said it was a secret national laboratory working on atomic weapons. At the time, my entire impression of atomic bombs was based on the black-and-white photographs in *Life Magazine* of a mushroom cloud—all that destruction below, those surreal shapes exploding upward. My personal exposure to those dreadful possibilities was limited to the fourth grade, when we children crouched under our wooden desks and covered our heads. Our hands had to cover our eyes correctly or else we repeated the drill. Certainly we wouldn't want to be blinded by the flash.

Uncle Win married a girl from Tazewell, Virginia. She was his third cousin. Such linkups weren't unusual when people from "old families" married in our part of the country. Uncle Win had no children, and his sole hobby appeared to be driving around southwestern Virginia, western North Carolina, and eastern Tennessee looking up family connections in county courthouses. He compiled family history from Bibles and courthouse records of births, marriages, and deaths. Then he wrote his findings on a large window blind, unrolled on a tabletop for writing.

Mom's family history came from Mamma Clay's oral recollections, which were vague at best. Maybe that's because her own father rode with Quantrill's Raiders. After the Civil War, people didn't talk openly about that group. In addition, both Mom and Dad were connected to the DAR in several ways. That was considered important. It was clearly understood that we were proud of our American and Southern backgrounds, and not necessarily in that order. The family tree, in Mom's pointy handwriting, always hung on a wall near the Jackson and Clay family crests. After all those distant names, over all those generations, I was the sole name-carrying male from Dad's family, and it was clear that one of my obligations was to maintain the name.

Mom made it clear that there were more immediate problems. "I'm worried about Daddy," she said. "He's drinking heavily."

My memory flashed back—so many nights his drinking ended only when he passed out in the chair, or collapsed on the floor.

She continued. "Before he retired, he would get cleaned up and go into work the next morning. It's different now. He doesn't go to the Elks Club often, which is good. He doesn't drink there. He does it here. But once he starts, he can't stop."

"What about the next morning, Mom? What about then?"

She nodded slowly. "He wakes up and starts drinking again. He doesn't have to go to work, so he doesn't get cleaned up.

"Does he eat anything?"

"Sometimes," she said. "But not much. At first, he would do this for a day or two. Then he would stop—get himself together. But the binges have gotten longer and longer. Last week, I had to call an ambulance. He was in the hospital for three days . . . had the d.t.'s. I'm scared."

"I would be too."

She looked away, then directly at me and said, "He can't go on like this."

I remembered the legal documents and asked, "Is everything all right from a legal standpoint?"

"Legal?"

"You know. All the legal stuff you went through with Hoffman Daley. That attorney. Did everything get done?"

He's Dad when I'm an adult emotionally. He's Daddy when I'm not.

"Did Daddy sign the papers?"

She leaned forward and lowered her voice. "Yes. Everything is in my name."

At that point, Dad walked into the kitchen. Seeing us on the back porch, he came over to the door and cleared his throat.

"Harumpf. Good morning. I hope you had a pleasant night. How are the kids?"

"Hi, Dad. They're fine. Callie took them over to Mrs. Carver's for breakfast. How're you this morning?"

"I'm fine." He hadn't acknowledged Mom yet.

"Jim, would you like something to eat?" Mom asked.

"You-all go ahead," he said. "I'll get some coffee and read over the paper."

Mom picked up where we left off. "We're in good shape. We seem to have more now with our Social Security than we had from Gibson's and the county." She meant her job as a county public health nurse.

Sounds from the *Today Show* on Channel Six came from the TV room. Mom leaned back and seemed to relax. It was one of those rare times, an adult-to-adult conversation with my mother.

The grapevines were just starting to leaf out. Little blades of fine verdant grass were appearing in the lawn.

"Do you remember the times I went to the state public health convention in Charleston?" she asked.

"The what?"

"Public health conventions. Seminars on health care developments. New procedures. Those sorts of things. We had to have continuing education to maintain our certification." She paused and looked back toward the kitchen. "They would begin on a Thursday and end at noon on Saturday. Christine and I would go together."

"Christine?"

"My friend Christine Blakely. You knew her. We went together. I would drive one year, she the next."

I remembered Christine. She was another RN with the county public health department. She and Mom were about the same age. "Is she still working?"

"No. Christine retired a year after I did. She still lives here in town. We see each other at the grocery store from time to time," she said.

"Well, anyway, we went every year for several years. I enjoyed learning about the newest developments."

Mom took a slow sip from her coffee cup, then put it back on the saucer carefully, as if she were weighing something. "Doctors were also at those meetings, you know. They had to go to seminars to keep up just as we nurses did."

I began to pay more attention.

"Friday was the social evening, with a nice dinner, a speaker, and various awards—that sort of thing. There was music and dancing. Some of the doctors at the convention brought their wives. Others came alone. Most of the nurses didn't bring their husbands, of course."

Mom took another sip and glanced back toward the kitchen. The TV volume was loud. Wisps of Lucky Strikes smoke were visible. A fresh wave of the smell reached us.

"There was a prominent doctor from Clarksburg, and he always would ask me to dance. It was a little embarrassing because no one asked Christine to dance. But he would come over to our table and ask me to dance."

I didn't know what to say.

"Every year."

She didn't want me to say anything.

That evening, I told Callie what Mom had said. "When she was telling me the story, her face was almost a blank reflection . . . like she was faraway."

"She probably was," Callie said. "I've noticed the same thing. A certain distant, faint look. Almost like a Mona Lisa mask."

On those trips back to Princeton—home, as we always called it, I tried to reconnect with Buddy Lewis. It was akin to taking a sip from a fountain of youth. He worked for the state, something to do with tax licenses for businesses. I called him at home one of the first evenings.

"Jimmy, you've just gotta stop by the office. I drive around the county a lot. You know, gotta check out things first hand. The next two days I'm in the office to put all the stuff into our files. All the paperwork shit. Can you come see me there?"

My next afternoon was free. "How about three, tomorrow?"

"Perfect. Just ask for me."

The office was in one end of the Mercer County Courthouse. From the outside, the century-old structure looked the same as it did when I left. Seventeen years earlier, a whole new life. All the smaller doors had been locked, and signs instructed people to use the massive main doors at the ends of the rectangular building. Out on the street, the "Mercer County Sherriff" door looked exactly the same.

The building had an old Southern courthouse look and feel: floors of heavy wood, old and solid, worn smooth by countless shoes; heavy old planks, fitted by hand; ceilings 14 feet high, with huge industrial fluorescent lighting fixtures; heavy-paned windows. In the main corridor, beside the entrance to the office, neatly ordered signage stated "West Virginia Business Licensing." The door itself was heavy, well built, turn-of-the-century. I turned the smooth metal handle and walked in.

A reception area, similar to a line of tellers at a bank, lay in front of me, with three spots for the people to pose their questions, pleas, or whatever to the authorities. At three in the afternoon, only one other person was there.

"Yes sir?" The woman is older. "Can I help you?"

I don't know. Can you? I'm a hopeless grammarian, but I keep my tacky thoughts to myself.

"I'm here to see Buddy Lewis."

"May I have your name, please?"

That's better.

"Jimmy Jackson," I say, reverting to the way I was known in high school. A flicker of recognition registers.

"Just a minute," she says, with the familiar accent and cadence. She goes to a door at the rear of the large office area. Almost immediately, Buddy comes out, walking at a brisk pace.

"Why, it's Jimmy Jackson," he says, loud enough so that everyone in the office hears him. We do the little manly hug and pat. "Come on back to my office. We can talk there."

"Well, goll-ee, Jimmy," he says slowly, as he offers me a chair. A Gomer Pyle impression that isn't.

"Did I used to talk like that?" I ask.

"Why, hell yes. You were a hick, like I still am. You know, I'm really into girl groups now. Drove up to Cincinnati a month ago to see this one big show. Doo-Wop Girl Groups. Helluva a name, huh? They do these dance steps, all dressed up in flashy skintight gowns that practically glow in the dark! Lots of great T 'n' A. Stuff jiggling in all the right places. They had—I'm telling you, Jimmy—*all* the moves."

The torrent continues.

"God, I was in Heaven. I don't know where they find these women! You know, there had to be at least one of them from the original group, to be able to use the name, but the original ones looked pretty damned good, too . . . well, most of them. And the others! Let me tell you, they'd knock your socks off. Other things, too."

"Who was there?" I ask, when he pauses for a breath.

"Oh shit—I mean, sorry. Let me think. There were the Bobbettes, the Chordettes, the Ronnettes, Rosie from Rosie and the Originals . . . Do you remember that awful sax solo in the middle of 'Angel Baby'? Let's see . . . oh, yes, the Shirelles."

"The Shirelles? You mean 'Soldier Boy'?"

"Oh yeah!" Buddy says, again nearly shouting. "Remember this one? 'Baby it's you, dun dun dun dun dun dun dunn, di dun.'"

He's on a roll, in vicarious Heaven. "I drove straight back from Cincinnati after the show! Can you believe that? Didn't get home until three-thirty in the morning! Totally psyched. Bought thirty bucks worth of tapes. Listened to 'em all the way back. That's how I kept awake."

"So how's the band doing?" I ask. "You still playing?"

"Yeah. I probably should get out of that, but it's so much fun. Carl Hyatt has a cover band. We do O.K. . . . mostly just the old hits. Try to sound like the records. Carl's good, talks to the crowd, pretty good singer, good keyboard guy. I play drums, of course. Peppy Blake still plays bass. Another guy you probably don't know plays guitar, sings some too. We do a lot of high school reunions and weddings, plus gigs at country clubs. The high school kids are all into other stuff. They don't go for the oldies."

"And," I interrupt, "you even have time for a job."

"Yeah, plus as much golf as I can work in during the summer."

"Still driving Caddies?"

"Hell yes. I just love Caddies. Always have. This one has the damndest sound system. Just had to have it."

"How is Arcie?" Buddy hasn't mentioned him.

"He doesn't play with us any longer—we're too small a fish. But as far as I know, he's fine. Arcie asks about you every time I see him. He's working for the new Forest Products Research Lab out near the Turnpike. It's a new state facility—a Senator Byrd gift—they develop new products based on trees and forest products. Arcie still plays around the area, you know. Weekend stuff. He's with a group out of Bluefield called the Soul Brothers. How about that! I'm pushing fifty-plus and playing with Carl and 'Coverall,' and Arcie's a 'Soul Brother'! We do more white stuff and they do some serious James Brown and Wilson Pickett tunes. He's always working on a new project. Says this one's going to go."

He pushes over a metal chair in my direction. "I'm so busy here, I can't even goof off. We handle business licenses and tax stamps for the whole county. I'm out driving all over the place three days a week, then here in the office two days to write everything up, you know, document things. They're working us to death." With that, he opens one of the large flat pull-out trays to display neat blue line prints and property plats.

Suddenly he's businesslike. "There are all sorts of guidelines from the state. You know, Charleston," he says, glancing over his left shoulder, like Charleston is just over the next hill.

It's time to leave. We've had our session. I'm caught up.

"Tell your folks hello for me," he says. "I always liked your parents."

We retrace our steps through the labyrinth of paper, desks, and filing cabinets.

He and I go back quite a way. "Take care of yourself, Buddy."

"Don't worry. I'll never change," he says.

At the front of the office, things are busier. People now are in lines for the three ladies to handle their matters. One last glance back, a last wave, and I'm out into the great granite and high-ceilinged hallway.

Chapter 27

MY SECRETARY TELLS me Callie's on the line. Hopefully Kenny isn't involved in another disciplinary problem at school. Line two is blinking.

"Hi Honey. What's up?" My tone is automatic. The report on my desk dominates my attention.

"Your mother just called."

New bookings were bad last month. The graph is headed in the wrong direction.

"Are you there, Jim? It's your dad."

Now I concentrate. "What do you mean?"

"It's his drinking."

"What does Mom want me to do?" We've got customers coming in. I've got to visit Chrysler in Huntsville next week.

"She's afraid he might die. You need to call her. Listen to her. She needs you to listen. *You're the son.*" Her voice is reasoned, steady.

"When does Mom want me to call?"

"Now," she answers. "He needs to go to the hospital."

"To sober up—dry out?"

"Yes."

"Can't he just do that at home?" My comment is as much a question as a would-be command: Just do that at home, dammit. *What's the matter with him!*

"Jim, call your mother." That ends the conversation. It isn't an intimate discussion between two life partners. It's more like a professional counselor talking to a client. Callie is the professional.

The familiar numbers: 304 area code, 425 for the Princeton exchange, then four digits.

"Hello." It's Mom's characteristic cadence.

"Mom, it's me, Jim," I say. "Jimmy."

"Hi, Jim," she says, using my grown-up name, as she calls it.

"Callie just called me here at work. What's the matter?"

"I'm worried about Daddy. He's in bad shape."

"Drinking?"

"Yes. He hasn't eaten anything for several days."

"What!" I blurt the word out. "Nothing at all?"

"Hardly anything. I fix him things but he just sits in his TV chair, you know the one—says he's not hungry." She pauses. "He's been drinking for a week."

I can't believe what Mom is telling me. "Where does he get it?"

"The taxicab company. I'm afraid to pour it out. Daddy gets angry if I try to talk to him. He hasn't changed clothes, has on the same pair of pajamas and his housecoat. He hasn't shaved. Jimmy, he looks terrible."

We're back to Jimmy now. Mom is taking charge.

She continues. "I want you to call Aunt Molly and see if she can come over. I need her to go to the house and see Daddy—see him like he is. I think he's under some sort of delusion that no one knows. It's gotten much worse. He's close to alcohol poisoning."

"Why don't you call an ambulance? Have them take Daddy to the hospital right now? It sounds terrible!"

"That's what I have been doing." The words are in slow motion. "For several months." Several months? "I haven't wanted to bother you. I know you-all are busy with your own family. Daddy has been in the hospital two times since Christmas. Once he starts, he can't stop by himself. He had bad d.t.'s last time."

He has pretended for years no one knew. Especially his family. One delusion after another.

"Aunt Molly needs to see him whimpering and blubbering, all messed up," she continues. "It won't be pretty."

Suddenly I feel removed from my world—detached. Just then a small bird lands on a tree limb outside my office window. It's March, still cold in Pennsylvania. The bird fluffs out its feathers, seems to shiver, then flies off. The limb is barren again. The conversation with my aunt already is forming in my mind.

"I'll call Aunt Molly right now. Then I'll call you as soon as I have something. It'll be a real shock to Daddy—his sister seeing him like this. Don't straighten up the house. O.K.?"

"It's the right thing to do." She says the words clearly.

"I'll call you," I say and put the phone down. I don't tell her I love her. Air hugs. Stupid.

Aunt Molly's phone number is in a small book with all of the family phone numbers and mailing addresses. I punch in the 540 area code for southwestern Virginia.

After four long rings, someone picks up the phone.

"Aunt Molly?"

"Ye-es." Two syllables. I recognize her voice from that one word.

"This is Jimmy. Jimmy Jackson." I've always been Jimmy to my aunts and uncles.

"Oh, Jimmy. Why, yes. Jimmy, I just knew it was you right away." With Aunt Molly, once she starts, she doesn't stop for some time. It's as if she wants to make sure she gets the maximum human intelligence transferred before she stops. "It's so good to hear your voice. You must be at work since it's a weekday. I was just mentioning to your uncle Carl that we haven't heard from Sara or Jim in quite a while."

She takes a breath, but before I can say anything she keeps right on. "We're getting ready for another spring planting season here in Poplar Hill. I suppose you know I'm sixty-three and Carl is sixty-five, and I just don't know how much longer we'll be able to keep doing this. For one thing, we have such a large garden here behind the house. Of course, we get such nice vegetables. Last year, we had to throw away so many good tomatoes and squash! Well, actually, I took them into Pearisburg and gave one mess after another to the food bank. I wanted Sara and Jim to drive over and get some but they never came. Everyone is so busy these days. It's a shame that none of our boys wants to take over the farm, but that's the way it seems to be going now with the young people. It's just so much work and the financial return is so unpredictable. You know, it's understandable. After all, they *have* gone to college, and—"

"Aunt Molly."

"Oh, yes, Jimmy. I'm sorry. It seems these days that I get to talking and just keep right on."

"That's O.K. I'm glad you and Uncle Carl are doing well." I pause to collect my thoughts about how to get into the request. Mistake!

"Well, thank you," she says. "We're just fine. How are you and your family? Where are you? I can't seem to keep things like this straight any longer."

"We're fine," I say, jumping in before she can begin another thought. "Aunt Molly, I called to ask you for a favor."

"I'll try to help if I can."

"It's Dad. Mom just called me. I'm still at work. I have some bad news."

"Is James all right?" His sisters call him James within the family.

"No, he isn't." I say. Plow on before she can take over again. "Dad has been struggling with drinking, especially since he retired from Gibson's. He always has had trouble with drinking, but he'd always get up the next morning, clean up, and go to work."

"Well . . ." Her words are spaced, deliberate. ". . . James always was a drinker, even as a teenager."

"He's in bad condition. Mom is afraid he won't last another month. Mom and I—both of us—need you to go over to Princeton. Walk in their front door. See him the way he is. It's important he doesn't know you're coming, or he'll try to clean up. Hide how sick he is."

"I'm aware that he had a . . . problem. But it seemed that he was, well, stable. What would I be able to do once we get there? Neither Carl nor I are trained in medical things."

"The main thing is for you just to be there. See him. If he doesn't get help, he won't be alive in another month. It's a terrible way to live, and it's certainly not fair to Mom."

"Oh, no. That's right." There's certainty in her voice. "I'll call Danny and get cleaned up. Danny and I will drive over to Princeton as soon as we can. Carl's out in the pasture, so I won't bother him. I reckon we can get over to Sara's by three this afternoon." Danny, her son, works as a probation officer for Giles County and is trained in substance abuse.

"Aunt Molly, be prepared for an ugly sight when you get there." Based on Mom's details, I can picture him: unshaven, blubbery, without a bath for days, in filthy pajamas, weak from too little food and too much bourbon, encased in his blue haze. The whole house reeking. "Dad's probably going to break down and start crying when he sees you. He'll be ashamed. It'll be a mess."

"That's all right." Her voice is soft and caring. "I've seen a thing or two in my time, even being a country person. And whatever I've missed, Danny has seen it by now."

"Aunt Molly, I can't thank you enough." It's all I can offer. "I'll call Mother now and let her know to expect you later this afternoon."

"That's all right, Jimmy. That's what *family* is all about."

Family.

I call Mom back. "Be sure to call me at home tonight. Hopefully, Dad will be in the hospital, be all right. I'm so sorry I'm way up here and not closer."

"Should I plan on calling an ambulance?" she asks. "With Danny's help, maybe we can drive Daddy to the hospital."

I hadn't thought of that. "Ask Danny. See what he thinks. If Dad can sit in your car, then you should be able to take him to the emergency room. If you think he might faint or vomit, then don't take the risk. If you aren't sure what to do, call an ambulance. They can handle anything."

"All right," she says. "I will. Bye now."

At that exact moment, a tiny bird, perhaps the same little bird that flew away earlier, flits back into view. It alights on a branch, fluffs up its feathers, and starts to chirp away in a little-bird song.

I call Callie. "I talked with Aunt Molly. She and Danny are going to drive over to Mom's this afternoon."

"What about later?" she asks.

"Later? What do you mean?"

"Your dad is a serious alcoholic! He can't continue like this. Do you know how hard it is for the human body to detox from high levels of chronic alcoholic content?"

"You're right. I feel like I'm so far away. More than just distance."

Her voice is firmer. "Jim, it's not only your parents."

"I know. I know. I'm going to come home. Is that O.K.? I want to come home." It's all I can say.

"That's good. I'll be here." Her voice is warmer.

She's waiting just inside the old kitchen door. For the first time in a long time, we actually hug, a good, simple, warm, emotional, connection of two people who need the comfort of each other.

I go over the phone conversations with Mom and Aunt Molly. Callie already has noticed so many signs of Dad's problem. I've learned not to notice. It's easier, safer.

"Here's some lunch. Sit down and relax. It'll do you good." She serves us soup and salad. We both have a glass of white wine. It's nice being alone and actually paying attention to each other.

Afterward, I clean off the table while she stacks the dishes. She's wearing a blouse and skirt that flatter her well-proportioned figure. We make love reasonably often, probably more overt sexual gratification on my part. My sexual desire for her remains strong, one positive in a marriage pushed to the breaking point by focus on career, plus my growing estrangement with Kenny and Katie. I walk over to her and wrap my arms around her. She moves backward, into me, and I move my arms from an embrace and cuddle her breasts. She feels firm, vigorous.

She turns toward me. We kiss and move from quiet intimacy to a rhythm of sexual foreplay. I run my hands over her. As she nestles her head on my chest, I pin her against a counter.

"I need to make love to you," I say.

We stumble from the kitchen, through the living room and up the stairs.

"Let me see you, as you undress."

"That makes me nervous," she says. "You've seen me before."

"No. Take off your clothes. I want to see you."

She removes her blouse, carefully placing it in her small closet. Her dancing and extremely active exercise program keeps her as trim and fit as any athlete. Her stomach is absolutely flat.

"You're so beautiful."

She comes to me, wearing only her satin underwear. Her breasts press against my chest while I stroke her back. It's wonderful, just as it's always been. But as much as I love Callie, and need her, we're coupled physically but not emotionally. I love her according to the rules of my family. She slides off the bed and takes her clothes to the bathroom, looking straight ahead.

My work papers are spread out over half the kitchen table that evening when Mom calls again.

"Daddy is in the hospital. He seems to be stable. I'll go back first thing in the morning."

"Thanks, Mom. It's good to hear that. Did Aunt Molly make it?"

"Yes, she did." Her deliberate tone of voice is steady. "When she and Danny got here, Daddy was asleep in his chair, in front of the television."

"How did he look?"

"He was in his dirty pajamas. Hair uncombed. Needed a bath, had a five-day stubble—looked awful. I heard a car pull up and thought it might be them. As I said, Daddy was asleep. He had the television on so loud. I shook him by his shoulders and got him awake . . . sort of. He was groggy. Then he saw Aunt Molly. He tried to act normal and apologized for the way he looked. When he tried to stand up, he fell. He couldn't get up."

"Was he hurt?"

"No. He was just sprawled there, right at her feet. And then he started crying. It took all three of us to get him back into his chair. You know how he is. He just whimpered and blubbered. He kept blowing his nose but the mucous kept running down his face." She paused. "Aunt Molly was really sweet. She put her arm on Daddy's shoulder as he sat there crying. She kept saying everything would be all right, and he had to make some changes, real changes . . . but that short-term, he had to get to the hospital and get some help, as she phrased it. Jimmy, I don't think Aunt Molly and I could have moved him by ourselves. It was Danny, mainly, who lifted him so we could get his face cleaned off. Somehow, we got him into the car and drove him to the hospital. Fortunately, he didn't throw up on the way over there."

"That had to be a terrible experience. Mom, I'm so sorry."

"Daddy was so ashamed . . . all this in front of his sister. We got to the emergency entrance and I went in—they brought out a wheelchair to get him. The ER doctor gave him a shot and put him on some sort of intravenous drip. I did the paperwork while they got him into a room. He went right to sleep."

"Did Aunt Molly stay long?"

"About an hour. The house looked terrible—I haven't cleaned it in weeks. The whole situation is a mess. Jimmy, I'm really tired. And on top of all that . . . when we got back to the house, for some reason I lost my balance between the car and the porch and fell down right there in the front yard. It was embarrassing."

"Don't worry about that, Mom. You have a lot going on."

"I just don't know what I would have done without Aunt Molly and Danny."

"You get some rest now. I should come down there and help you. Would you like us to come?"

She answers immediately. "I think he will be all right now. It's all right now. I need to call Susie and let her know what has happened."

It took a week for Dad to become stabilized and return home. But this time was different. He agreed to go to Fellowship Hall, an alcoholic rehabilitation center in Greensboro, North Carolina. Mom drove him there, and he was admitted on an in-patient basis for six weeks. I was only a remote spectator, getting news from Mom—or from Callie, who talked with Mom.

Things seemed to be on the right track. I didn't go back to see either Dad or Mom during this time. For some reason, this seemed acceptable. Mom kept insisting that she didn't need me to come. So I didn't.

CHAPTER 28

BY THE SPRING of 1984, the situation with our kids was even more trying. It was no doubt mostly my fault. My inability to engage was a serious flaw.

When Katie was a freshman at a women's college in Spartanburg, S.C., the "Daddy-Daughter Dance Weekend" illustrated the point. Someone had determined that staging the affair in the gymnasium for the girls and their fathers, many of whom had never danced a single time in their lives with their daughters, would anchor a positive bonding experience. Katie and I managed a few awkward fast dances and formal waltzes. The event transitioned into stilted introductions, clusters of coeds chatting amongst themselves, and groups of "daddies" making boring conversation about their golf games, or wagering on the outcome of the upcoming South Carolina-Georgia football game. The best I could do was a one-way conversation with a wealthy apple grower who lived near Winchester, Virginia. He had flown to Spartanburg in his private jet, and could talk only about his orchards and other possessions.

Katie had insisted on going there to study opera. Our sweet, young girl from Pennsylvania, the would-be Wagnerian mezzo-soprano, was miserable in a sea of sticky-sweet Southern girls. "Daddy, all these girls want is to marry a rich Wofford or Furman boy and be the wife of a lawyer or doctor." She cried the entire weekend.

Following that first year in South Carolina, she enrolled at the Philadelphia School for the Performing Arts, then at the nursing program at Thomas Jefferson University, both in center-city Philadelphia. We helped her select a nice apartment in the theater district. After neither of these programs clicked with her, we insisted that she default to Bucks County Community College for a year to settle down, and in addition give our budget a rest from premium college expenses. She got her own apartment, and was working and living on her own while she figured out what she wanted to do. During this period, she met a nice young man and seemed serious about him.

Kenny was drifting fast into troubled waters. He defiantly resisted authority, both at home and in school. We spent more and more time in sessions with the school's disciplinary authorities. Eventually, he was shuttled to an alternative school where he sat sullenly and completely disinterested until he dropped out. For four months, we didn't know where he was, or even if he was alive, until the phone rang early one day.

"Collect call from Savannah, Georgia. Will you accept?"

"Dad, it's me, Kenny." He was sniffling, trying to conceal tears. "I've been following the Grateful Dead tour. Been working a little—selling stuff at the shows. People have been nice . . . took me in." He started crying. "I want to come home. It's cold. I spent last night with my guitar in the rain, under a billboard." It breaks my heart to think about how hard it was for him (and for us).

Not even 17, now he was back in the area living in a hovel of a low-rent dump outside Doylestown, working in a dangerous machine shop. All this seemed impossible. It was what he said he wanted to do. We had little influence with him. It rips my heart out to write this, but it was the way it was. At least he was alive and we knew where he was . . . sort of.

Joey, somehow in all this madness, seemed to follow an easier path. I really don't know how. For the life of me I don't understand all the dynamics that took place within our family. I recall once when he was eight or nine . . . I came home to a caldron of difficulties and angst on the part of his older brother and sister to find him alone in the living room quietly leafing through the pages of the *Wall Street Journal.* Nothing ever seemed to faze him.

Looking back, we were trapped in a web of dysfunctionality. I survived it, and probably caused more of it, for the lack of a better description, by tuning it out. My escape was work. When I got home, I'd go up to the third floor, past Kenny's room with his things everywhere and art, poems, and writing all over his walls, enter my world of ham radio, put on those earphones, and fly away. By not being there and dealing with things, I could survive. By the same method of escape, I was a major part of the problem.

In the midst of all this, the phone rang one spring day, a soft and warm Saturday morning, at the old farmhouse on Landisville Road. Callie answered—she always did. I've always resisted the phone at home. It must stem from the connection to work issues and demands, which so often were delivered over the telephone.

"George Tucker . . . it's so nice to hear your voice. It's been quite a while," Callie says into the phone. It's our little system to let each other know who's on the line. "Yes, we're still here in Pennsylvania. I guess you can tell that from the area code." She's listening again, then responds. "I'm glad to hear that. Oh yes, congratulations on everything!" Again the room is still. "I will," she says. "I know you want to speak with Jim. He's right here with the newspaper and a cup of coffee."

My mind is alert. "Good morning."

"Jim, this is George Tucker. How're you doing?" His voice is familiar from my former life at Motorola: no regional accent, confident, business-like. George grew up in Phoenix, worked hard, put himself through Arizona State. He has done well—a good guy all around. He'd been my direct boss for a while and we always got along well.

"Hi George." My voice seems foreign to me. I'm in the third-person now, listening to a person who sounds like me talking on the phone. "We're fine. How about there, in Phoenix?" Return serve.

"Glad to hear that, Jim. Things are super. In fact, maybe a little too super. Actually, the reason I'm calling is that our business units are really growing, and the guys in Austin asked me to call you—see if we could get you to come back to Motorola and give us a hand."

The words ricochet around my head. George had been promoted to president, the head man at Motorola Semiconductors! Callie is looking over, waiting to catch up on the conversation. My expression must be somewhere close to glazed-over.

"Wow, George." My emotion is real, verging on immature. "It's great that business is so strong." I recalibrate myself: things come into focus, my head is clearing. "You probably remember that Callie and I were big fans of Austin. I know from my business here that you guys are booming. My group competes with the Austin guys at Chrysler. So I run into my old Motorola buddies all the time!"

He laughs. "Yes, I know, I know."

My group currently supplies the electronic architecture in Chrysler's engine electronics module, but Motorola is pushing hard to bump us out with their microprocessor.

"Jim, the business is growing so fast we can hardly keep up. How about coming down and talking with Glen Williams? You know him. He's now general manager of the Austin operations. It's the fastest growing part of our semiconductor business."

The word "our" resonates. Something inside me wants to be part of that again.

"George, you caught me a little off-guard." Callie is looking at me intently. From my end of the conversation, it's not clear to her what is being said.

"I'd like to tell Glen you'll get back to him," he says. "Let me give you his number. Mine, too—if you have any questions."

"It's really good to talk with you. It's been a while . . . You know, I've always felt good about Motorola." Send a positive signal.

She watches me write down numbers on the sports page.

"That was a surprise. What did George want?" She knows he isn't calling on a Saturday morning to ask about the weather in Pennsylvania.

"He wants me to call Glen Williams and talk with him and the guys in Austin about coming back!" It's as if I'm outside my body watching myself say these words.

"Really! That would be fantastic!" She never liked Pennsylvania. Too many bad memories. My work situation is bad and getting worse. Family tensions are suffocating all of us. "Why didn't you tell him yes, right then and there, on the phone?"

The courtship was quick, the decision never in doubt. In many ways it was as if we never left. I felt like a lost brother returning home. Motorola's top financial guy in Austin was a close friend from our time together in Phoenix. He drove me back to my hotel after the interview and we stopped for a beer. "We're growing so fast we don't know what the fuck we're doing!" We laughed like the old days. "You gotta come back."

I did.

By early July we'd moved to the hill country west of Austin. Work came first, but that was the way it had always been. Things were booming. The industry was on a big up-cycle, one good opportunity after another.

Back in Pennsylvania, Katie had gotten on track after zig-zagging earlier. She graduated summa cum laude in English from Temple and started work in a small company that published specialty magazines in art and the high-end jewelry business.

She now was engaged to her beau, the young man from Philadelphia named John. "Mom," she confided in Callie, "Back when I worked in that restaurant—the Italian place with a tough shift manager—I had a problem with one boss. John told the guy he'd beat the shit out of him if he ever treated me badly." John offered her what I wasn't able to, attention and unconditional approval.

Kenny, amazingly, survived the drug culture and dangerous small machine shops of suburban Bucks County. I wasn't able to communicate with him, and it seemed I was his father in name only in terms of our lack of any real relationship. Callie spoke on the phone with him often, and provided the family glue. Eventually she helped him move to Austin. He was closer, at least geographically. But he struggled with jobs he hated. He pursued music, and at first, busked on Sixth Street in Austin. With a natural talent for music he wrote his own songs, played lead guitar and sang in a progression of rock bands as he became better known.

Joey, the youngest, moved with us to Texas before his freshman year in high school. He glided through high school, doing well in academics, as well as enjoying an active social life. He played on a very good basketball team, captained the state-championship debate team and went off to Palo Alto for college.

Over the next 10 years, Mom's health declined precipitously. At the start, when she began to have balance problems and her facial expressions became static, she told me "Uncle Carter says I have Parkinson's syndrome, but I'll be all right." Not so. Inexorably, she progressed to the full-blown disease—finally unable to care for herself. Eventually, in a gut-wrenching family decision, she was moved from the home on North Walker Street to the Princeton Health Care Center. How would Dad be doing living by himself at home? It must be hard after 50 years of marriage to see your wife losing her health. At age 82, he now had to drive across town to visit her in a nursing care facility.

It would be our first trip to see Mom at her new home. We were just east of Knoxville when we called Wendie and his wife from the car.

Connie answered. "Wendie's taking a nap, but you just *have* to stop and say hello. We're only a few minutes off of the Interstate near Bristol." Her directions led us by Kings College and the bucolic countryside to a modern group of condo units overlooking a small lake.

The complex had a nice look of understated affluence, a small gem of modern architecture on a country lane in the rolling hills of eastern Tennessee. After all, Wendie had risen to managing editor of the *Bristol Herald Tribune*. In addition, he'd operated a successful printing business for years. That wasn't surprising. He had talent, a certain élan. He was quiet and smooth, a step ahead of most of the high school group.

We parked, then stiffly got out and stretched our legs. Callie put into words what we both were thinking. "What sort of shape will Wendie be in?"

Our steps clicked on the concrete walkway and echoed off the brick walls as we approached. The resonant two-note doorbell sounded only once before Connie opened the door. Perfectly dressed, she contrasted with the two of us, rumpled and bedraggled.

After the initial hugs, we followed her inside to the living room. It was perfect, if immaculate is your thing: formal furniture, white carpet, lovely paintings on pale walls, and a dominating white grand piano. A large picture window on the far wall framed a serene lake with a canopy of graceful willows on the banks.

"Wendie and I always like to come home after work to a quiet and pretty setting." Suddenly I recognized the familiar scent of his Winstons as she spoke. "I'm a music teacher at King College. There are times I need peace and quiet." Classically coiffed and outfitted, she smoothed her skirt over the sheen of hosiery and sat with her legs pressed together. I couldn't help but notice the striking high heels.

Wendie was taller than I remembered. Heavier too, stiff as he approached.

"Well, well, well. If it isn't my old neighborhood pal, James Clay Jackson," he said, extending his right hand. A cigarette dangled from his left. He hugged Callie. "Please make yourselves comfortable. It's nice to see you—well, at least it's nice to see you, Callie. Jimmy, I hate to admit it, but it's good to see you as well. How long has it been?"

"Not sure," I said. "You been to any of the class reunions?"

"Nary. Not a one."

"Amazing. On the run from the law?"

"One might think that," he quipped. "Really, I've lost touch with most everyone."

"You did manage to show up at our wedding in sixty-two as I recall."

"An old memory through the haze. Tried to warn you. Did my best." There it was, that same half-smile. "But you married a good girl. Seems to have turned out well."

"My best man, as I recall."

"True," he said. "No booze there in the Church—a shame. Yet I suppose a small hindrance to ensure your marital vows went off properly. Brought my own meager supply. Added it to the Coke—hid in the bathroom to perform the dirty deed. Ah, yes . . . speaking of that elixir, that very essence of life, I have an adequate supply here."

He turned and struck a theatrical pose. "Fair ladies, what may I offer you? Coffee, tea, or . . . oh that's such a tired line. A fine adult beverage?"

It was hard not to find Wendie charming, even as the smoke enveloped him. During the next hour Callie had a small glass of white wine and some crackers. I had a beer. And he made quick work of two large tumblers of one of his fine adult beverages, chain-smoking the entire time.

We reminisced about the old days. Wendie hadn't kept up with most of the old group, so I updated him about what I knew. Arcie's name came up, of course, but since Wendie didn't have the unique relationship that Arcie and I shared, I limited it to his job at the Forest Products Lab plus his music in the area.

The serious conversation centered on Wendie's terrible automobile accident. Someone ran a traffic light. He was in a coma for two months.

"You know, the consensus of the medical community was that the condition would be permanent," Connie said. "Wendie defied that. He clinically died twice—they restarted his heart each time."

"Yeah, I guess you can say that," Wendie joked.

I sat there, not knowing what to say.

They recounted how he endured a slow and painful rehabilitation program. Somehow he'd come through all of that. Come out of it to this.

He was unable to work for so long that the Bristol newspaper moved on with a replacement. Since then he'd focused on his printing business—reported that business was good.

We said goodbye. There was that same familiarity: a certain way of expressing himself, the different manner of dressing, the mischievous smile, the way he combed his thin straight brown hair, our little code words.

They stood at the condo entrance as I glanced back. "Do your lungs burn as much as mine?" I asked Callie.

"My eyes, too. I couldn't have stayed another minute," she admitted. "I can't wait to get these clothes off and into a washing machine."

"Between the chain smoking and the non-stop drinking," I said, "It's a crap shoot which will get him first."

With the car windows open and the air conditioner on maximum, we passed the "Welcome to Virginia" sign with the red cardinals perched on a dogwood branch.

Interstate 81 tracks the Shenandoah Valley northeast from Bristol, past the old Confederate salt works at Saltville, and intersects at Wytheville with Interstate 77, which comes up from Charlotte and heads north toward the West Virginia border in one of the most spectacular stretches of Interstate highway east of the Rockies. Parallel ridges run as far as the eye can see from the three and four-thousand foot summits.

The vista and scope are breathtaking. "I feel like I can see all the way across the southwestern slice of Virginia into North Carolina," Callie says as the road crests over Brush Mountain. From there the highway continues to Big Walker Mountain, with a tunnel right through the massive ridge itself, then on to East River Mountain and the even longer horizontal shaft there. Big Walker and East River mountains are so steep, with no passes or gaps, that the road builders had no alternative but to bore right through them.

Between these last two summits is my old Boy Scout camp swimming-pool nemesis, Wolf Creek, which had cut a major water gap through one of the intervening ridge lines between Big Walker and East River Mountains. The water gap is just wide enough for the creek and the Interstate highway to snake through.

Following the water gap, the road once again gains altitude. It's as if we're on a gigantic launching ramp. The Interstate tilts upward toward the top of East River Mountain, looming darkly ahead in the late afternoon clouds. We've gained 1,000 feet of elevation when the stark concrete outline of the tunnel entrance appears, a half mile ahead.

Inside, our headlights snap on. Two lanes of cars and big trucks drive side by side for a mile in the narrow roadway, a half dome overhead, sooty from diesel exhausts. Water trickles sporadically from the tiled sides as fluorescent lighting creates a cool, barren appearance. A tiny spot forms in the distance and grows as we near the northern end of the tunnel. The border runs along the top of the ridgeline far above. This is one of only two Interstate highway tunnels between states. The white dot increases in size until we flash out of the tunnel into blinding light and pass the welcome sign, "West Virginia, Almost Heaven."

The Carver family's modest home is overflowing with relatives and the warm ritual of hugs—real hugs. Her family has few boundaries regarding coming over. On occasions the small living room will be full of people, some actually still dropping in, when the eleven o'clock news comes on the Bluefield television station. I retreat into our small bedroom to escape.

I'd called Dad to let him know we arrived safely and would see him the following morning. His house is the opposite. No one ever comes when we visit.

Naturally, Callie's mother insists on sending breakfast to him. We pull into the driveway—the two little parallel concrete strips now are cracked. They look old, seem smaller than I recall. Dad is inside, sitting in his favorite chair, the same one. The *Daily Telegraph* rests on his lap. The television, the same old one, is loud, as usual, and a curl of smoke—it looks like the same one—rises from several cigarettes in various forms of decay in a large glass ashtray. The chair has extensive burn marks. That the house never caught on fire baffles me.

He clears his throat, the common harrumph he always utters before answering the phone or greeting someone.

"Hello, Jim . . . Callie." He'd switched over to Jim sometime in my 20's. "Good to see you-all." His voice hasn't lost its resonance. The accent is perfect for educated and blue-collar alike. People would trust this man, and would buy a car from him.

"Hi, Daddy." The word comes unconsciously. We shake hands as he remains seated.

Callie walks over to his chair, leans over, and gives him a sort of combination hug and pat on the shoulder. "How are you, Jim?"

"I'm fine," he says, his voice competing with the TV. "And how're you-all?"

"We're fine," she says.

"And the children?"

"They're fine. They send their love." The standard reply.

"How is Mother doing?" I ask. "Does she like it at the new facility?"

"Well . . . I think so. She has a semi-private room. Right now there's no one else there. She says the food is pretty good. I go out there every day and see her."

"That's good. We're looking forward to seeing Mom and her room . . . the whole facility. What's a good time to go?"

"I think the visiting hours are pretty flexible. Something like nine in the morning to eight or so at night. You can go there pretty much at your convenience. I usually go out after breakfast. Mother usually has taken her breakfast by the time I get there." Dad's family "took" breakfast.

The nice-to-see-you-again greeting is short. We bring in Angie Carver's breakfast, more like a feast for a multitude. Dad has another cup of coffee and a muffin. It barely makes a dent.

I stand up, stretch, and say, "I think we'll run on out and see Mother."

"That's fine," Dad says. "I'll be right along."

The entrance is in the center, with one wing and hallway to the left, and an opposite and symmetrical structure to the right. The grass is mowed and neatly trimmed. The heavy glass door leads to an unoccupied desk, with a "Visitors Sign In Here" sign.

The corridor to the left is the Alzheimer wing, a stark reminder of which is a large red button on the wall alongside the sign to "Ring for Assistance." Two people stand stiffly in the background, there but not there. The right corridor leads to the medical wing. There are no "senior retirement living" facilities here. All the residents require medical assistance. We walk down the spotless corridor into a large airy atrium and sitting room. Residents sit on chairs and sofas. Some are in wheelchairs. It's a cheerful area with green plants and a pleasant open feel. Magazines and newspapers are everywhere.

"There she is," Callie says. "Over there." I'm not prepared. She's alone in a chair, a walker nearby. Her handsome face is tilted to one side.

"Sara! It's us, Jim and Callie," she says, rushing over. Mom grimaces as she strains to look our way.

Her voice is weak. "Oh, Jimmy, Callie. How nice to see you. I've been looking forward to your visit."

I stand there, not quite knowing what to do. "Hi, Mom. How are you?" I give her my best Jackson family stiff hug and peck-style kiss on her cheek.

"I'm fine, I guess." She seems subdued, unable to smile through the Parkinson's mask. But her eyes tell the story. "As you can see, I'm having a little trouble getting around. But I still can go to the dining room for meals, and do enjoy getting out of my room and coming here to our atrium. Isn't it nice? I have a walker now."

We were in town six months ago. They were still living at home, but it was obvious Mom was finding it harder to get around. Dad couldn't take care of her, and if she fell, it wasn't clear he could get her up by himself.

Callie rubs her neck and shoulders with cream. Mom's mental condition is good but the deterioration in her muscle control is frightening. She says Dad comes out every day. He sits with her in the atrium and often eats the midday meal with her. She still is able to feed herself, but her fingers and hands are stiff and starting to balk at responding to her mental instructions. Her back is stooped, the disease pronounced. She can walk by herself for short distances. But she feels more comfortable with her walker.

"It takes me a while to walk out to the sunroom and to my meals, but I'm determined to do that."

Callie is so much better than I am at emotional and physical closeness. She wipes Mom's nose and mouth, loving every minute of the connection between them. We go through the run-down on the children.

Mom is the sole surviving member of her immediate family. Now she's failing.

A voice interrupts us. "Mizz Jackson, it's time for lunch." The aide, a cheerful young black woman, stands nearby. "Would you like something to eat? Why, of course you do!"

Mom twists to look at her, unable to raise her face.

"Is that you, Angeline?"

"Why, it is. Are these good-looking folks your family?"

"Yes," Mom answers. The word is delivered proudly. "Yes, they are." Stated elegantly. "My son, Jimmy, and his wife live in Texas."

"Mizz Jackson is doing fine, just fine," she says, with a bubbly, positive voice. "She's one of my favorite residents."

We're standing, so Mom isn't able to tilt her head and see us as she speaks. Projecting her voice in an effort to be heard, she says, "Angeline is a sweet person. She helps me with my food. I have some trouble swallowing it anymore."

"Why, you just don't give yourself enough credit," Angeline says, now stooping, so she and Mom are on the same level. "Let's show your son and his wife what a good eater you are."

I help Mom to her walker, and she shuffles slowly out of the atrium and down a short hallway to the dining room. At a table, Angeline helps her into a chair, then says, "Now you wait here, and I'll be right back with your meal. You-all go ahead and sit with her, and we'll get your meals in a jiff."

"You know what I like, don't you?" Mom asks slowly. Her voice is so soft it's hard to hear.

"Of course I do. You just wait here and talk with your family."

Dad appears a moment later.

"Jim, don't you look dapper," Callie says. And he does, in his tweed sports coat with leather elbow patches, shirt and tie, and brown slacks. Only a few dark burn spots give away the cigarette damage.

He actually laughs. "Thank you." Then turning to Mom, he asks, "How do you feel today, Sara?"

"Oh, about the same," Mom replies. "About the same." Then she brightens. "I'm so pleased to have Jimmy and Callie here."

Angeline returns with Mom's special food, plus three additional trays on a cart.

"I saw you come in, Mr. Jackson," she chirps. "You and Mizz Jackson certainly have a fine son and daughter-in-law." She pauses while laying out the trays. "You *are* going to have lunch, aren't you?"

"Thank you, Angeline," Dad says. "That's mighty nice of you."

The three of us sit down, and Angeline slides a chair up next to Mom. "I'll just help Mizz Jackson."

Callie won't think of that, of course. "Is it all right if I help . . . help with her lunch? Are there any special instructions?"

"Not really. She's got special foods, you know, things she can eat without a whole lot of chewing—things that'll go right on down and digest easy. Just go slow and make sure she doesn't try to eat too much, too fast. I'll be here if you need help. Just ask anyone."

Mom struggles. It's hard for her to hold her utensils, and she has trouble with her glass. Dad becomes frustrated when she drops food or fumbles with her fork. Her fingers no longer have much strength or flexibility. Every bite of food, in form ranging from a small bit of bread, a neatly-cut green bean section, or a minute nibble of chicken breast, is the focus of a concerted effort. Mom's battle of mind-over-muscle leaves her exhausted. Her head is drawn down toward her right knee all the time now. I can't imagine what it must be like—inside your own body but unable to control your arms or legs or fingers. She's 77. Not *that* old. It's clear her health is slipping away, controlled by the insidious effects of this horrible disease.

Suddenly, a flash of her old self emerges through the neurological facial veil that masks her emotions. She wrenches her face upward a bit and says, "I want to show you my room." We have to help her up. It's no longer something she can manage by herself. She steadies herself and then pushes her walker slowly down a hall leading away from the dining room. After what seems like forever, we come to room 307 with a small sign that reads "Mrs. Sara Clay Jackson, Princeton, W.Va." The other nametag is blank.

"Here we are." Her voice is soft. "My room . . . I hope I'll get better so I can go back to live with Daddy."

The heavy hospital-style door opens smoothly. Inside are two beds, an austere chair beside Mom's bed, as well as an exact match on the other side. Mom has the side away from the window, where it's easier to get in and out. She seems to like it. The windows frame East River Mountain, tall and hazy to the west.

She sits heavily. We help her move her legs into a comfortable position and Callie massages them, which pleases her. Finally we help her into bed, so light, a shell of her former self, as we say our goodbyes and promise to come out around supper to see her again. Her eyes close. She falls asleep almost immediately.

"Dad, are you going to stay?"

"No, I'll go back home. You-all want to stop by the house for a bit?"

We owe it to him. We were there for such a short time that morning. "We'll follow you," I say.

One reason to follow him back to the house is to see how he's driving. Actually he does just fine. We don't have to deal with the tricky issue of wresting the car keys away, depriving an aging man of his independence—at least yet.

The three of us sit in the kitchen and talk. It had been a major decision to move mother from home, but the care she's receiving seems excellent. Everything appears to be going well with Dad . . . until I peek into the downstairs guest bedroom. It's full of boxes—20 of them, each from Universal Nutrition Corporation of America. Every one labeled identically: "Nutritional Supplements." Stacks of them! In the basement, there are even more, along with cartons of "Caribbean Treasures" and "Genuine Las Vegas Prizes."

He's still in the kitchen. "Dad, what are these boxes in the bedroom and the basement?"

"Oh, those. They're vitamins, things for better health." His smile is forced, now morphing into a smirk. "You know, a gentleman of my age and stature needs to take care of himself."

"Are you actually taking them? I mean, are you using any?"

"Not yet. Haven't started."

"There are enough of those things to last you for a hundred years. What are those other boxes in the basement?"

"Things I won," he says, suddenly defiant. "Prizes. Consolation prizes from when I bought opportunities to win a first-class cruise in the Caribbean."

"A cruise?"

He straightens up, looks straight ahead. The smirk is gone.

"A cruise."

"And what are these?" I hand him an opened box, one of the shipments from the Las Vegas Prize Company: plastic plates and cups; domes that snow on a tiny skater when turned upside down. Kitschy.

"Are you ordering these?"

"Those're prizes."

"Prizes?"

"A sweepstakes—an opportunity to win a hundred-thousand dollars. I bought some chances. The odds were good."

"A hundred-thousand dollars! You must have bought a lot of those chances."

"Some." He looks right at me. His voice is rock-steady.

"Are you buying these at the Elks Club?"

"No, no. Nothing like that."

"Then how are you buying them?"

"A representative calls me—vice president of sales—makes me aware of major opportunities."

Callie's been watching up to this point. "Jim, do you feel these are good decisions?" Her tone is courteous. Somehow she can remain calm.

I'm having a hard time containing myself. "The guest bedroom and the basement are crammed full of boxes like this. Full of junk!" My voice rises—so much for a measured approach.

He reacts angrily. "It's not what you say. It's what I said—nutritional supplements, craft items, consolation prizes."

I turn to her. "Come. Take a look."

"All this stuff!" she says. "There must be 30 cartons. They all say supplements."

"Wait until you see prize central down in the basement," I say.

Cardboard boxes are piled five feet high down in the dampness. Callie opens a box with the cheap plastic plates and cups. We stand there in the musty air, surrounded by the stacks.

"How much do you think he's spending on this stuff?" I ask. "All junk. This is the sort of thing we saw in *Parade Magazine*. What did they call these things? Boiler rooms? They run scams on older people."

"Your mother always kept her checkbook in the drawer of the side table near the television," she says. "See if he's writing checks."

"How is he able to write checks? I thought Mom blocked that back when he had gambling problems." Then I remember. When Mom's health problems required her to go into the health care center, their assets were divided—all but the house, which remained in her name. CDs and other savings were separated into two equal portions. Hers drew down to the minimum and triggered Medicaid payments. So Dad now has his funds under his signature control. He also has his Social Security.

Back up the narrow steps. The checkbook is in the same drawer. Inside, in his characteristic jutted handwriting, he has recorded checks totaling over $25,000 to various companies—all with "Las Vegas" somewhere in the name—over the past four weeks! The records are meticulous. His half of their financial assets, not counting the house or car, was only $46,000 to start with. Over half of his savings is gone.

I stalk into the kitchen, checkbook in hand. He still appears upset. It's about to get a lot worse. I try to steady myself. My father and I have never really had much of a relationship, not a single meaningful conversation other than the one after my stupid road racing incident.

"Dad, the checkbook."

He looks at me defiantly. In my entire life, I've never seen him show real anger.

Until now.

"Give me that. That's my business."

I resist an impulse to shout, but take a breath instead. "You've written checks for over twenty-five thousand dollars to two or three companies in Las Vegas over the past month or so. Do you realize that?"

For a moment, he doesn't react. Then, "It was an investment."

"An investment?"

He won't concede. "An opportunity. To win a large sum of money."

"That represents over half of your entire life savings!" I say. It's hard not to shout. "Do you really think that was a good thing to do?"

"The way it was presented to me, yes."

"Daddy! The papers have stories about these people in Las Vegas. They call older people, you know, retired men and women. These things aren't legitimate. It's a con game."

He bristles. "That's your word, Jimmy. It was my decision. You have no right to interfere."

Callie sees us revert and motions for me to back off. "Jim, you can't afford to be spending thousands of dollars a month! At this rate you won't have any money at all in one more month!"

"I'll have my Social Security," he counters.

"That's right," I say. No one can take that from you."

Right then, my first attempt at an actual adult conversation with my father is interrupted. The old green phone rings. Instinctively I pick it up and answer, sure it's Callie's mother wondering how our visit with Mom has been.

"Hello."

A man's voice. "Mr. Jackson?"

"This is Jim Jackson." It's true.

“Good morning. This is Ted Stephens. We spoke yesterday.” The voice is professional, smooth. In the polished West Coast non-accent, the name is pleasantly generic.

I get the drift.

“Mr. Jackson,” he continues, “we have a new product here, one that I’m sure you’ll find interesting. We’ve put together a special limited participation opportunity for a grand prize of five-hundred thousand dollars. The thing that makes it so interesting is that only one thousand chances will be offered. Each chance is only a thousand dollars. I recommend you consider five of these. Mr. Jackson, the winning investor can live in luxury the rest of his life.”

“Mr. Stephens, do you realize my father is eighty-two years old? He’s just wasted half his entire life savings in the last month on scams like this?”

“Who is this? I want to speak with Jim Jackson.” The polished voice shifts to the defensive.

“This is Jim Jackson. His son. Get off the phone and never call my father again. I’m going to report you and your lousy outfit to the legal authorities.”

The line goes dead. I stand there stiffly, the phone still in my hand. Finally, I put it down slowly and look at Dad. “That was someone, gave his name as Ted Stephens. No telling what his real name is. He wants you to spend another five thousand dollars on a raffle for half a million dollars.”

“That might be a good opportunity,” he says. “It depends on how many tickets they have.”

“My bet is that no one ever wins a cent. They probably have consolation prizes—more snow globes.”

He doesn’t give an inch.

“This is a professional con game.” I lower my voice, try to sound conciliatory. “These types prey on older people—people who don’t get a lot of phone calls and feel lonely. They’ll continue coming after you until you have no more money. Then they’ll move on.”

He sits in his chair, his eyes glaring straight ahead, averting me. I've never interacted with my father this way. He clears his throat. "Jim, you have no right to interfere with my investment decisions."

I'm trying to be tender, to share empathy. This isn't something we've ever done. *Hesitate and take a deep breath.* "Dad, these are not investments. I'm sorry, but we can't let you spend twenty thousand dollars a month on vitamins and raffles. You only have that much more in your checking account. Don't you see that you'll have no savings at all in another month?"

He slouches but stands his ground, or more exactly sits his seated position.

"It's my money, my decision."

"No, it's not. This is illegal. They're cheating you. It's against the law."

We face each other.

"I'm going to keep your checkbook. We can't allow this to continue. Tomorrow first thing I'm going to the bank and close this account. There might be checks that haven't cleared yet. We can stop payment on them."

He pulls out a cigarette, lights it, and draws deeply. The smoke courses through the kitchen. Later, I call Susie and tell her what we discovered. She has the power of attorney for both Mom and Dad. The whole thing is a shock to her.

Callie and I went down to Princeton Bank and Trust Company at nine o'clock sharp the next morning. Susie faxed her POA and we managed to block two checks for a total of $5,000 that hadn't cleared yet. We closed out the account and set up a new account in her name. There were no other bills other than local utilities, and these along with local taxes, were routed up to her. Dad's Social Security checks were rerouted to Susie's bank in Columbus, Ohio, and she maintained a modest amount in Princeton so he could make routine cash withdrawals for personal daily needs.

I updated Mom when we went out to see her the next day. She was sad for Dad but understood. It was fortunate that they both had signed a POA for Susie. That had been 10 years earlier. I didn't even know about it. Dad brooded and was sullen the entire time we were in town.

On our last day, we said our goodbyes to Mom, who sat there with her expressionless face, drawn to her right. Callie told me that Mom asked her if we would move her to a health-care center near us. She asked my wife, not me. I didn't feel it would be fair to take her away from Princeton. Dad would have to stay by himself, or move to Texas . . . live in a room in the independent senior living wing of a retirement home while Mom was in the associated medical wing. That seemed too traumatic. It also meant they would be 1,300 miles from my sister. He still lived at home and had a handful of family and friends left. In that time and place, it didn't seem the right thing to do.

Now, I'm not sure.

Chapter 29

MOM'S CONDITION DETERIORATED. Badly. Except for a lock of brown hair at the nape of her neck, my mother now was completely white. Her head drew even farther down and to her right. Her face was frozen into the appearance of a grimace.

Dad was becoming more forgetful all the time. Mom was nearly 80—he almost 85. Be without parents? I'd never known anything else—Mom and Dad were constants.

I'd transitioned from being their child, then becoming a husband and parent myself, to now parenting my parents: Mom the sick, dying child; Dad the irresponsible child, as distant to me as my older son. We had to discipline my father—take away privileges with money. I never knew an in-between state when they were vital and vibrant adults, people I could get to know on an adult-to-adult basis. I was too busy.

Their loss.

My loss.

A few months later—early in the morning.

Callie struggled to wake up, reached beside her for the phone. Who would call at this time? "Hello. Oh, hi Susie. What?"

She sat up in bed. "What? Say that again." Her face went ashen. "That's terrible. I'll let you talk with Jim." She handed me the phone. "Your mother."

I tried to clear my head. "Susie?"

"Jimmy, it's me, Susie. The health care facility, the place where Mom is staying—they just called." There was a pause. Her voice broke. "Mom died this morning."

"She died? Mom?"

"An hour ago."

Just like that.

"Susie, I didn't think she was that . . . I mean I didn't think she was close . . ." I can't say it.

"Oh, Jimmy, Mom was going downhill fast. When the kids and I were there a month ago, she couldn't swallow. They weren't able to get her to eat anything, even purees and liquids. We went to tell Mom goodbye."

I didn't know what to say. *They were saying goodbye?*

"I looked in her eyes. The children held her hands. Jimmy, it was terribly hard. She knew."

She knew. They knew. I didn't.

Callie and I flew back. Our three children all came in. Mee-Maw was a special figure to all of them. Her sewn, painted, and carved crafts were treasured Christmas and birthday presents. She played the piano and ukulele for the kids, even recorded special "live performances" on an old cheap tape recorder. All this, plus her corn dodgers and baked cottage cheese and heaps upon heaps of good fried chicken. Mee-Maw was the wonderfully dippy one, the theatrical one, the grandparent with the creative artistic relationship with the kids.

Fortunately both Mom and Dad had gone to Seaver's Funeral Home with Susie and me a year earlier. It seemed like an academic exercise at the time. I wanted it that way.

Susie and I alternated pushing her around the casket display center in a wheelchair. That alone was a strange experience. She would stop at a casket and ask us what we thought. "What about that, Jimmy?" How does a child answer that question? Daddy picked out one as well. Susie wrote the checks, a pre-paid package deal. Now there was no need to do anything except to call Seaver's. One phone call, that's all.

More people were at the funeral than I had expected. Mom's friends—those who still could get around—were there. There were a few from her public health department days, along with some from the church, her circle mostly. Callie's folks and many of her relatives came. Her mother looked weak. Dad's two surviving sisters made the trip from Virginia, along with their children. Of course Susie and her family were there. All in all, 50 or 60 people. The new minister at the First Methodist Church didn't know Mom well, since her health had gone downhill about the time he came to Princeton. He'd been out to the facility and had spent some time with her, yet his proper but prosaic eulogy didn't reflect her as a real person. She didn't look like herself either: Her skin was frozen, taut.

Mom had kept a journal. She didn't add to it every day, but earlier in her life she had written a poignant entry saying she wanted to be remembered as someone who had laughed and cried, who lived and loved, and was loved. I read that line verbatim at the service. Katie sang "Amazing Grace." Kenny played her ukulele while the rest of us sang "She'll be coming 'round the mountain when she comes." That would have pleased her to no end.

She was buried in the Jackson family plot at the Saltville cemetery: old and traditional, with weathered stones going back to the late 1700's. The day was gray, gloomy. Mom's final resting spot was with a family who questioned whether she was "proper" enough for their own. Mom had been so alive.

One space remained—for Dad.

Following Mom's death, Susie, Callie, and I convinced Dad to move to the Methodist Home in Glenwood Park, a 10 minute drive from Princeton. After all, both my parents had been members of the church for many years. Dad had enough money to afford the move, with the portion of his savings we had blocked from going to the boiler room in Las Vegas, as well as his Social Security.

The facility consisted of an assisted living wing and a medical wing, with a large and friendly dining room in the center. The residential part included a quiet, pleasant main area with sofas and chairs, tables for board games, plenty of books and magazines, plus newspapers from regional cities. The lovely site was set in a leafy forest, at the end of a long driveway, a single-story facility with trim grounds and walking pathways. It would be a perfect location for Dad.

His room was just a short walk beyond a small sitting room and library section. I doubt that he ever spent much time at all in either of those areas, but he liked the food and made friends with other gentlemen. They sat together at meals.

Susie and her husband, as well as Callie and I, spent a week going through the house on North Walker. One of Mom's paintings depicted lovely seagulls, in country-art style, the lines perfectly done on a piece of smoothed driftwood she found when she and Dad visited Uncle Carter after he retired in Florida. Such delicate lines—the birds seemed alive. On the back: Sara 1979. We took it back to Austin.

We moved a few pieces of furniture from the house out to Dad's room, along with clothes he needed, some of the few we found that weren't full of burn holes. He seemed pleased.

We finally cleared out the house and put it on the market.

Once Mom died, the mortality dominoes started to wobble. Callie's mother looked pregnant even though she was 69 and weighed

90 pounds. Angie had experienced ovarian cysts for years, but for some reason the family doctor in Princeton always advised against a hysterectomy. When a lesion appeared in full force, her doctor insisted it was "only a hernia." No scans, no x-rays. No thought process.

Callie flew back home and blew up. She was strong, insistent, buoyed not only by natural nurturing tendencies, but also by her undergraduate and graduate education in Social Work at the university in Austin—she'd gone back to school when Joey went off to California for college.

Her mother got scans. It was a tumor: A big one, stage-four ovarian cancer. The oncologist put it candidly to the siblings, "Your mother has two, maybe two-and-a-half years max. We can treat her but it's a malevolent and aggressive form of cancer. It's a killer." Angie went on a strong regimen of chemotherapy—drugs designed to attack the cancer cells, but not *quite* kill the normal tissue. Amazingly, though so small and frail, she responded well to the procedures, and in the fall of 1994, the lesion decreased to a pecan-sized mass. A surgeon removed it and did a complete hysterectomy at the same time.

She completed her treatments. By late 1995, her hair was coming back in and she felt good. She was in remission according to all the marker tests. The two-year point was critical. If she could remain in full remission for two years, the statistical probability started to look up. People had beaten the dark cloud. It was possible.

Meanwhile, Dad seemed to like living at Glenwood Park. The Methodist retirement home had a nice feel about it. Lovely tall hardwoods shaded the immaculate grounds, which included comfortable sitting nooks with chairs and benches located in a park-like setting.

Crisp echoes clicked off the polished floor as I walked alone down the long hallway to visit. An etched brass sign next to his room silently announced: "James Jackson, Princeton, West Virginia." The door was slightly ajar. I knocked.

Harrumph.

His familiar voice follows, "Come in."

"It's me. Jimmy," I say, still standing in the hall. *Why do I use Jimmy?*

He doesn't. "Oh, Jim. Come on in."

Dad sits by his window, in that same old familiar chair. The *Daily Telegraph* is spread out on his lap. He looks good. His flannel shirt goes well with his slacks. Suddenly I realize that I'd never seen him in a pair of jeans. He has on his trusty tweed jacket with the leather arm patches. He's clean-shaven. He could sell someone a new Buick right then and there.

The room itself is comfortable yet professional, with a standard institutional bed and a hospital style bathroom with handrails and an easy-to-reach tub and shower. Furniture from the North Walker Street house provides a homey, well-worn feel—very well-worn—with the cigarette burn carry-overs. Fortunately he can't smoke in his room, a safety issue. A smoking area is designated away from the rooms, on a screened porch.

"How are you?" he asks, remaining seated. I lean over. We shake hands.

"Things are good. And you?" A typical non-conversation for us. "You reading the paper?"

"Just glancing at it." he says.

"Anything new?"

"No, pretty much the same thing."

"How are things here?"

"Fine," he answers, with the broad "F-eye-n" sound, the way each of us would speak our entire life.

"Food all right?"

He perks up. "The food's good."

As far as I can tell, Dad has no lady friends . . . not that I'm looking for them, or would care. He's 87. Although he looks spiffy on the outside, clearly his dementia is worse. He takes on an earnest yet distant look, glances at his watch, looks at me, and asks, "Now, Jim, when did you say you had to leave?" He isn't trying to get rid of me. It's just that his capacity to carry on a conversation doesn't extend far beyond that.

"Have you met some people?" I ask.

"Yes, I have."

"And?"

"Met several people . . . the men at the dinner table. One's a retired judge, another's a retired pastor. I believe the third is . . . you know, I'm not sure what he did." The three meal settings are the social highlight of every day, when Dad and three other men, all in their mid-to-late 80's, sit together.

Suddenly my mind switches to Mom—gone, buried at Saltville. It isn't right that Daddy is my one remaining parent, the increasingly fragile symbol of my own mortality.

"What do you-all talk about?"

"Well, I suppose we really don't do too much talking," he says. "Mr. Saunders—he's the retired judge—he doesn't hear very well. Mr. Andrews is a former minister. He watches television in his room. We mainly talk about the food, you know, the meals. Weather, too." He pauses, "Now I remember. The other man's a doctor, a medical doctor. He came here only recently, a bit younger than the rest of us. Dr. Bailey, Sam Bailey. Used to practice near Beckley."

Dad sits back in his chair. He's capsulated his shrinking universe.

"Go on and finish the paper," I say. "I'll just sit with you."

He leafs through the sports section. The Bluefield Beavers football team is the headline: "Beavers Top Big Creek with Big Plays." They always were good in football. Some things never change.

Out the window, the fall foliage is past prime color season. The big hardwoods are nearly bare.

Have my father and I ever had a single real conversation? That can't be literally and factually true. He did come through to get me off the hook after the road racing arrest. But that was him talking and me listening. I can't recall a shared experience, actually *talking* with him. Not a single solitary real conversation. The family *duty* thing wells up inside me again. He has done his duty. Here I am. I'm his required male offspring, with an education, a career, who has two boys and a daughter. What more did he need to do?

"When did you say you have to leave?" he repeats.

"Do you have visitors?"

"From time to time, yes."

"Glad to hear that. Who's been out to see you?" I try to be friendly, disarming, mask my feelings.

"Well," the word is drawn out slowly. "Mr. and Mrs. Carver come out occasionally." Dad never refers to them as Jake and Angie, at least to me.

"They are considerate people." I lean back a bit. "Anyone else?"

He's silent.

"Anybody else?"

"I'm trying to think. There are others, but right now I can't think of their names."

"Aunt Molly and her family. Have they been over?"

"Oh, yes. She and your uncle Carl were here on one or two occasions. They drove over."

"That's nice," I say. "How about Aunt Emily?" She and Molly are the two youngest, the only other siblings still living.

"No, I don't think she has been here. I'm not sure. You know, most of our friends are gone." There is a sense of loss now. To be fair, at 87, most of his friends *are* gone now, or are in poor health and unable to get out and around. But it's clear he doesn't have many visitors.

"Does that bother you?"

"What?"

"Not to have more visitors?"

"I have everything I need here."

"Do you miss Mom?"

"Yes." It was slow and drawn out. He pauses, "Yes, of course I do."

It always bothered me that Dad had been critical of Mom when her health was failing. He bordered on verbal abuse when she dropped a fork or spilled food.

"Sara," he would say, an edge to his voice, "Sara, be more careful."

"Do you believe you were a good father?" I ask him.

The room becomes absolutely still.

"A good father? Why yes, I would think so. You and your sister never did without."

The words start to flow, words that matter to me but have been unspoken for so long. "You came when I got my Eagle Scout award. You got your picture in the paper. You came to my high school and college graduations. But you weren't there for the little things." I try to keep the emotional walls from crumbling all at once. "You never played sports with me. You never saw me play a single Little League game. Never showed me how to work on a car. How to polish my shoes. How to shave. How to use the twenty-two I got for Christmas when I was fifteen. I just went out by myself with that new gun. There just wasn't any interaction. None."

Neither of us speaks.

I swallow hard. "Daddy, do you remember sitting at the kitchen table drinking bourbon and Coke until you would pass out?"

He stiffens. "There are some things I'm not proud of." His face shows nothing, but there is emotion in his voice.

"You used to holler out 'Hey, Joe,' over and over—carry on a one-way conversation with someone named Joe. Who was Joe?" I ask. My voice cracks.

"I did that?" There is a flicker of something, a ghost of recognition. He says no more.

He looks away, out the window. He might be wondering what else he had said, even though there had been nothing. "Your mother and I did the best we could."

That triggers it, the missing emotional connection. I want to say "Mom was always there. But not you." *Be blunt. Just say it.*

But I can't. I just can't say the words.

So here we are, my father and I, in the last part of the ninth inning of his life, me at 53, having our first and only discussion about my feelings . . . my father, who has been missing in action my entire life.

It's too late.

The sun streams in through the window. The atmosphere in the room is thick and brittle. He clears his throat again. "I would say I was a good father. You and Suzanne never went without." *That again.* "You both received an education."

"That's correct. But I . . ." I'm searching for words now. "I just have to say I resent the way you treated Mom at the end. I resent the fact that you and I never had a single real conversation. I don't think you wanted—or at least you weren't able—to give me much guidance growing up. I can't express myself well. I don't know what I don't know. All the experiences between you and me that we never had. No baseball tosses. No fishing or hunting trips. Never a family vacation. To be honest, I don't ever remember our family ever eating out in a restaurant."

"We drove to Charlottesville and Danville on occasion," he says. The tone is defensive.

"Yes, we did. But they always seemed like family assignments—always trips to the relatives. It was expected. I got to look at the photographs and the family tree, to have it made clear that of the seven of you, the four girls and three boys, I was the one offspring to carry the name . . . It was my duty to, you know . . ."

A single intense beam of the afternoon sun spotlights the tiny specks of dust suspended in the air.

"Daddy, I don't even know what I missed."

Then I hear myself saying words I've suppressed for years. Words that seem to come from someone other than me.

"I don't respect you."

"I'm sorry to hear that," he says. He actually says it professionally, as if he'd lost a sale.

It's my one actual attempt at sharing feelings. It's a lousy way to end our single father-son dialogue.

A minute later, we shake hands and say goodbye.

Chapter 30

ANGIE CARVER'S CANCER came back in 1996. It returned aggressively as a metathesis in her liver. The tiny lady swelled up like a balloon. There was no misdiagnosis this time. They removed the tumor along with a portion of her liver. To the amazement of everyone, she was able to tolerate both the surgery and a powerful experimental chemo. She lost all of her hair again, and her weight dropped to even more elfish dimensions. But the cancer markers in her blood dropped back to normal. The entire family celebrated. Our children came back again and got to spend quality time with their remaining grandmother who was thrilled to be "cancer-free" once again.

We were relieved. She appeared to be heading in the right direction. Yet her oncologist was candid with Callie and her siblings. The probability of a lengthy remission at that point was exceedingly unlikely.

"Treasure the good days."

Of course we all went out to see Dad as well, "Gramps" to the kids. He had aged dramatically. After all, he was now 88 years old. But this was different: He was unshaven and disheveled, dressed in his pajamas and a robe, his hair uncombed. It was so unlike him. He appeared confused, surprised to see us even though we called before leaving the hotel. Every few minutes he asked us how long we could stay. His deep memory—those early years—still hadn't left him. In sharp detail he could describe the yard and interior of the home that his father, my grandfather, built on the farm at Broadford, Virginia. Yet it was more obvious than ever that his short term memory was gone. He was heading into his final time with ossified arteries from all those years of smoking and drinking.

The children paid polite respects to a shell of a grandfather they (and I) had never known as a person. As we closed his door, he sat by the window in his room, confused and unkempt, the afternoon sunshine pouring in through the leafless hardwood trees.

That was the last time I saw him alive. The phone call came in December, at the same time the kids were visiting us in Austin for Christmas.

After lunch, Dad had walked by himself back toward his room. An aide saw him "in distress" and helped him sit down on a chair in the hallway. After a few minutes, he said he felt he could continue. The aide helped him to his feet and he walked a short distance before collapsing. He was dead when the doctor arrived. It was his heart. They said he didn't suffer. I dealt with Dad's death the same way I dealt with his life, as far as our relationship had been. I didn't.

The kids remained at our home in Austin while Callie and I flew back. It was a chance to spend some rare time together. Katie, now in her early thirties, was married. She and her "young man," now her husband, appeared happy. She was editor of a glossy magazine for the fine jewelry trade. Kenny was writing music, playing with his own rock band in Austin, and beginning to transition to recording and mixing music. His goal was to have his own studio. Joey had completed the MBA program at Stanford, and was engaged to a girl from from the Northwest. He was firmly a West Coast man by now.

All arrangements were in place. Thank goodness for that. The service was small and quiet. Unlike Mom's funeral, there were no jokes, no laughter, no outpouring of fond remembrances. No tears either. Few people of Dad's age came, of course. Most were gone now. His family was represented by his two remaining sisters and their children. The largest single contingent was Callie's family. Everyone quietly paid their respects and left. The Methodist minister hardly knew Dad at all. We drove over to Saltville and watched as he was buried beside Mother in a short, emotionless service. The final plot in the old Jackson section now was complete.

I felt exposed.

The focus now was on Callie's mother. Her remission was holding. She had started to gain back her weight. Her hair had come back, though with less of the black that was inherited from her parents, both of them a quarter Cherokee.

The inevitable next development came several months later with a phone call from Mr. Carver. "Mom's cancer is back."

Callie sensed the resignation in his voice. Her mother was weak from experimental chemo drugs, a last chance the family had hoped might work. The specific problem was massive bacterial infection. The oncologist said large doses of antibiotics might help her to beat that. Mr. Carver asked how long that would last. The doctor looked directly at him and said, "It will come right back."

By this time, little Angie weighed at most 75 pounds. She'd lost her hair for the third time.

"Do you want me to treat it?"

Mr. Carver didn't even look at his children. He faced the doctor and simply said, "No."

Her last week was dignified, even pleasant. The end was beautiful. She was surrounded by her family: people who were taught to love the Lord Jesus, treasure babies, hug one another, visit frequently, and call all the time to "check in." She was completely lucid. She laughed. She cried. A man whose gaunt Appalachian features were etched into a face hardened by the sun and hard labor knelt at her bedside. With tears running down his face, he prayed and thanked Angie and Jake for the food, clothes, and money they had provided so many times when he was out of work and had, literally, nothing. Everyone in the room cried. Those were acts of kindness that so symbolized the two of them. She died in her sleep that night. Mr. Carver was by her side.

The community outpouring that ensued was, by any measure, the largest seen in Princeton in years. No one could remember anything like it. The normal folk were there: People who appreciated quiet acts of generosity; parents of little children watched over by "our Angie" in the nursery of the First Christian Church for over 30 years; neighbors who had been driven to a doctor's appointment, or who had been surprised when Jake and Angie knocked on the door, unexpected, at five o'clock with a home-cooked meal just when the cupboards were bare. They remembered. The funeral home's parking lot filled up and officials stood out on the Athens highway directing traffic.

Callie anchored the receiving line with her dad, her brother, and her younger sister. They cried, hugged, remembered. She was the perfect oldest adult child for the family. As her husband, I felt it was my responsibility somehow to support her. That was impossible. In light of Dad's spare funeral service and my own shortcomings in terms of emotional openness and vulnerability, it would have been a task of Herculean difficulty if . . . if I had been able to do it.

I wasn't. She didn't need me. I sat along the edges with our children and got up every so often to say a timid hello when one of the people I knew came along.

By ten o'clock, the last visitors filtered out. Only the immediate family was together. There was a closeness I never had.

Mr. Carver lived nearly three more years. The official medical statement indicated a heart attack. That's partly true. He really died of a broken heart.

Part 4

Pipestem State Park
Southern West Virginia

Chapter 31

WE WOKE UP early Saturday morning. Oldie rock and roll music from last night still filled my head.

Shadows and distorted morning light confirmed starkly how far our room was set back, under an overhead walkway, next to the elevator. It was as if we were in the innards, the maw, of something.

"Claustrophobia Central" included a low-end coffee maker along with two sealed portions of coffee, packets with fancy names for a quotidian mixture, probably from Viet Nam, with little bits of leaves and twigs ground in along with the beans. The machine hissed and gurgled while coffee spat out into a paper cup. Sitting in the single chair, a floor lamp over one shoulder in the otherwise dark room, I leafed through the main handout from Friday night.

The brochure included bios based on comments we were supposed to send in. I read it from start to finish as I exhausted the inventory of ground-up more-or-less coffee. I hadn't taken it seriously. My remarks were shallow. Tell your life story in three lines: *Veni, vidi, vici*. A "non" in front of one or more?

"You up?" The voice emerged from beneath a clump of dark blankets.

"I am."

"Sleep O.K.?" the voice asked.

"Yes." My libido increased whenever we traveled—especially in hotel rooms—but last night we both went right to sleep. She has never been a morning "let's make love" person, unlike me. "You want to take a shower first, or do you want me to?" I asked.

The bed covers stirred. "I will. Just a minute till I wake up."

Someone put a lot of effort into the booklet. A collage on the front and back covers featured popular culture icons of '59 and '60: Elvis and Ann-Margaret, with a slim and neatly attired Elvis in a suit and tie; the Everly Brothers; John Wayne all dressed up in Western garb, looking like . . . well, like John Wayne; Nancy Kwan on the cover of *Life*; Ike and J.F.K.; movie hits including *The Alamo* and *Spartacus*; and popular media, such as Dave Garraway's TV show and *Boys' Life* Magazine. There was the seal of the new state of Hawaii, as well as the emblem of the fledgling American Football League, which supposedly was doomed right from the start. A new-fangled contraption, an eight-speed bicycle by Schwinn, was featured. Who'd ever want eight speeds on a bike?

Callie came out of the bathroom wearing only a bra and panties. My attention immediately switched to seduction.

She rebuked me. "Don't even think about it. Take a shower and get cleaned up. I'm going to Princeton to see my sister."

"Not even an innocent hug?" I asked, rising from the chair.

"There *is* no such thing as an innocent hug in a situation like this," she said, leaving no room for misunderstanding. With finality, she pulled on a blouse and a skirt. Clearly I didn't generate reciprocal feelings, so I gathered my unkempt self, tiptoed into the small, hot, and humid bathroom, and began a hoped-for transformation to humanity.

Large windows offer a grand view of the Appalachians and make the main dining room a compelling feature of the Pipestem Lodge. At this time of day, the river below remains cloaked in a fluffy chord of fog, a milky-white link fading out of sight as it winds its way toward the Bluestone Gorge Bridge.

"Here's your table," the young woman says. Her name badge reads, "Juanita, Hinton, West Virginia."

"So you're from Hinton?" I ask.

She looks to be in her mid-thirties and has that drawn facial appearance you sometimes see in Appalachia.

"Yes sir, all my life." The accented 'R' and the broad 'I' stand out.

"Ever heard of a nightclub in Hinton called the *Pair-A-Dice*?"

"Paradise Club?"

"It sounds like the word 'paradise,' but it was spelled like 'pair-a-dice.' You know, gambling." I'm not making myself clear. This isn't going anywhere.

"No sir. I sure haven't," she says. "Where is it?"

"I don't think it *is* any longer," I say. "This was back in the late fifties."

"Oh," she says and laughs. "Well, I wouldn't know about that! Have a nice breakfast."

So much for that. How does it feel to be old?

After breakfast, Callie leaves for Princeton. The room quickly closes in on me, and I leave thinking there must be some of the old gang around. Finally, at the snack bar off the lobby, I locate Donnie Davis and his wife.

"Donnie!"

"Jimmy, come on over. Sit down."

"Where is everyone?"

"Don't know. We slept in. Haven't seen a soul today. This isn't the hottest social area, that's for sure. But we missed breakfast and it's too early for the dining room, so I'm going to get something."

"Real committed foodie, aren't you?" I ask.

"Mainstreet U.S.A. all the way."

The door opens. Marnie Bowland Santoro sashays in, flicking a cigarette outside, a little smoky cloud slinking along behind her.

"Ain't it just a nasty habit," she says as she sits down. "It's my vice, at least one of them."

"You're just full of vices?" I can't resist.

"Oh you just don't know," she rasps. "Actually, I talk a good line, but I'm a simple kept woman, and by an *Eye-talian* at that! Gawd, I've smoked like a chimney all morning—gotta take a break."

"Is Tony here?" I ask, somehow remembering her New Jersey husband's first name. They own a nightclub in Florida. He seemed nice, never said much at our other reunions—looked like a man who could take care of himself.

"You know, he came five years ago. It's a bitch to go to your spouse's high school reunion. He said for me to come by myself this time. Actually it's more fun because he just sits there not knowing anyone. I feel bad for him."

"Want something?" I ask. "Be glad to get it. Big spender. We're at a food cornucopia as you can see."

"Like shee-it," she says, smiling. "See, I can still talk with an accent. I *will* take a coffee. I'm a slow starter when it comes to food. Just live on nicotine, I suppose. I'll get something later."

Donnie turns to me. "I haven't seen Wendie. Is he coming?"

"Wendie Johnston . . . didn't you hear he died?" Marnie says.

He looks stunned. "Wendie? What happened?"

"Someone sent me an obituary," she continues. "Said he died after an 'extended period of poor health.' I think that was the phrasing."

She turns to me. "Jimmy, weren't you a pall bearer?"

"Yes. The funeral was in Bristol."

"Someone told me Wendie'd gained a whole lot of weight. Said he always had a cigarette in one hand and a drink in the other." Marnie keeps in touch.

"Not at the end. But let's just say he didn't have a healthy lifestyle," I say, looking down. "He was my closest friend growing up. Best man at my wedding." Words start to pour out. "He started as a sportswriter, his real love. Went on to be the editor of the *Bristol Courier Journal* at a young age. Became nationally known by developing some sort of style guide for the design and layout of newspapers. Forty papers, coast-to-coast, adopted it. He used to speak at conventions. Was a judge for national awards for newspaper layout." I hardly stop for breath, not looking at them any longer. "The guy had so much talent. He wrote the most amazing letters—he had a knack for words and the English language, that's for sure. He had way too much potential to end up not taking care of himself."

All three of them stare at me.

"Sorry. I get carried away."

"Hell, I can't take any more sad stories," Marnie says. "I need a drink."

"You mean a drink at the non-existent bar here at the lodge?" Donnie says. "You'll have to use your private stock."

"That's O.K. Hey, we run a club. I *have* private stock—from our bar."

Things lighten up after that little séance on my part. Donnie and his wife get something and Marnie nurses several cups of black coffee.

By five o'clock, Callie is back. "When do you need to be there?" she asks. "They'll take a group picture. It's usually the first thing they do, while the light's still good."

I rummage around in the reunion folder. "Six, outside the snack bar."

"You'd better hustle. They're not going to wait for you."

I put on my high-tech uniform: khaki slacks, a blue button-down shirt open at the collar, and a blue blazer.

"Those colors make your blue eyes radiate," she says.

"You're just trying to seduce me. I know the game."

"It's easy."

"I plead no contest."

A low series of risers have been put in place, and it's the usual "taller men in the rear, women in the front." Melvin Grubb, the ageless photographer from Bluefield, is organizing the shoot. It takes talent to get a big group to look at you, not blink, and appear pleased to be there. Somehow, after only a few shots, Mr. Grubb seems satisfied.

The nametags include a copy of our senior-class photographs. Some people look similar, while some bear little, if any, resemblance of that earlier phase of their life. One person still easy to recognize is Mack Andrews, who's talking with Buddy Lewis. Mack still has that same glistening black hair, although nature and time have infused enough gray to produce a striking mature look. He married a local girl and ended up working his entire career for a high-tech firm in Florida. He's retired now. Life seems to be good—he's the same, just without the hot car. He said that he and Margie Rey dated—he brought it up—until she went off to BYU. That seems so long ago.

Buddy Lewis' hair is slightly thinner. He hasn't gained weight, still looks good. "I'm excited about tonight." Buddy still has that same airy and exuberant manner of speaking.

"Still into the oldies?" I ask.

"Are you kidding? Am I still alive? Just got back from Roanoke—you know, one of those fifties and sixties reviews. Ain't nothing like it."

"The original groups?"

"They look and sound just like the originals, right down to every song being two minutes and twenty seconds long. Just like they were. The Four Aces, in person, right there in front of me. Can you believe that?"

Buddy gets a dreamy look. The Four Aces could be doing "Rock and Roll Waltz" in his mind. "They did those cool sideways-steps, you know, two to the side, one back, one forward, then two to the other direction. I was in heaven. The place was full. The only problem was that the women were old and overweight, and the guys were losing their hair. Shit, I was the only one there who looked normal!"

"Hey man, still back in the fifties."

Buddy laughs. "Never left 'em. You-all have fun tonight. I'm gonna sit in with the band at some point. It's all set up. Arcie's going to sing too. He won't be around for the meal and the program—said something about another commitment—but he'll be here later. The band wants him to come up, do some oldies. 'Mustang Sally,' a couple more. Really something, ain't it. It won't be the real thing since Coverall is more of a rock band than an R & B band. You know, no horn section. But it'll be O.K. I gotta run now."

Buddy goes over to his table, and Mack is off to find his wife across the room. With all the chatting going on, I haven't staked out a table. It'd be a bummer to sit with people we hardly know.

"Jimmy. Over here." Slate's waving. "Two seats. Got you covered."

We're the last people to sit down.

One of our classmates gives the invocation. He's impassioned, a minister in Beckley. It's lengthy, including a three-minute word-for-word reading from the Bible. Thoughts of Sunday mornings at the radio station flood back. I can look down at the floor only so long. Not a soul looks back at me when I peep and look around. Welcome back to the Bible Belt.

The program includes a memorial service. Donnie Davis presides. "I ask your cooperation as we honor and remember our classmates who are no longer with us. I'm going to call out each name. As their name is called, one of our classmates has agreed to come up here to represent him or her." He pauses. "Please keep them in your thoughts and prayers. Now, in memoriam, Harriet Lee Blakley."

The lights dim. The room is subdued. A woman I don't recognize rises and walks slowly to the front holding a small candle, as yet unlit. The names and the solemn walks continue. Finally, the Js and the name I'm dreading to hear: "Wendell Louis Johnston."

Callie whispers, "They didn't ask you to represent Wendie?"

Marnie Bowland stands and walks to the front.

Slate looks at me and whispers, "I didn't know."

Suddenly I was at Wendie's and Connie's . . . that last visit. Once again, Connie sat beside the white grand piano. She hadn't changed since the last time we had seen her, four years earlier. She'd filled out a bit in an attractive yet proper way, always in control.

This time something was different. I didn't smell the scent.

"I know you want to see Wendie."

Not a single fiber on her or that formal chair was disturbed as she rose.

"How is the rascal?"

"He's doing fine." She pronounced the word with the flat "eye" inflection, but with precision. "He's downstairs. We use the downstairs as our living space these days. Wendie says I keep this area too formal. But that's just me, I suppose." Callie and I stood, too, joining her.

"Our little lake there," Connie said, motioning past the window. "We used to go there and walk. But he hasn't been able to do that since his fall. They didn't know if he would make it. It was after the car wreck, after he left the newspaper and was working full-time with his printing company."

He had written me about it. Wendie wrote the greatest letters.

She smoothed her skirt. The three of us started in unison, the music doyenne and the two travelers. The stairs were bisected by a large landing, where the steps turned so that we ended up exactly beneath the area where we started. An apparition that looked like Wendie was sitting in the room.

"Jim, Callie, it's been a while. Welcome back to God's country," the apparition said, maintaining a sense of humor.

Wendie rose unsteadily in front of a huge chair. He had filled out in a way that made both his height as well as his girth more noticeable. His face was a rubber mask inflated from within, lips pronounced. It was uncomfortable to watch.

"Sit, please," he said and plopped back down. "As you can see, I'm not in the greatest physical shape of my life."

Callie leaned over and gave him a hug, straining to reach around him. I sat across from his commander's seat. The room was all orange, a shrine to the University of Tennessee sports programs.

"Welcome to my world. As you may have noticed, I follow the Vols closely."

"Why would anyone think that?" I say. "Just because you have orange everything and a picture of Coach Fulmer on the wall."

"Always a perceptive sort," he quipped.

"How have you been?"

"To be candid, it's been a tough two years. After I confounded the doctors and actually survived that damn car wreck, I almost got back to what passes for normalcy in my case. A bit off the track for most people, I might add. Then I got up one night to go pee and fell over our dog. He was asleep on the floor. Fell hard into the chest of drawers. Broke my shoulder. That really messed me up."

Connie leaned forward. "It's awful what he went through. He had a stroke. A blood clot formed. His heart stopped. It's a miracle he survived—I mean, once again."

"You used to chain smoke," I said. "No more?"

The air is clean now.

"Ah, you noticed," Wendie replied. "After almost forty years as a loyal customer for those damn things, I'm now a former smoker. I miss 'em every day. The doctors demanded it—something about not lasting another year if I didn't mend my evil ways. Booze too. Stopped cold. But if you wish to partake, I still maintain a proper supply for visitors. Just say the word."

I shook my head. "Driving." If there had been constants in Wendie's life, they were smoking and drinking. And words.

"Good idea," he said and reached down beside the commander's chair to a small cooler. He fished out a Diet Coke from several cans buried in ice cubes.

"My new addiction." He held it with both hands and popped the tab. There was the brief but familiar *whoosh*. "Like one of these?"

"That's all right. Trying to quit."

He grinned and took a long swallow from the can. "A man's gotta be addicted to something, Jimmy."

"You feeling better?"

"Well, er, I, er . . . yes." He'd launched into the old Wendie-speak. "A qualified yes. But most of the time, to be honest, I can't walk upstairs without resting on the landing over there. Just don't have the stamina. It's a bitch."

Wendie and I are both in our mid-fifties, yet he's in this sort of shape!

When it was time for us to get back on the road, he got up, stiffly reached for a cane near his chair, and managed to walk back upstairs. We had to wait on the landing for him to catch his breath.

"Tell your folks hello," he said as he shuffled to the door. "I've always been very fond of them, especially your mother."

"She's not doing well. Callie's folks go out to see her every day. The Parkinson's is a lot worse. She can't feed herself any longer. It's hard to see her like this. But what the heck, it gives me a chance to check up on my old best man. He needs to take good care of himself. Is that a deal?"

He leaned on the cane. "That's a deal. Anyway, the Vol nation can't survive without me."

Still that old twinkle.

"I'll send you my good wishes from over here," he said, as we reached the door.

Connie looked worn out, in an elegant kind of way. Wendie still leaned heavily on his cane.

A year later, we got Connie's email. He was in the hospital. That, in itself, wasn't a huge surprise. Wendie always had recovered in the past, somehow brushing aside crisis after crisis. This wasn't his first. He'd do that again. Wendie was a constant, a part of my existence.

"Wendie's in a coma," a later email stated. Several days later, "Good news, improvement in his vital signs." Good old Wendie, way too tough to fail. He'd make it through this. He always did.

A week after that, the phone call. "Jimmy, this is Connie. Wendie died last night."

Wendie couldn't die.

"He died? I'm sorry. After all this, it's a huge shock."

"His body had been through so much," she said. "The doctors said he simply wouldn't die. He wanted to live so badly."

He wanted to live. I have no doubt.

Connie asked if I would be a pallbearer. Of course. It was an honor.

The six of us remained outside while the funeral director pinned boutonnières on our suit coats. When we entered the main room, the size of the attendance, or to be exact, the lack of it, was surprising. For the most part, these were the same people who'd congregated back in the family section before the service. Where *was* everyone? Wendie had been a community leader, a high-profile editor of the major newspaper in the region.

I suppose the minister did a nice job. His generic words, soothing to friends and family, were recognition of Wendie's life and accomplishments. But they lacked Wendie's essence. The only way to have added that would have been for a stand-up comedian to do a bit in Wendie-speak. "Well, uh, um. Tell me again . . . um . . . what's the occasion? And why does everyone have on coats and ties?"

Out of the question. But in my private little world, that's what happened. I smiled and almost laughed thinking at what Wendie would have said if he could have given his own eulogy.

"Heh, heh, heh. Glad you could be here."

After the service, most of us drove in a short procession, not to a traditional cemetery, but to a granite-encased building, a repository of cremation urns. I was listening to a local FM station broadcasting Imus-in-the-Morning from New York. Wendie would have loved that.

We sat once more for a brief "urn-side ceremony." Connie hugged us. It was over.

The last name is called . . . Myrna Alice Walker. Someone gets up and walks slowly in the subdued light to stand beside the group, a semicircle now, each person with a candle. Donnie lights his candle and walks to each one, repeating the process until there is an arc of tiny stars.

"Thank you everyone," he says. The room lights come back up. My eyes are riveted to Marnie's candle, now extinguished.

People move back into the present. The din of conversation resumes. Food is brought into the room in large buffet-style chafing dishes. "We're going to go by tables," someone announces. "Check your number. It's located in the floral piece. O.K. now. Tables one and two start, then three, four. You've got it."

Slate points toward the central arrangement. "What's our number?"

I'm in the middle and turn the small metal blossom toward him. "Lucky number seven. You're the table captain. Lead us to the promised land."

"He's used to it," Ellie Gaskins says. "The front man. All those years with a guitar and a microphone."

Slate laughs. "Hey, I'm not even the best singer in our house. Ellie was a studio session singer in Nashville until the kids came along. You should hear her."

She blushes. "That was a long time ago."

"Believe it," he says. With that, he takes a handkerchief from his pocket and ties it around his head. "Hand me that metal flower with the number on it." Holding it behind his head, Indian-style, he slides the stem behind the headband. By this time table six is in line. "Table seven, on we go." We follow Big Chief to a smattering of boos and applause. That's Slate.

After the meal, someone goes through the "most" awards: most grandkids, most distance traveled, most years married . . . the same people win. The "business meeting" is brief. We vote to come back in five years, and do it again at year 50.

Donnie tries a few lame jokes about herding cats to pull this thing together.

"You know, cats. Dammit, we all were cool cats back in the day."

No luck.

"All right. It's settled. Now get set. We have a special treat for you. Please give a great big welcome to the area's favorite reunion band . . . Princeton's own Coverall!"

The keyboard player sits down at the electronic piano and leans into the microphone.

"Ladies and gentlemen, class of nineteen-sixty. Hey, you-all." The din starts to rise even louder. "Are you ready for some music? We heard this class has the best reunions. Everyone ready to party?"

A disorganized "yes" ripples through the crowd.

"All right. You're in the right place. I'm Carl Hyatt, and we're Coverall." With that, he hits the opening riff of the Jerry Lee Lewis song, "Whole Lot of Shaking Goin' On." They mix up the set with a few country standards like "Amarillo by Morning," plus the old Top 40 standards from the late 50's and 60's. They do slow songs like "Mr. Blue" by the Fleetwoods, and "Save the Last Dance for Me" by the Temptations. They do a great job on the Boxtops' "The Letter," one of my all-time favorites, along with "Woolie Boolie" by the coolly named Sam the Sham and the Pharaohs. I've finished getting ready to get the feeling. Things are good.

"We love to see you dancers out here," Carl tells us. "We hear you-all are the best Princeton High reunion class. You know, I tell 'em all that, but . . . for this group I really mean it. And I don't tell all of them that. And . . . this class has someone no other class can match. You know you have a drummer—heck of a drummer." With a theatrical gesture, he says, "Mr. Buddy Lewis!"

Buddy emerges from across the room in the center of applause and some commotion.

"Buddy Lewis, percussionist extraordinaire, former member of this band, come on up here." A burst of applause follows. "You dancers keep right on dancing. Buddy, I think you just might know this little tune that Mr. Buddy Holly and the Crickets, from Lubbock, Texas, made famous way back in nineteen fifty-seven. Get us started with 'Maybe Baby.'"

As I'm walking over to the bar to refresh Callie's soda water and my bourbon and Coke, Buddy is on it, just like he had been for years. When he's in the groove, and I've seen it over and over, he has a certain smile, a combination of focus, kinesis, and pleasure. He's feeling it.

"All right. Buddy. Let's hear it!" A nice round of applause ripples around the room. "You know, this class grew up back in the days of soul music."

A smattering of applause follows.

"Do you want to hear some real soul music, some good old-time soul music?"

Big cheer.

"We need to have a soul man—a man who can *bring* it. A man who can *feel* that great soul music! That right?"

Bigger cheer.

"All right, folks. You-all *know* who I'm talking about. So get on your feet, put your hands together, and welcome Princeton's own—this classes' very own—Mr. Arcie Peterson!"

It begins at the very back of the room. An opening in the crowd develops and then continues along the entire length of the dance floor as Arcie moves forward. His tuxedo, black bowtie with a formal white shirt, black slacks, and shiny shoes are fit for a star. His hair falls below his ears, straightened. Finally, our hero emerges and stands triumphantly in front. The crowd is his crowd. Tonight, we are his people.

"Thank you," Arcie says. "Thank you so much. Thanks to Carl and Coverall for that super introduction and all the great music so far." Then, glancing back, "And how about our own Buddy Lewis!" In the lights, the sweat beads on Buddy's forehead. He's in the moment, the moment of yesteryear. This is his tour, his own version of the doo-wop acts.

Arcie looks over at Carl and nods. He's ready. I've seen it.

The synthesized keyboard delivers a loud, raspy, organ sound, and the lead guitar simultaneously hits the lead-in riff to "Mustang Sally." The place goes nuts.

We have the feeling. We do. Arcie does a good version of Wilson Pickett's classic from '66. But reality sets in as the song progresses and it's obvious that Coverall isn't Wilson Pickett's house band from Fame Records, and that Arcie, our own music man, isn't Wilson Pickett. Still, it's a good moment. The band immediately segues into a second Wilson Pickett hit, the 1965 "In the Midnight Hour." Arcie starts strong, but soon enough his voice stretches and strains. By the end, some of the magic is waning as the clock nears the actual midnight hour.

Arcie raises his hands. "Thank you all so much. I'd like to thank Carl and the band for allowing me to stand in like this. It was fun. It's still some of the best music around." People start drifting back to their seats. Some start to leave. "Let me announce, with great pride, that my new CD is out. It's available for purchase. I have a few here, or you can contact me at home. Give it a listen. I know you'll like it."

A smattering of clapping drops off, then Carl picks up his microphone. "We have a little reunion of your old high school band, the Roadsters, here tonight. We do—three of the original five." He turns around. "Buddy, a drum roll please . . . We have the founder and lead guitarist. Is Slate Gaskins in the house?"

Slate looks at Ellie. "This wasn't part of the deal. I don't remember any of those songs. No way."

"Slate," Carl continues. "Our lead guitar player just happens to have an extra guitar tonight. Amazing how that happens. We've even got some words printed out. Take one song and get warmed up. Both of you can play."

Slate slowly gets up, still wearing the headband from the table numbering plan. He walks to the stage, swings the guitar over his shoulder, adjusts the strap, and plugs in the audio cable. He says something to Arcie off-mic, and when Arcie gives a thumbs-up signal Slate goes over to Carl, who takes the microphone and announces, "Will Ellie Gaskins please come to the stage." She does a double-take, then walks up and stands alongside Arcie, who says something to her.

Immediately, there's a one-two, one-two-three-four and the band launches into Sam and Dave's 1966 hit, "Hold On, I'm A-Coming." The electronic organ sound is a decent approximation of a horn section—if you imagine hard enough. Arcie now seems stronger. Ellie easily picks up Sam Moore's tenor part. From the start, she has good harmony and pitch, backing up Arcie on the refrains. She clearly becomes more comfortable as the song progresses.

"How about that Mr. Arcie Peterson!" Carl shouts. "Don't forget Arcie's new CD. And how about Ellie Gaskins on backup. Ellie, so we don't continue to surprise you, come over here and get the words. There, that's good," he says as he reaches out and hands her a sheet.

She nods and walks back to Arcie. Always the class act, he gives her a polite little bow as the band kicks off into "Soul Man," another Sam and Dave hit. Again, the organ sound synthesizes a horn section with the familiar opening notes: dooh do do dooh, do dooh, dooh do do dooh, do dooh. . . .

Arcie starts out as before, with the main lead. Now that she has the words, Ellie picks up and sings the complete tenor track. People start to notice. Snippets of "Did you know she was this good?" ricochet around the crowd.

By the end of that song, Ellie's is the more pronounced voice. The tenor pitch dominates in a situation like this. But it's more than that. Her voice is strong, pitch-perfect, and gaining in confidence. Arcie, on the other hand, is tiring, his voice stretched.

The band takes a final bow. Buddy's face is dripping with sweat. Slate once more is the front man guitarist. We all stand and cheer. Arcie is the first to leave the stage.

On the way out, Arcie stops. "Call me," he says. "Lunch. Before you leave."

"I will."

He says nothing else. There is a sense of resignation. With a tap on my shoulder, the black man in the white sports coat is gone.

Chapter 32

SUNDAY MORNING FORCES itself into my consciousness. The morning after the night before is accompanied by a headache, neither unexpected nor terribly bad. The sound of bathwater, along with a flat and empty place next to me, signals Callie is up. Our little cavern still is shrouded from daylight by the thick drapes.

Now *that* was a high school reunion.

At some point, the grating irritation of a hair dryer completes the process of waking.

"Good morning, Sleepyhead," she announces as she sweeps by me in her silkiness.

"Come here, you vixen." My morning surge of testosterone takes over.

"No way, lover boy. I'm all clean. We need to get ready and head back to Princeton."

We pack, straighten up the room, and navigate the dark corridors for another late breakfast. Several couples who were at the reunion are sitting separately. We'd had enough reunioning so to speak, so with polite waves we acknowledge one another but sit apart. Once again, there's plenty of room by the gorge-side windows. The spectacular view of the Appalachian ridges, trailing off into the distance to East River Mountain and the Virginia border at the summit, frames our next-to-last day in the area.

Although I separated myself from religion years ago, both of us enjoy Sunday morning services at Callie's family church, the First Christian Church on Straley Avenue. It's an old-line mainstream church, but not one of the grand five-column edifices. You've got to seek it out, two blocks off Mercer Street. It's a compact, brick structure with beautiful stained-glass windows all along the sanctuary walls. Scenes depict Jesus with small children, peaceful birds, and wonderful miracles—all with splendid rays of the sun at attractive angles.

The services are broadcast on 1490 radio. That reminds me of Sundays at WLOH, as well as Mr. Emory, my mentor and key influence, who designed and built the equipment that enabled the original broadcasts from the First Methodist Church in the 50's and 60's.

We're early. The parking lot is less than half full. Callie's high heels are a bit tricky, so we walk slowly down the old sidewalk, at places cracked and canted. She seems to know everyone. For me, most of the faces are only vaguely familiar. Inside the church, the greeters—men as usual—say hello. They wear boutonnières, are conservatively dressed, and have timeless Sunday morning pleasantries about them. The same as it always was. More pews are empty than full. We slide in next to one of Callie's cousins and her husband. Only a sprinkling of young families sit among the mostly older congregants.

Memories flood back: soft organ music, Sunday morning handshakes, "church smiles," and nicely dressed people. Gary Warren, the minister, is in his late 40's and has a beautiful singing voice. He welcomes everyone and proceeds through the announcements, prayer lists for the sick, and concerns for servicemen and women serving the country. Ladies' circles, choir practices, and a young persons' bus trip all are mentioned.

We haven't been there recently and didn't see him prior to the service, but Gary mentions us by name. His sermons always are interesting, with a blend of timeless philosophies and Christian teachings, as well as the history of the Biblical lands at the time of Christ. He doesn't blame, never threatens. There is no mention of vengeance, of boiling cauldrons of liquid sulfur just behind the door to hell.

The scripture is from First Timothy, an extremely short Gospel in the New Testament. I read the entire book—there are only two pages of it—as he speaks. Here was a man who was in prison somewhere in the Roman Empire, most likely sentenced to death for his blasphemous support of a prophet in Judea who was causing problems to the ongoing provincial administration in that remote area. The theme is patience. His sermon deals with the need to have thoughtful restraint in all things we do. He uses First Timothy as an example of that characteristic.

First Timothy is so short that I also read the equally brief book of Second Timothy. It includes passages of the Bible that thinking people must ignore, or at least rationalize: Women must not receive an education, must not be teachers of men, must not be leaders in the church.

The service comes to an end in a reassuring manner when the pastor walks from the pulpit back to the church entrance, pausing on the way for his wife to join him and walk hand-in-hand. Callie and I remain to exchange greetings with several friends. When we finish, we're practically the last people in the sanctuary. The minister and his wife are standing by themselves, and Callie and I walk over. We've developed a casual but sincere friendship with them despite our infrequent visits. He's a Virginia Tech football fan, so we have that in common as well.

I tell him how much I enjoyed the historical aspects of his sermon. He nods.

Then, "I read ahead of the scripture . . . Second Timothy as well as First Timothy." He listens, says nothing, displaying patience, in accordance with his sermon. "Second Timothy has some explicit directions on how to establish a church."

"Yes, that's correct," he says. "Paul was a traveling man, a most unusual man, on his own then. It was important to have structured guidance on how to establish this new phenomenon."

"How do you, as an educated man, a man of faith," I say as politely as I can, "reconcile these instructions along with the clearly stated directions that women not be educated, not be teachers, not take positions of authority in the church?"

Both Callie and his wife now are listening. He laughs easily. "Oh, that," he says. "Good points. People deal with that in different ways. Some take it literally. Not in our church. The thinkers and sages, plus mere mortals like me, choose to interpret the Bible's passages such as these in a way that separates what we would characterize as eternal truths from customs of the day. Biblical acceptance of slavery is a good example of this. For me at least, these passages, although explicitly and clearly stated, reflect the social mores at the time. Those are not considered eternal truths."

"So, it's open to interpretation?"

"Keep in mind that everything we read in the modern English language version has been through at least two complete language translations—Aramaic to Latin to English—and then through a thousand years of change in the English language itself, from the Anglo-Saxon Old English roots to the present form. It's important to seek the meaning, the intent, independent of shifting cultural customs and norms. It's neither simple nor easy to do. As one of my professors at seminary used to say, 'Beware of absolutes. There are few.'"

"This church is fortunate to have you as their pastor," I say. "I hope they understand that."

He shrugs. "You're very kind."

He seems somehow to sense I'm dealing with a broader issue. I may not understand it myself.

"Patience," he says softly, extending his hand.

I'm crystallizing my demons in my own mind: the way my father and I ended our relationship, the way I may be extending that very legacy to my children.

"It allows understanding," he concludes.

On Monday Arcie and I meet for lunch. He pulls in right on time, driving a big Caddy, six or seven years old. The car is spotless.

"Enjoy the reunion?" he asks.

"It was a bash. On the serious side, the candlelight memorial ceremony impressed me. We didn't see you before the big intro."

He nods. "I missed the program and the meal—to be honest, a cost-saving move. I'm selling 'Nevermore' when I can. Got a new CD in development—always a new project."

"You still working? I mean outside the creative space?"

"No. Finally checked out—retired from the Forest Products Lab. The state was looking for some cutbacks. It's not bad, a situation I can live with—got health coverage plus a more or less decent pension plan. I have time for the music. But no more touring, at least until one of the CD's hits."

"Good deal. Did you have fun with the music thing at the end?"

"Oh yeah. Always. I got a kick outta the band reunion bit. Most of that was planned, of course. Carl wanted Buddy to come up and play some. They called me and asked me to sing a couple of numbers."

"Arcie, you were looking sharp. The whole wardrobe. White tux. Fancy bow tie. The real deal."

"Oh yeah! Gotta do it. Gotta see if the old guy still can put on a show."

I don't push it any further and am ready to move on when he says, "Slate's wife can sing."

"Did you know she was going up there?"

"The whole bit with Slate was a surprise. Something Carl ginned up. Slate walked over and asked me if she could sing backup—said she was pretty good." He looks straight at me, as if he's looking for a comment.

"Someone said she used to do studio session work in Nashville."

"Yeah. Hey, it's all good, you know," he says with a smile. "For the old times."

"So what else you up to?" It seems a good time to change the subject. He perks up, turns in his seat, his eyes bright.

"You know, Jimmy, I'm worried about our community here. I mean the black community. When I was a kid, we didn't have trash on the street, beer bottles lying around . . . all that stuff. If I mouthed off or didn't go to school or church, my dad or one of my uncles would bust me one. It's different now. I just don't know."

Two men, now in their 60's, connected by a thin but real web of long-ago experiences. One is white, the other black. Here we are again. We're talking social values, or the lack of.

"We didn't have our rights then," he continues. "That damned segregation. Swimming pool and movie theater access, restaurants, even separate schools before the Civil Rights laws. It was easy to stick together 'cause white society kept us out of the way—kept us down. I got involved with some of that. Most of the stuff was over in Bluefield . . . more TV and newspaper coverage. We had that one big demonstration in front of the Monarch."

"I remember."

"You know, I didn't follow up the way some did. The N.A.A.C.P. honcho in Charleston wanted me to go on bus trips, meet some people . . . get more involved. I just wanted to play music. Believe it or not, the guys in the Roadsters—those long drives with you when we used to talk . . . all that helped me. Just like walking the protest lines with the sign. I could have done a lot more, I suppose. Part of me knows that.

"Things have changed—don't get me wrong. I still have a black minister and black neighbors, but it's different. Some things are better and some things're not. Something's added now, but something's lost. We got something, something that was absolutely necessary, but ended up losing something as well, something that was strong and important, the glue, the binding."

He pauses, waiting for some sort of response. I have nothing but the slow and sure transition in my own thinking over the years.

"I just don't get it. We've got young men in our community—I'm talking about teenagers, twenties, that age—who've got nothing. Nothing! Dropped out of school, don't have a job. They hang around and make fun of anyone who stays in, can speak an entire sentence with decent grammar. These guys, they're dealing drugs, doing mischief, getting girls pregnant. It pisses me off to see that. Some have flashy cars, do the jewelry thing. For a while, it looks like they're doing great. Looks like that to some of the young people in the community. Of course, most of them get shot in some drug deal, or do serious time. It's temporary success, but it seems to make an impression. Quick money, easy way to hustle. Beat the man, you know."

"Your community isn't the only one with these problems," I say. "They grow out of desperation, lack of hope." My words seem academic.

"That's right. But we've got to help ourselves. In the end, you've got to help yourself. Anyway, I work with the high school guys. We meet on Sundays, sort of man-to-man stuff. I have a little street-cred left after all these years of trying to do music . . . on the road, here in the area. That's one reason I'll never stop my music work. It's good for me and good for other stuff as well." He smiles. "It used to be good to pick up women, too. I've done my share of that."

The pressure pops. We both laugh out loud. People look at us.

"Arcie, somehow I never doubted that."

He turns serious. "I can talk to these guys. Anyhow, that's what I do."

"You're O.K. It's good—the community stuff."

"You know, we all do a little something, Jimmy. Hopefully it adds up. I will say I'd like to make a CD that takes off and sells a million. But . . ."

"Never say never."

"That's right. That's the motto of my life. Never quit."

Chapter 33

AT DUSK ON our last evening in Princeton, a distortedly enlarged sun is setting rapidly over East River Mountain. Half of it still straddles the summit, the other half already gone. There is ineffability in the timelessness and inherent majesty of never-ending ridgelines.

"I keep thinking of that last day with Dad."

There's a clear edge to Callie's voice. "Oh, that again."

"You know, that last time we talked to any extent at all—"

"Are you going to replay that again? I've heard that story too many times. The damaged you, getting in the last word."

"I don't . . ."

"Are you proud of that?" Her interruption is terse.

"I don't know what I feel."

"Don't give me the same old thing," she says. "Big drama. You got in that final cutting remark. You seem to be O.K. with it. With never having had a relationship with your own father. In fact, you seem to relish it. Don't be proud of the emotional barrier you developed around yourself. It wasn't limited to your dad. It's a wrapper you use to seal off the world when you don't want to, or you can't, deal with it. The kids and I have seen it for years. It has been, and it is, a problem." She glares at me.

"My medicine. Without the pills."

"That's right. But it's not healthy. Is that the way you want to leave it with your children? When you're eighty or ninety, a frail old man?

Even right now? Have them think of you the way you thought of your father?"

"No."

"Don't you think your dad did the best he could?"

She looks directly into my eyes. I'm unable to speak.

"What's important is the way a family loves one another, protects the children, gives them a blanket of security and confidence. Hopefully, someday you'll come to understand your dad better."

Words now come. "I'll never know what I missed."

She puts her arms around me. "He did the best he could."

It was good to be back. But even though Callie and I still are "from there"—we always will be—we no longer "are there," on many levels.

The last sliver of the sun slid silently down and out of sight. An intense orange-red aura lingered over the now-dark ridgeline. The stillness of the evening surrounded us.

The reunion was a good one, with the usual backpatting and once-every-five-years updates. Seeing Buddy again, others as well. It was settling somehow to watch Arcie chase his dream, deal with non-stardom in one way, yet realize he had moved over to another track. Our friendship was a meaningful bond, an awareness of a relationship that changed me—probably both of us.

The memorial service allowed me to say goodbye, finally, to Wendie. I forgave him for allowing himself, so unique and talented, to live in a haze of intemperance—at least until the effects were irreversible. I released him. I released myself.

Somehow those important closures with my generation crystallized the loss of my parents. I never knew them beyond a superficial closeness when we were older. Perhaps I could have bridged that with Mom, but her Parkinson's ended that possibility.

With Dad, I was a complete failure. I thought he bore the responsibility, it was his fault.

I was wrong.

THE AUTHOR

Photo credit: James Minor

James Kennedy George Jr. grew up in the southern Appalachian Mountains of eastern Kentucky, southwestern Virginia, and southern West Virginia. He is retired from a successful high-tech career in the semiconductor industry, and lives in Austin, Texas with his wife, Diana.

CPSIA information can be obtained at www.ICGtesting.com
Printed in the USA
BVOW061337020312

284145BV00002B/108/P

9 781468 529678